DARK STORIES FOR THE MIND: A DREAM OR A NIGHTMARE

WRITTEN BY
KEITH STARBLUE

Dark Stories For The Mind:
A Dream or a Nightmare

Copyright 2017 by Keith Starblue

ISBN-13: 978-0692127520 (Keith Starblue)

ISBN-10: 0692127526

The characters and events described in this book are fictional. Any resemblance between the characters and any person including their names, living or dead, is purely coincidental.

All rights reserved. The author has all rights to reproduce any and all content at their discretion.

Because of the mature themes presented within, reader discretion is advised.

Dark Stories For The Mind:
A Dream or a Nightmare

Tapped
Chapter One:

Welcome to Dark Stories For The Mind, Volume Two.

The mid nineteen nineties. "What is this spot between my eyes?" Sid asks himself as he looks into the bathroom mirror. "It wasn't there when I went to bed. Weird. It's red and it sticks out. People will look at it and wonder what it is. I must have pinched myself or slept on one of my knuckles. What can I do? It is what it is and I'm running late. Glad it's Friday. Hopefully this spot will fade away before my date, my love making with Eileen. Wonder what she cooks for breakfast, don't matter I'll be long gone and asleep in my own bed way before that."

Sid finishes his bathroom time. He pours himself a cup of coffee and makes himself two pieces of toast with strawberry jam. Sid eats. Sid drinks. Sid takes a piss. He washes his hands, he re-brushes his teeth and heads out the door to drive to work.

Sid is in sales. Sid sells very well, actually Sid is almost great. If he gave up women he would become great. Sid knows this and says to himself, "Forget that. I love to get laid. I like to get laid every night. I am a man that is full of passion. I have even slept with the boss' wife. After that I received a raise from my boss with a smile on his face."

Long thing to say to oneself but for Sid it is sound. Sid pulls into the same gas and stop he does every morning and buys himself a fancy large coffee to take with him to his office. Sid flirts with the sexy tight pants wearing Sherry. Sherry flirts back naturally then she sees the spot between Sid's eyes and she tampers her flirting down. Sid notices this and feels like placing his hand over his eyes.

Back in the car Sid puts on his glasses on this very dark cloudy September day. "Damn I'm too good looking to have a spot between my eyes. Sherry, how many times have I made her purr? I can't believe the look in her eyes. She was turned off."

All day long people looked at the spot between Sid's eyes. To Sid this day became the worst day of his professional life. All his clients and their aides stared at the spot between Sid's eyes. After lunch Sid said enough is enough and went to his Doctor's office. Sid's Doctor, after trying to talk Sid out of it, sent Sid to the hospital to take some tests. These tests took a long time which made him cancel his date with Eileen.

The next morning Sid woke up and did his morning thing. In the mirror he looked closely, the spot between his eyes has almost faded away. Sid cheers himself on. Sid hurries up and makes a call to Eileen for a re-date tonight. Eileen makes him suffer a little bit before she tells him what she's going to do to him later tonight. Sid says goodbye to Eileen with an erection in his pants.

Later that night Sid feeling so great about feeling relieved about the spot between his eyes fading away, makes him make love to Eileen three times. One time too many which knocks Sid out and makes him spend the night with Eileen.

Eileen does her best, I'm a great woman to be with the next morning bit. Sid smiles not wanting to rush towards the door. The confused couple eats breakfast, they say goodbye and Sid drives home in a pretty good Sunday morning feeling mood. September turns into middle October and the spot reappears between Sid's eyes three more times. All three times these spots only lasted about a day before they faded way.

Sid went to his Doctor, they talked about his test results. he could come up with nothing why these spots would show up and go way just as fast. Sid's Doctor, Doctor Coffee suggested that Sid make an appointment with a Psychiatrist that might help Sid from another direction. He then gives him her card.

4

October turns into the beginning of November. The spot keeps coming back. Sid wants answers. Sid has become really tired of this damn spot. Sid reaches into his wallet pulls out the card Doctor Coffee gave him and then makes the call that will hopefully lead to his cure.

November, 9th. Sid is sitting in the waiting room of Doctor Stacy Quarters' office. Thoughts of why am I here flood Sid's mind until the receptionist tells him Doctor Quarters is ready to see him.

Sid looks over at the door that leads to the unknown and away from safety, it looks twelve feet tall and kinda blurry. Sid looks back over at the receptionist, he thanks her and gets up from his chair. Eighteen steps (Seventeen and a half) Sid opens up the door. Second office down the hall on the left side, standing by the entrance to her office is a business sexy dressed lady with her hair put up and held in place with a pencil.

Sid forgets what and looks at her like he wants her instantly. She notices and blushes with a I got you glare in her sexy, blue eyes.

Sid is having his quick moment when she speaks to him, "Hello I am Doctor Quarters. Are you Sid Smith?"

Sid finishes with his quick moment and replies eagerly, "Yes, yes I am Sid Smith. It's nice to meet you Doctor Quarters."

"It is nice to meet you Mr. Smith. Please come into my office and have a seat."

Sid walks towards a not moving out of the way into her office Doctor Quarters. Right before Sid is upon her she smiles and steps in front of him. Doctor Quarters turns her back to Sid and walks first into her office. Sid looks from Doctor Quarters head to her ass in a heartbeat and enjoys what he sees, it is fine.

Doctor Quarters walks around her desk and sits down in her chair. Sid walks in and looks for the couch.

"No couch Mr. Smith."

A surprised Sid responds back, "How did you know I was looking for a couch?"

Doctor Quarters laughs a little cute laugh and happily responds back, "Everyone that walks in here looks for a couch. You are no different Mr. Smith."

"Sid, please call me Sid. I guess that is true about the couch. This is all new to me. I was expecting..."

Doctor Quarters interrupts Sid, "What were you expecting Sid?"

Confused, Sid looks at Doctor Quarters, "I don't know what I was expecting Doctor Quarters."

"Well relax Sid your mind is in great hands. Please have a seat in whichever seat you want."

There are two chairs in front of Doctor Quarters' desk. They look closely alike but do not match and one is a little taller. Sid picks the taller one and sits down.

"Interesting? You picked the taller chair Sid."

A more confused and looking around Sid says, "Did I pick wrong? Should I have picked the shorter chair?"

"It's not a question of right or wrong Sid. It's a question if you want to be up higher than your problem. Look at the chair beside you Sid, look at the shorter chair. That is where your problem is Sid. It is lower than you. Remember this before we get started, you are higher than your problem. Remember and believe this Sid and together you and I will control your problem."

"That sounds... I guess control would be nice. What I really want, what I really need Doctor Quarters is not control. What I need Doctor Quarters is to defeat... destroy my problem."

"I see Sid. I have to tell you I have concern with you wanting to destroy your problem."

"Well I don't know any other way Doctor Quarters. I want it gone and I want it to stay that way."

"What do you want gone Sid?"

"The spot between my eyes."

Doctor Quarters looks at Sid closely, "Sid you do not have a spot between your eyes."

"Well, not right now Doctor Quarters but very soon the same spot will reappear right between my eyes. It is red and ugly. The only good thing is that it is not very big. But still, it sticks out like a beacon and I hate it and I want it gone forever."

"You hate the spot between your eyes Sid?"

Sid blinks a few times, "Yes I hate it."

"You hate the spot that only you can see Sid. When did it go away? Was it there yesterday?"

"No it was not there yesterday. Let me think. It was four days ago, or was it five? Doesn't matter, it will come back, I know this for sure."

"I see Sid..."

Sid interrupts Doctor Quarters, "Doctor Quarters, I'm not crazy or making this spot up. Other people have seen it."

"Please Sid try to relax your defenses. I am trying and willing to help you. It is all up to you Sid, if you allow me to help you remove this spot from your life. I have to understand, so I have to push perhaps push hard to get the answer I need to help you. You must understand this."

"Doctor Quarters, let me explain this spot of mine better."

"Yes Sid, please make clear to me about your spot."

Sid looks at Doctor Quarters, she looks hotly intrigued and skeptical at the same time. Sid shakes his head a little bit and laughs putting his hands to his face to cover it up.

Doctor Quarters watches Sid, then she quickly responds to his gesture, "Please Sid, don't cover up yourself. You have to be willing to face your problem with your eyes wide open, to the very normal possibility that your spot, the spot you hate, is all in your mind."

Sis removes his hands and shakes his head no to Doctor Quarters. They look eye to eye for a moment before Sid blinks.

Sid smiles, he sits back in his chair to gather himself, "Two months ago I woke up one morning and when I looked into the mirror I saw a spot between my eyes. The next day it went away.

"Just like that, the spot was gone?" asks Doctor Quarters.

"Yes. No big deal. Then it came back three or four times from that early day in September until October. I said enough of this spot and I made an appointment with my doctor, Doctor Coffee.

Doctor Quarters nods her head yes in recognition, "I know Doctor Coffee. He is of great quality. Did Doctor Coffee see this spot?"

"Yes he did. By luck the spot was between my eyes on the day of my appointment and on my next appointment when we talked about the test results."

Doctor Quarters gestures to the phone, "So Doctor Coffee can confirm that you indeed had a spot between your eyes two times, is that correct Sid?"

"Yes Doctor Quarters. The second time is when he told me to contact you."

"You contacted me right away?"

"No, I waited awhile."

"Why because I'm a woman?"

Sid looks at Doctor Quarters, she is looking back at him like do not lie to me.

"No Doctor Quarters, I waited because I wasn't sure if I wanted to talk to a Psychiatrist. It does not matter to me if you are a woman or not."

"Very good Sid. I'm glad that you did not lie to me. We can go on now, please continue."

"That's it Doctor Quarters. The spot came back about four or five days ago, I called your office and made an appointment to see you today."

"I see. It's unfortunate that this spot did not make itself present today. I think this is where we should stop today. I tell you what Sid, when this spot returns I want you to come to my office that day. If I can see this spot for myself I feel I will be able to help you more."

"Should I call first Doctor Quarters, to make a appointment or just show up?"

"Yes call first, that way I can put on hold what I'm doing when you show up. We will not need long. If I see this spot with my very own eyes then we will go on from there."

Early morning, two days later Sid sees the spot between his eyes once again. Sid walks disgustedly to take a piss. Three hours later Sid's spot is being inspected by Doctor Quarters for longer than Sid expected it to be.

"Sid this spot... I don't know. You sure you did not do this to yourself? Or let someone do this to you?"

"No and no Doctor Quarters. I hate this spot remember?"

"Okay, I believe you. I want you back for an appointment as soon a possible. I will cancel appointments for you Sid."

"Why would you do this for me Doctor Quarters? Is it my spot?"

"Yes it's because of your spot... Sorry Sid I'm excited. I've seen this same spot in between your eyes before on someone else."

"When? Did anything happen with their spot?"

"I don't know. What I meant to say is, I have seen a picture before with someone who had the similar looking spot between their eyes."

"Nothing else about them Doctor Quarters?"

Doctor Quarters looks away from Sid, "Please if you know anything Doctor Quarters tell me."

"I know one thing Sid. It is a little hard to believe."

"What is it?" Sid asks with his heart racing.

Doctor Quarters, lets out her breath and says, "Aliens."

"Aliens? Are you talking about Aliens from outer space Doctor Quarters?"

"Yes Sid. Yes I am."

Sid laughs like you are crazy lady, "Well Hell, it's been fun but I think this is my stop so long Doctor Quarters."

"Mr. Smith, I expect you to take this very seriously. I'm not saying to you Aliens to make myself amusing to you. I am a doctor. I take my profession very seriously and with a lot of respect. I am not playing games with you Mr. Smith, I assure you this..."

"Please Stacy calm down. I didn't mean to upset you. You have to see it my way. I'm a simple man. I work hard. I play hard. I have sex four times a week and my life was simple and fun until this damn spot starting popping up. So when you say Aliens, I have to say to you, I'm looking for more of an Earthly cure."

Doctor Quarters looks at Sid and then she steps closer to him making Sid back up against the wall. (The two of them are talking down the hall away from her office.)

Pressed against Sid, "You know Sid you are a smart ass. A very good looking smart ass. I'm not going to take that from you. I'm in charge when you come to see me."

Sid is turned on and feeling weird as well, " Doctor Quarters, I..."

Doctor Quarters puts her finger to Sid's lips, "Quiet Sid. Let me help you to be quiet."

Doctor Quarters takes her finger away from Sid's lips and replaces it with her lips. The two kiss only long enough to touch lips three times. They pause and look into each other's eyes. Passion is burning and their next kiss reflects this passion perfectly.

11

Doctor Quarters pulls away from Sid, "What are we doing Sid? I can't help myself. I want to lose control. It's been such a long time, almost a year since I've made love."

Sid smiles like oh yeah, "A whole year? Come here Stacy, let's not waste another minute. I want to be the man to touch your beautiful body for the first time in so long."

Stacy licks her lips and nods her head yes. "Okay but not here. How about you come back after hours and we can make love on my desk?"

Sid is smiling ear to ear, "That sounds perfect Stacy."

Stacy kisses Sid and places her hand between his legs and gives him a squeeze. Stacy pulls away and laughs, "That is Doctor Quarters to you Sid."

"Even when we are making love on your desk Doctor Quarters?"

"Yes Sid. Especially when we're making love. I have such plans for you Sid."

"I'm all yours Doctor Quarters, until tonight. Do I need to bring anything?"

"Yes, a bottle of wine and an overnight bag."

"Wow, that's hot. Wait a minute what about my spot?"

"Do not worry Sid I am your psychiatrist first. I will help you as a patient that needs my medical help. As a woman, I'm going to use your body for lots of pleasure. I've been so lonely, it's been so long. You would not deny me some needed pleasure, would you Sid?"

"No, never Doctor Quarters. I want to feel and taste your sweetness. You are such a fine and sexy lady."

"Call me Stacy from now on Sid, unless we're making love. I mean this Sid, I want this Sid. You are to be the sexy patient that walks into my office for help but when you see me, you can't help yourself, you rip off my clothes and make love to me on my desk."

"Because you are so beautiful and untouched, sexy Stacy?"

"Yes Sid. Please Sid tonight be perfect for me. I want hot lust that lasts for hours. I wish it was tonight right now, kiss me Sid."

Sid and Stacy kiss while touching every body part of the other they want to touch. They are not paying attention when Stacy's receptionist Gail walks up to them.

"Excuse me Doctor Quarters, Mr. Green is getting impatient. What should I tell him?"

"Tell him I will be there in a moment. Get him a bottle of water that will keep him busy for a minute."

Gail just stands there looking at her boss, not saying anything.

Stacy looks back over at Gail and smiles at her, "Is there anything else Gail or do you want to join us?" Stacy says to Gail very sexy and confident.

Gail blushes and walks slowly over to Sid and Stacy. When she reaches them she pulls Stacy away from Sid and kisses her, after that she kisses Sid.

"Please you two be gentle with me. It's been over six months since I've made love."

Sid and Stacy look at the other and laugh. "Damn Sid you lucky man you. Two fresh hot beautiful woman to enjoy in one night together. Could your night get any better?"

"I happily think not Stacy. Forget my spot."

"No way Sid. If it wasn't for your spot, this would not be happening to you. Is that not correct Gail?"

"What spot Doctor Quarters?"

Sid and Stacy laugh as Gail looks at them as if they are weirding her out.

Sid gives Stacy a goodbye until tonight kiss and then he kisses Gail the same way.

They both say goodbye to him one more time and then they kiss each other again.

Sid turns around three times as he is walking away to see if his two dates for later tonight have stopped kissing. The third time they stop kissing and look at him with faces touching, both saying at the same time, "See you tonight."

Sid says see you tonight in happy response then he turns around and walks away and out of the building.

Sid heads to work and puts in about five hours before he leaves early to get ready for his double date.

Sid goes all out making himself look as fine as he can. Sid looks into the mirror and sees his spot and says to it, "You're a damn ugly spot you but it seems you have brought me some luck on this Friday night."

Chapter Two:

Sid is finishing up and ready to head out the door when his phone rings.

"Hello?"

"Hello Sid this is your sexy date tonight Stacy."

"Hello Stacy, how sexy are you dressed for me?"

"I'm dressed to kill Sid, just like Gail is. Here say hi to her as I touch her breast."

"Hello Sid, this is Gail. Come over quickly, I'm drinking and I want a man to sit on top of and kiss."

"I would love that Gail..."

"Hello Sid, this is Stacy again. Change of plan. We, Gail and I are in my apartment. Come to us, come find us."

Sid listens as Stacy hangs up on him. Sid smiles and then he frowns.

Sid to himself, "These ladies are hot. These ladies are beautiful. I have to find them. How am I going to do this? I have no idea where Stacy lives. Call me ladies."

Sid puts his phone back on the receiver and it rings. Sid smiles and says, "Hello sexy," into the phone.

A man's voice says to Sid, "Sexy? What kind of number did I call? Are you one of those nasty sex numbers? Well go screw yourself with no goodbye from me."

Sid pulls his phone away from his ear and gives it a dirty look. "Stupid, ass faced, bastard. Call me and give me some shit out of nowhere." Sid hangs up his phone and stares at it.

Nothing. Five minutes and nothing, no calls. Three minutes later while Sid is walking back from grabbing a beer his phone rings.

Sid puts his unopened beer down and answers his phone, "Hello?"

"It's you again. Why are you answering my girlfriend's phone? Where is she? Let me talk to her, you weirdo." The same man from eight minutes ago yells at Sid.

Sid is pissed, "You stupid idiot. You have the wrong number. Your girlfriend is probably out fucking somebody else. By the sound of you, anybody would be better for her. Next time you want to call me, call yourself instead and then hang up on yourself. You stupid idiot."

Sid hangs up to Stupid Idiot telling him to do painful things to himself in many different ways.

Sid walks over to his beer and opens it up. Sid is just about to take a drink of it when his phone rings. Sid stops himself from taking a drink but too slowly for a single drop of beer falls to the floor. Sid looks at the drop of beer on his floor as his phone keeps on ringing. Sid is just about to move when his phone stops ringing.

Sid is just about to take a drink of his beer when his phone start rings again. Sid says to himself, "One more time." Sid picks up his phone and says nothing.

"Hello Sid?" Stacy says to Sid with a big question mark at the end.

Sid's blood stops boiling as the thought of having sex with two ladies comes very sexy fast back into his mind.

"Hello Stacy, what is your address?"

"Where were you Sid? I called and called."

16

"I was here Stacy."

"Yes but your phone was busy. Were you talking to one of your lady friends?"

"No Stacy, I had the misfortune of talking to a wrong number. Twice."

"Well Sid that is over now. The right number is calling you. Do you still want to have sex with Gail and I?"

"Very much so Stacy. I would love that. Give me your address and I will be over as fast as I can."

Sid is about to walk out the door when his phone rings, "Goodbye, Stupid Idiot." Sid says with a spring in his step.

Sid to himself, "This is going to be fun and interesting. I've had two ladies at the same time. Stacy and Gail have not been two ladies before. I don't know why, don't really care, they're hot. There is something... If it is all fun and exploration, I'm up for anything. The something, I think I'm being played. Why? Has to be because of my spot."

Twenty minutes later, Sid is knocking on Stacy's door. Sid listens for footsteps. Sid starts to feel even more turned on when he hears two sets of foot steps walking towards the door from the other side. The door opens up and standing there is Stacy and Gail dressed in leather teddies, with long boots included. Stacy is wearing black and Gail is wearing red.

"Come in man with the amazing spot." Stacy and Gail say to Sid at the same time.

Sid breathes in fast and lets it back out as fast, "Ladies, you look so lick-able tonight. Thank you for inviting me over, here is a lovely bottle of wine for us to share. For sexy fun the lady that gets closest to the number I'm thinking, gets to be kissed first."

17

Stacy shakes her head no, "Sid get in here and kiss us both. Me first, Gail first, we don't care. We've all ready started without you. Taste one of us taste the other on our lips... Stop staring and walk in here like we are in charge."

"Ladies move your sexy bodies over a little bit so your male for the night can enter freely and spread out."

Stacy and Gail, look at the other and touch the tips of their tongues together. Sid watches, while unzipping his pants. Stacy and Gail look back over at Sid, they grab him quickly and pull him through the door.

"He's so fine Stacy. I want him first."

"This fine man is mine first."

"Ladies please." Sid says as he is being pulled into Stacy's apartment. "Ladies tonight it's not first then second. No,no,no, sweet ladies, it's one for a few moments then the other for a few moments. And ladies I can do this all night long. The hotter you two ladies are the better of a man I will be for you two."

Two drinks drank and a third drink being poured for Sid by Stacy as Sid is kissing Gail while playing with her ass.

Stacy brings Sid his drugged laced third drink and he downs it in two gulps. "That's a good boy Sid now it's my turn to be kissed. Let's go lay on my bed."

"Lead the way Stacy, come on Gail let's follow Stacy."

Gail takes Sid's hand and walks with him to Stacy's bedroom. In the bedroom Stacy and Gail make a standing Sid sandwich. They keep this sandwich tightly in place as the the three of them dance to the unheard music of love and lust. Sid's buzz is changing, the room is staring to spin. Sid to himself, "I'm being played."

Sid's clothes are being taken off him by Stacy and Gail as they are talking to him and to each other.

Stacy to Gail, "You were so great today. I just loved it when you said like you were clueless, "What spot?"

"Thanks, I can't believe this is happening. We've waited so long for one like Sid to come to us for our help."

Stacy grabs Sid by his face and says into it, "Yes you did, didn't you Sid? You just came to us like you were destined to. I told you Gail, one day someone like Sid would come into our lives. Someone that remembers being tapped."

Sid tries to speak but he can't form the words as he is laid naked on the bed. Stacy makes smaller Sid rise up and say hello. Sid in and out of consciousness enjoys Stacy as she makes love to him. Twenty minutes later Sid feels himself ready to finish. He hears Stacy say to him, "Give it to me Baby, I want to feel your love, give me your seed."

Sid has no control of himself as he gives Stacy what she wants. Sid feels Heaven as Stacy takes her right fist and beats it down sexually upon his chest.

"Thank you Sid, thank you for choosing me to carry your child. I will raise it with lots of love as you live out the rest of your life on another planet."

Gail out of patience says to Stacy, "Get out of my way, it's my time to be chosen."

Stacy gives Gail a dirty look and gets off Sid slowly. "There you go Gail, what a ride Sid is. You can tell he's been touched by Aliens. No normal human man has ever felt this great to me."

Gail smiles and makes smaller Sid rise up once again.

Sid's mind is trying to grasp what is happening to him as Gail makes love to him. In Sid's mind, "These two ladies want my child as I live on another planet?" Sid tells himself that he has to stop Gail but she feels so good and knows how to move like an angel on top of him.

Gail to Sid, "Give it to me better. I know you like me better. I'm more special ain't I Sid?"

Sid can say nothing as Gail goes into overdrive on top of him. Stacy has heard enough and yells out to Gail, "Shut up Gail, you bitch. How dare you tell Sid that you are more special than me".

Gail stops making love to Sid and says to Stacy calmly, "You had your turn. Shut the Hell up and let me have my turn the way I want it. Sid is the best I've ever had and your big mouth is pissing me off."

Stacy storms out of the bedroom in a rage. Gail looks down at Sid and asks him, "Where were we sexy?" Then Gail re-begins her one of a kind love making to Sid until he can't hold back the urge anymore.

Fight between ladies is avoided as Sid is tied naked to the bed. Gail is on the bed with Sid rubbing his body as Stacy is attempting to place him under hypnosis.

The urge to take a piss is compelling within Sid's mind as Stacy pushes harder and harder at it. Sid begins to feel his thoughts slip to the back of his mind. Stacy has eased Sid, he feels comfortable and relaxed as he opens up his mind to her for exploration.

Stacy talking to Sid, "Sid I want you to go back in time. I want you to take me with you to a night before you woke up the next morning having your spot reappear. Any night you choose Sid. It is all up to you. Just relax and find the night you want to take me back with you to."

20

Stacy gives Sid a moment to think about a n ght he wants to share with her. "Sid have you found a night yet?"

Sid says nothing as he passes by nights before the spot reappeared to find the perfect one. The one he woke up during the night and was made to forget.

Stacy to Sid, "Sid are you alright? Can you hear me Sid?"

Sid finds the night he is looking for and replies, "Yes I'm fine Stacy, I found the night I want to take you back with me to."

Stacy and Gail look at the other and smile, "Great Sid take your time, tell me at your own pace."

"Yes Stacy I will. It was an ordinary night, I got back to my apartment about an hour or so before my bed time. I had a great date that night. Her name was..."

Stacy interrupts Sid, "Never mind her name Sid, tell me about you alone in your apartment."

"Yes Stacy. I fiddled around for about an hour not ready for sleep because I still wanted to have more sex with the date that you don't want me to mention."

"Okay Sid you were still horny for your slut, then what happened after that?"

"I went to bed and tried to fall asleep. Two hours later I was in between sleep and consciousness when something enter my bedroom and joined me on my bed."

Stacy excited asks Sid, "What was it? What entered your bedroom and joined you on your bed Sid?"

"I don't know, I can't remember but I feel it's very important that I do. I can almost see but there is this veil in front of him or her. I can't see through it."

21

"Focus your thoughts past this veil Sid. It is the Aliens' block that they placed inside your mind. Clever, very clever these Aliens are. Do not worry Sid, together you and I will remove this veil so you can see clearly."

"I see something Stacy. What is it? It's on top of me, get it off, it's cold.

"Don't worry Sid this is only a memory within your mind it cannot hurt you. It can seem as real to life but it is only a memory. You are stronger than your memory. Take a deep breath and try again Sid."

"It's on top of me... It's not a veil blocking my view Stacy. It's bright, this thing on top of me, it is bright like clear light. So bright it hurts my eyes to look at it."

"I want you to pause what you are seeing Sid. Now remember before you look at this Alien on top of you, you can make the light less bright. Use your memory to your advantage. Move your head a little bit maybe you will able to see around this bright clear light."

"Yes Stacy, I will try. Wait a minute, I can see its face, it's a kind face. What is it doing? It's bringing one of its long fingers to my face. It placed it right between my eyes. Something is happening. My memories... It's like it's tapped into them. This creature is siphoning my memories! No it is leaving them in place, this creature is reading my memories Stacy."

"Calm down Sid, relax. Now tell me what this creature with a kind face looks like. What is it? Is it an Alien?"

"I don't know Stacy. In my memory my body is moving around, like what this creature is doing is bothering me. Wait a minute, I'm awake. The creature is looking down at me. It pulled its finger out from between my eyes. Its face does not look so kind now. It does not like that I'm looking at it."

22

"What is it Sid? Tell me, tell me now."

"Stacy. Stacy this creature is trying to use a finger on its other hand on my spot. I'm awake more now, I'm fighting back. We are struggling, it is so much stronger than I am. It lunges its finger at me, I moved just in time, it missed me. Off me, it is off me... It's floating above me, it has wings. Stacy this creature is not an Alien it s an Angel."

"What? No way. You must be mistaken Sid. There are no such thing as Angels. No Sid what you're looking at is an Alien from another planet."

"No Stacy, it is an Angel. In my memory now, I'm getting out of my bed. It is next to my ceiling speaking words I do not understand to me. I can see it as clear as life now Stacy, it has lowered its light. Stacy it is an Angel, a golden winged Angel was in my bedroom, gathering my memories. What does this mean Stacy?"

"I don't know Sid. You are suppose to be the one that brings me the proof I need that Aliens exist. I cannot accept that you are seeing an Angel. It must be another block in your mind that the Aliens placed there. Yes another block that is it. They don't want you to remember them so just in case you get a memory back they make you see something your mind can grasp to be true instead of seeing them."

"I don't think so Stacy. The Angel is flying down to me in my memory. It is smiling and holding out its hands in a gesture for me to come to it..."

"I am not scared as I walk over to it. I have reached it now. The Angel pulls me towards it. Its wings, it's wrapping its wings around me. Everything is bright now, too bright, I can't look at it anymore."

"What is happening now Sid? Where is the Alien?"

"I don't know Stacy. It is gone, my memory has ended. There is nothing left to see but darkness."

"Okay relax Sid this is almost over with. Now Sid before I bring you back, I want you to make sure for yourself that what you believe what you saw was an Alien not an Angel. Can you do that Sid?"

"No Stacy I can't. What I saw was not an Alien from outer space but an Angel from Heaven."

"That is very unfortunate Sid. I was hoping that I could make you change your mind. Now you leave me with no choice Sid. I'm sorry."

"What do you have to be sorry about Stacy?"

"This Sid. Gail get away from Sid and spread your wings. I want you to wake up now Sid, look at us, see us as the Angels we truly are."

Sid comes out of his hypnosis clear of mind. But what he sees brings forth sudden euphoria within his mind.

"Before I release your soul from your body Sid, I want you to know I tried my best making what you think you've seen was really an Alien. Even going as far as the both of us having sex with you. I wish things were different Sid especially after I release your soul from your body."

"What's wrong Stacy? I'll be okay, won't I?"

"No Sid. I have very bad news for you, your soul is to fall to Hell after you die. Oh well I guess there is no reason to put this off any longer. You were so close Sid, a few more good deeds and your soul would have made it to Heaven. Too bad I have to end your mortal life before this could happen, goodbye Sid." Sid falls down dead and his soul falls to Hell without incident.

Empty Hands

Randy is walking down a cold damp alley in New York City. Down on the world is the thoughts inside his mind. Randy wants, needs the big score with lots of payoff in the end.

Let's check out what's going on inside Randy's mind. "Damn them for not including me, I could have done the job. I'm all about the job, I am the job. Stupid bastards, I hope they get busted."

On and on complaining about the world is all there is to be heard. So we'll let Randy hear his own thoughts as the story shifts to a pair of gloves that needs to be found. Three months ago in this same alley a man named Benny laid on the ground bleeding to death from a bullet wound to his stomach.

Benny was a thief, a very good one. Benny had a secret, a pair of gloves he found five years ago. These gloves are very special for their wearer, they have the power to provide what their wearer desires or needs at any given time. Benny always needed tools to help him enter any place or buildings. Benny's needs never caused harm to another person physically.

One night, like so many other nights in other people's lives, the night Benny lies dying in an alley, he did something different. Benny told the gloves he needed a gun instead of a key. Of course a key would have done Benny no good but if he would have told the pair of gloves he needed the key instead of a gun, a cop would have not shot him in his stomach.

Benny, before he died took the gloves off his hands and tossed them away from him. When they landed on the ground they disappeared. Benny laughed then he died. Three months ago turns into this night as the gloves reappear ten feet up the path that Randy is walking.

25

"What's that? Gloves? They look new. I don't need gloves I need money." Randy kicks the gloves out of his way and keeps on walking while he repeats out loud, "I need money."

Pete watches Randy walk away. "Damn. I guess there's no reason to rob a man that screams out to the world that he needs money. Well what now? What did he kick out of his way?"

Pete walks up to where the stranger paused and spots the pair of gloves about six feet away from him to the left.

"Gloves? I lost my gloves awhile back, I could use a new pair. Why not? Might not be money but my hands are cold and now they can be warm. Life is a trip, I need money."

Pete walks over to the gloves and picks them up. They're a little dirty so he shakes them off. Pete slides his left hand into its glove then his right. The gloves are warm and soft which make Pete smile until his stomach rumbles.

"I'm so hungry, I could go for a thick cheeseburger." A ten dollar bill appears in Pete's gloved left hand. Pete freaks for about ten seconds then he smiles very greedily.

"How about fries and a soda, maybe a slice of pie? Can't forget the tip. They work so hard for so little money."

The ten dollar bill has company join it when two more ten dollar bills appear on both sides of it. Pete smiles even greedier as a very big light bulb pops over his head.

"I could use a castle to live in and many cars to drive," Pete looks at his gloved left hand and watches as the thirty dollars become nothing in his hand as they disappear.26

"What the? Not my thirty dollars! I'm so hungry." Pete says to himself then he says this out loud, "I'm sorry. Forget about the castle and the cars. May I have my thirty dollars back?"

Nothing as Pete looks back between his gloved hands. Pete is about to give up when twenty dollars appear in his left hand.

Pete says to his gloves, "Thanks gloves. I have learned my lesson. I won't be greedy, I'll just ask you for what I'm truly in the need of."

Pete is about to put his twenty dollars into his left front pants pocket when he hears from behind him, "Give me your money or I will shoot you in your head."

Pete does not turn around as he hands his twenty dollars to the man that is standing behind him. "Very good. Now don't turn around and you will stay alive with your stupid looking gloves on your hands."

Pete listens to the man walk away from him then he hears the man run off like a thief in the night. Pete is pissed as he turns around to see no man at all.

"Damn. I can't believe this. Me, I get robbed? This is not my night." Pete's frown turns into a smile as a fifty dollar bill appears in his left gloved hand.

"That's what I'm talking about. Hello precious, you're going into my pocket this very second. Ain't no one going to take you away from me."

Pete walks out of the alley a rich man in his heart. He finds a small diner and orders himself a half pound hamburger with extras of everything, a large order of onion rings and a chocolate shake. Pete eats his food, which taste delicious, all is perfect in Pete's world at this moment.

Pete puts his new gloves under his pillow when he goes to sleep in his cheap one room apartment. The next morning the first thing Pete does when he wakes up is put his hand

27

under his pillow. To Pete's happiness the gloves are still there.

"Yes there you are you wonderful pair of gloves. Let's go out, let's find out what I will need you to give me today." Pete cleans up and leaves to grab a quick, small breakfast. In his gloved left hand before he enters the diner appears a ten dollar bill.

Pete to himself as he enters the diner and after smelling coffee and bacon instantly, "Breakfast money, money left over from last night. I wish I knew my limits. How much money can I make my new gloves give me today? This I need to know very much. I want pancakes. I want bacon. I want a glass of milk and a glass of orange juice. I like today, today is going to be a great day."

Pete eats his breakfast, taking his time, talking to strangers with a good morning to you look in his eyes. While Pete has his back turned away from his table, a young lad of eight on his way out of the diner with his family picks up Pete's gloves from off his table and walks away with them placed under his arm.

Pete is none the wiser, as the mother, after they are out of the diner asks her son where he got his new gloves as she takes them out of his hands. The lad does not answer and just shrugs his head, like I don't know. The mother is not happy with her son as she tells him that he has no idea who wore these gloves as she throws them on the sidewalk about five feet away from the entrance of the diner.

The family walks away as Pete looks for his gloves. Pete is standing tall looking around the diner as a passing poor man picks up the gloves and puts them on. One minute down the sidewalk the man with the new gloves turns around and walks back towards the diner. The man stops eight feet from the diner and takes off his gloves and stuffs them into his two front pants pockets. He walks into the

28

diner, Pete looks at him then he looks around the diner some more.

The man that is very happy about his new gloves that just gave him a twenty dollar bill, looks at Pete and knows that his new gloves belonged to him just a few moments ago. The look of panic in Pete's eyes is a clear giveaway. The man that has money on him for the first time in a long time smiles at Pete and sits himself down at the counter.

Just a man looks at the waitress and is about to order a hot coffee when she stops him by asking him if he has any money. Just a man smiles and shows her his twenty dollar bill with pride within himself. Out of the corner of his eye the man that just ordered breakfast sees Pete with his head hanging low walking by him and out the door.

"They were yours, now they are mine. Stupid fool must have let them slip out of his pocket. Not me. No not me. I will be more careful, yes indeed I will."

The man that paid for breakfast inside a diner instead of searching a garbage can for his breakfast today, looks up at the sky and says out loud, "Today is my day."

It is two hours later and just a man lies dead on the ground from being hit over his head with a brick until he died. His head is a bloody mush as a friend of his starts to put on his new pair of gloves. A man with money, a man with a life off the streets screams out to him from behind his back. "Someone call the police, that man just killed the other man!"

The man is scared, he drops his gloves on the ground and takes off running for his freedom. Todd walks over to the dead man to see what a dead man looks like close up. Todd looks at the dead man's bloody head and shakes his head no. For no reason at all but just to do it Todd picks up the gloves and walks away from the dead man with them placed under his arm.

29

Later that night Todd is sleeping in his bed while the gloves he took from a murder crime scene are placed on the small stand next to the door of his apartment. Todd does not hear the lock of his apartment door being picked.

Pete still down on the world enters Todd's apartment very quietly. Pete closes the door and looks down at the stand next to the door and sees his stolen gloves.

Pete to himself, "I can't believe it, my gloves. The asshole who owns this apartment must have stolen them off my table. I knew there was a reason I picked this apartment building and this particular apartment. Should I punish this man for stealing my gloves? Forget it, I have my gloves back and that is all I care about. Whoever you are you are one lucky bastard."

Pete leaves Todd's apartment without incident. The next morning a freaked out Todd looks around his apartment for the gloves he took from a crime scene. They are nowhere to be found. Todd gives up and walks over to his door to leave. He is just about to grab the doorknob when he notices that it is unlocked.

Todd to himself, "Did I leave it unlocked and someone walked in and stole my gloves? Or did someone break in and steal only my gloves? Couldn't have been the police. They would have woken and arrested me. Who would break into my apartment and steal my gloves? Man I think I'm going to be blackmailed. Why didn't I just leave those damn gloves where they laid on the ground? Why did I have to be so stupid? What the Hell am I going to do? Should I call the police? Yeah and tell them what? I'm so screwed."

The next morning is much better for Pete than it is for Todd. The sun is shining, it's damn cold this November day but the sky is clear and blue. Pete is walking down the sidewalk passing everybody by like they are not even there. Those that notice Pete talking to himself loudly without a care in the world, all think he is crazy but one man, who paid attention very closely to what Pete said while passing him by. Magic gloves, Money and how to get it?

Pete to his gloves out loud for them and the rest of the world to hear, "Did you leave me my gloves? Am I not worthy? I have to be, I found you again for a second time. Did you lead me to you? I had no idea that you were in that apartment." Pete chokes on his words and stops walking. The man looking for magic and money stops following Pete and hangs back looking around.

"I'm your servant am I not, my gloves, my very special gloves? Yes I am and I do not care. Give me wealth and I will help you get to the others you want to get to. Do with them as you may and then come back to me and give me more riches. You need some blood wiped up, it will cost you extra. For extra, I'll wipe it all up. Like this fool that is following me."

Pete looks at Pete a man that looks nothing like him but does share the same first name. "Hello stranger I'm Pete, do you want your chance at a wishing well?"

Pete looks at Pete and softly replies, 'Yes I do Pete, I am also Pete. Small world is it not Pete?"

"Yes Pete, yes it is. Very wild that your name is Pete. Does not matter what your name is as long as it does not become mud. Am I right or am I right Pete?'

"No mud Pete, just call me superstar. Give me my chance Pete."

"Here you go Pete, put on these magic gloves, let them give you what you need."

Pete looks at Pete, he takes the gloves out of Pete's hand and places them on his hands.

31

"How does it work Pete?"

"Just tell them what you want and they will give you what you need at this moment in time."

"Okay Pete here it goes. Magic Gloves I want money, lots of money but first I need to know if my wife is true to me, that she can be trusted with all my new found wealth?"

Pete looks on at Pete. Pete looks down at the gloves in his hands. Nothing. Pete is starting to feel foolish for trusting a crazy person when a picture appears in his gloved right hand. Pete looks at the picture and gets very mad instantly.

"What the Hell? How could she? With her boss?"

"What is it Pete? Is that a picture of your wife?"

"Yes Pete. This is a picture of my wife in the nude fucking her boss."

"That's... That's really bad Pete."

"No shit Pete. Tell me something I don't know."

"Well at least you know now. What are you going to do Pete? How are you going to handle the answer to your wish?"

"Well Pete, I'm going to kill my cheating wife and her boss while they are fucking each other like the pigs they are. Do you have a problem with me doing this Pete?"

"No Pete, that is for you decide to do or not. I am just the man that allows a person like you a chance at something, whether it be nice or sad, good or bad. What comes after is in Fate's hands. May I have my Magic Gloves back?"

"Yes Pete, here you go," Pete hands Pete his Magic

Gloves back. "Thanks Pete, I can't believe my wife is cheating on me." Pete drops the picture of his wife and her boss having sex on the ground.

"You can try to find forgiveness for her Pete. It's not too late to change your mind. You can still not become a killer."

"Too late for that Pete. I've killed before, ten maybe twelve times or more. I was going to kill you and take your gloves. But since you said I could use them for free, I am at peace with you Pete. Long life to you Pete. Thank you for my chance. Too bad it really sucked bad."

Pete watches Pete walk from the sidewalk and straight into the road. Too bad for Pete that he wasn't paying attention for if Pete had been paying attention he wouldn't have been run over by a electric company's truck.

"Damn Pete you're all squashed. Dumb ass. Well gloves give me my prize." Pete watches as a thousand dollars appears in his right gloved hand.

"The right hand this time my money appears? I guess that means I'm damned, huh my Magic Gloves? Until it comes my time, let the good times role. Let's hurry up and find another person for you to judge not worthy. I want this thousand dollars to turn into two thousand dollars. Come to think about it my Magic Gloves I have all day. Let's turn this thousand into a quick ten thousand. What do you say my Magic Gloves? Do you have what it takes to keep going all day into the night? Just point me the way and let's get this new thing of ours started right.'

Pete this day did not make ten thousand dollars, he made seven. Pete was disappointed he wanted ten. The need to be never satisfied inside humans is the gloves bread and butter. Still this entity has to rely on humans to do its bidding. It wonders and does not care how long Pete will last. Some humans last a week, some a day. Some even

33

a year or more. In the end, they all get served a portion of death. They all die and the pair of gloves stays where they lie after a death or they disappear from sight.

There's not much more information about these gloves. Where did they get their power? Is the power inside them two different resentful souls working together in one conman goal? What year did they first appear with special powers? Have they always looked the same? Were they at one time or another something besides a pair of gloves? And why a pair of gloves? They can be separated.

All great questions for something you can converse with, get to know. Learn its high and lows. Not in these gloves' world. These gloves affect the minds of its human hosts. Greed from the humans and their ability to effect their thoughts makes easy days for the pair of gloves. Even if they only use the new human host for a few minutes before their check out time pops up, they always get what they want from them.

Pete lasted seventy three days before the gloves made two aces appear in the right one. Pete was playing poker when a player beside him that was losing big time looked down at the floor and Pete's jacket. In the pocket hanging out was a glove with two aces placed inside it. The man yelled out foul to everyone. Everyone turned on Pete really fast and they all together stomped Pete to death.

After Pete's death those that stomp him to death took a closer look at the two aces that caused all this to happen and they somehow had turned into a pair of two's. Everyone left except Jack. Jack, because of being really stupid, had to bury Pete all by himself.

Jack died three days later, then Paul had them. For some reason only men get to be chosen, perhaps it's because they are a pair of male gloves.

Fast forward three years, a man named Danny is choking

to death on a piece of meat. Danny stops choking and falls down dead to the floor. Nobody screams, some start eating their meals again. Another man named Jack walks by Danny's table, he picks up Danny's gloves and walks out of the restaurant with them safely in his left hand.

This Jack's specialty is ripping off ladies out of their money. The ladies fall in love with Jack. The ladies give Jack money to help him out of a bad situation. He is so happy with them, he is so loyal. They're going to get married. The ladies make the plans, while Jack runs off with the rest of their money. Never to be seen again.

The gloves like this Jack. His deep need for greed within himself makes him feel pure of all guilt from being greedy. This is a strange concept to the gloves that Jack possesses within him so they have decided to stick around with this Jack for awhile. It is no love feast. The gloves one day will make Jack die. It's only a matter of time before they make this death happen to this Jack.

Until this day comes to be, the gloves let Jack be Jack. They help Jack with his ladies and Jack helps the gloves bring their death to whomever is next on their list.

One last question. Are these gloves, gloves that Death misplaced somewhere on one of its stops of reaping?

The Summer Of Rex
Chapter One:

A small town in California, the early summer of 1988. Rex works at a small record shop, Jim's Rock and Roll Shop. Rex, Katie and the owner Rock and Roll Jim are the only ones that work there. Rex and Katie have had sex a few times. Katie feels a little love in her heart for Rex. Rex is young and hung with the idea of his love being simmered on the back burner until he feels it's time to be served. Rex also part times for a furniture store.

Rex went into this furniture store one day an hour before dusk looking for a bar stool. They had none. He talked to the owner's daughter-in-law, Dawn. After Dawn spoke with Rex while he was looking for his bar stool, she left him standing there to go convince Edna to ask Rex if he wanted to work in their store a few days a month.

Edna asks Dawn if she was out of her mind. Dawn told her to imagine a sale for the store titled ladies furniture sale day. There will be all kinds of ladies that will show up, some of them will be single and looking for love, perhaps even interested in buying a new bed.

Edna after looking at Dawn like she is a hussy, telling her that they are not that kind of furniture store. Dawn tells Edna that she is old and in her way. That it's time she had some free reign in the store or she might just have to tell George (Edna's son) that she is unhappy and she wants to move away. Leaving her old self to run the store without George's help.

Edna calls Dawn a witch. Dawn laughs and tells Edna that she is to come with her to see how the young do things. Edna follows a vixen that thinks she's going to take over her store. Fat chance in that witch, Edna says to herself.

"Did you say something to me Edna?"

"Yes Witch, I said fat chance."

"Don't call me Witch you worn out old bag. And fat chance in what?"

Edna keeps it to herself and says, "Fat chance that this young man will want to work for us."

"Well, you just let me handle that. All you have to do is agree with whatever I say. That's not too hard for you, is it Edna?"

"Well go on my child. Show me what you got."

Dawn looks confused, "Yes... Well... Never mind, just follow me."

By the time Dawn and Edna make it to Rex, he is making his way towards the exit.

Dawn calls out to Rex, "Rex can you come over here for a moment, we'd like to talk to you."

Rex turns around and looks at a very big smiling Dawn and a frowning old lady, "Sure, I'll be right there."

A few moments later, "Rex we'd like to offer you a job here at Big Mike's Furniture Store."

Rex knows why Dawn wants him to work at their store but he feels nothing coming from the old lady but hate, "Thanks Dawn, but I have a job already."

"We're not talking full time Rex just a few days a month."

"What do I have to do?"

"Dress sexy and act sexy while talking to lonely furniture shopping ladies."

"What? I don't know. Like how sexy?"

Dawn laughs a tiny, I'm sexy, look at me laugh and says, "As sexy as you can be would be just perfect Rex."

"So all I have to do is be sexy? Nothing else?"

"Well maybe a little more. You see Rex when a lonely lady walks in here, we want you to make her want you to look at her and to talk to her. You have to be willing to play a role. You will talk to her and convince her that whatever she is looking at is perfect for her. The great news is that you get ten percent from every sale you make."

"That sounds great Dawn. But I don't know."

"We'll do a trial run. Come back this Saturday and we'll see if my plan is a success just like I know it will be."

Rex agrees and shakes Dawns hand as Edna stares at the floor saying nothing.

"Here let me walk you out Rex," Dawn says as she starts walking towards the door not waiting for Rex's answer. "Watch the store Edna."

Dawn walks past Rex. Edna looks at Rex and gives him her hand, "Welcome to Big Mike's Furniture Store."

"Thank you." Rex says as Edna turns away from him and walks off without saying another word.

"That is one cold old lady," Rex says to himself and turns around to walk out of the store.

In the parking lot. "You know I have a great feeling about this Rex."

"I do as well Dawn."

38

Dawn looks at Rex as he is leaning against his car. His blue eyes and kinda long blond hair turns her on.

"Forget it Rex."

"Forget what Dawn?"

"Forget the beating around the bush. I can tell you like the ladies and you know how to turn them on."

"That is correct on both counts."

"Yes I'm sure. Anyway this Saturday I expect you to lay it on thick with your prey. Remember this Rex, even though they are your prey you have to be the nice and sexy man and not a predator. Do you understand the difference?"

"Yes Dawn, I think I do?" Rex says laughing as he says it.

"I think I better make sure for myself, f you can be the sexy stud I need you to be for the store. I tell you what Rex, after we're closed tonight about nine o'clock come back here. I'll be waiting in the back of the store. When you get here I want you to look sexy and try your best to turn me on."

"What happens after I turn you on, I go home?"

"No. We will make love."

"Am I on the clock?"

"What? How dare you! Who do you think..."

"I do not have to think Dawn, I know. You're hot, in your early thirties and wanting a younger man to give it to you like you've haven't had it in years. Mature is my specialty. It will cost you a hundred to find out. Dawn this is a one hundred dollar savings I'm giving you because you're my boss.

Dawn don't let this one time special price get away from you. This might be your last chance, to enjoy the extra savings."

"I want a kiss first, for free."

"Come on and get it darling, I'm all lips."

"You're all ass." Dawn says lowly.

"I missed what you said Dawn."

"I said pucker up and don't forget to use your tongue."

"Lay it on me baby."

Dawn rushes to Rex for her free kiss and enjoys it very much. Rex makes love with his kisses.

Dawn and Rex stop kissing, "I deserve you Rex, you know that? I'm a great wife. I put up with my husband's crappy old mom and dad. And George, what a man. He's pretty much my dog. Good thing for him I like my men to be my loyal pets."

"Is that a fact Dawn? Well sexy all I have to say, if it's between the two of us, I will not be the one that is doing the barking."

"Let me tell you something, you may get me to pay you more than I want to, but you will never get me to bark. Do you understand me?"

"Wow from sexy and hot to I'm out of here lady."

"Don't you dare leave," Dawn grabs Rex and demands another free kiss without asking him.

The two almost strangers kiss in the middle of the parking lot for all to see, including a staring at them from a front window Edna. Rage of betrayal for her son burns within Edna as Dawn and Rex say goodbye until tonight. Edna knows her son, that he is weak. This betrayal would break his heart, but it would strengthen his soul.

Rex slides Dawn's right leg from around his waist, her kissing lips will not let go of a sweet thing, like this hot young stud, she's going to ride tonight until she breaks him and makes him whimper.

Rex after kissing Dawn like she payed him for a kiss looks into her eyes and sees what she has in plan for him later tonight. Rex to himself, "This hot lady is going to go all out tonight. I better not smoke any weed that way I can go longer. I'll just drink a few beers to make her look even finer. This lady is going to go broke trying to tame me."

"Until tonight Rex, I just love your name, I'm going to enjoy screaming it out loud in passion."

"Looking forward to hearing you scream it Dawn. See you later tonight."

Rex gets in his dark blue 1973 Dart and drives to Jim's Rock And Roll Shop. About three miles down the road, behind him appears a bright yellow Bug. It is Tiffany.

Rex out loud, "Not again! Man this chick won't go away. What's she doing? Crazy lady, she's so close, I can't see the front of her car."

Rex speeds up to put some distance between him and Tiffany. Thirty five to forty five, siren comes on behind them. The police car is quickly behind Tiffany, she pulls over and the police car keeps going after Rex. Rex says, "Fuck," and pulls over to the side of the road.

Before the police officer can make it to Rex's car, Tiffany stops next to it,

41

she looks at Rex like he's the Rabbit that got away. Rex watches as Tiffany holds up a pistol and points it at him. Tiffany mocks Rex like she is shooting at him. The police officer is making his way too close, so Tiffany drops her pistol and pulls away. Rex looks in his rear view mirror waiting on his confrontation.

The police officer looks at Rex with no smile on his lips. Rex tries not to sweat knowing his weed is stuffed in his underwear. The two look at the other, Rex is the first to blink. "Out of the car." The police officer commands Rex.

"Why officer? What did I do?"

"This is not a you ask me questions kinda of stop. Get out of the car speeder. Let me see what kind of man you are."

Rex turns off his car and steps out of it. The police officer makes Rex wait to open his door all the way up by moving very slowly out of the way. Rex out of his car and standing on the side of the road, looks at the police officer waiting on him to do his thing.

The police officer yells out to Rex, "Hands on the car, spread your legs. After that do not make a move. If you move, I'll make you cry, I'll make you die."

Freaked out Rex says, "What?"

The police officer goes from cold as ice to burning rage as he pulls out his pistol and presses it against Rex's head. "Do you want me to shoot you?"

Rex, scared and pissed says nervously, "No, I don't."

"Then turn around and shut the Hell up."

The police officer pulls his pistol away from Rex's head so he can turn around and do what he was commanded to do.

Rex notices that the police officer is sweating and breathing heavy. After Rex is turned around with his hands placed on his car and his legs spread open the officer's pistol is placed on the back of his head.

"You piece of shit. You think you can fuck another man's woman and get away with it?" The officer asks Rex with his pistol hand shaking.

Rex gulps and wonders to himself which woman was his. "Look officer, I don't know what you're talking about. I have a girlfriend. I'm loyal to her. You have the wrong man."

"Bullshit you horny bastard. You did it, didn't you? You fucked my Molly. My sweet Molly, that tells me I have to wait until we get married before we can make love."

Rex thinks fast, "Molly? I don't know a Molly, do I? Wait a minute. Two weeks ago at a party at Jim's house, I had sex with Sara and her friend Molly at the same time. Oh fuck! Sara told me Molly was dating her brother. Damn it! Not only did I fuck this cop's girlfriend, I also fucked his sister at the same time. I wonder if he knows about that as well? What am I going to do?"

The police officer has waited long enough for Rex to answer. "Well puke, answer me. You fucked my Molly didn't you. Save your lies, you horny bastard, my sister Sara told me all about it. How you got Molly drunk and took her outside into the dark of the night and fucked her on the ground, like the animal you are. You're going to pay, you ruined my Molly. She was so pure, untouched and you had to taint her you nasty animal you."

Rex says to himself, "Think fast."

"Well answer me before I pull my trigger. You tell me the truth, I might let you live. If you lie to me, you're dead. Talk, tell me now!"

Rex looks up at the sun that is about to set in fifteen or twenty minutes, he knows that he has no choice. He hopes without much hope that the truth will set him free. "Yes I fucked Molly."

"You sorry bastard, I knew it."

"It didn't go down like you we're told."

"What? You trying to tell me that Molly wanted you?"

"Yes. And so did your sister Sara."

Peter the cop slaps Rex across the back of his head with his pistol. "Turn around, I want you to see me shoot you, you dirty bastard."

Peter helps Rex turn around, then he knees him in the gut and shoves him to the ground. "I've only had to shoot two other people before, you make number three. The other two were criminals. You are worse, you are scum."

"Wait man, wait. Listen to what happen, it's not my fault. No man could have said no to what I was offered."

"You lie, sex pervert."

"No, I'm telling you the truth. Sara was all over me on the couch. I was sitting between her and Molly. I was pretty much shitfaced letting Sara have her way with me. She stopped kissing me and let Molly have her turn."

"You lie!" Peter screams out and stomps his right foot down upon Rex's chest, three times. "You lie. You lie," Peter says as he starts to cry from a broken heart.

Rex coughs feeling the rising pain in his chest. "No, I'm telling you the truth. The three of us made out on the couch 'til Jim told us to take our fucking outside."

Peter looks down at Rex with eyes of tears and ask, "Who the Hell is Jim?"

"Jim is the one that threw the party."

"Go on. Speak the rest of your lies. Get them all out, before I send your soul to burn in Hell."

Rex looks at Peter and knows all is lost so he says to himself, "One for the road."

Rex clears his throat, "The three of us went outside where twenty or more people were partying. We picked a spot and laid down on the ground. I was shitfaced like I said so I let Sara ride me. When I had enough, I told her to get off and told Molly to take her turn. The funny thing is I didn't remember her name so I called your Molly you."

Peter pulls back the hammer to his gun. "Time's up."

"Wait there's more. Your sweet untouched Molly was not so sweet and untouched as she told you she was. Believe me I know women. Your sweet Molly, likes to get it on. So much so I told her to get off me and let your sister ride me until I finished."

Rex closes his eyes and says, "Fuck you pig."

Peter straights himself up and wipes his eyes so he can see the man he's going to murder with clear sight. Peter says to Rex, "My name is Peter, you asshole."

Rex laughs, opens back up his eyes and says, "Go ahead Dick, take your best shot."

Peter takes five steps backwards. Peter is in his own world, he see and hears nothing but what's in front of him. Too bad for Peter as a down the road watching all of this happening Tiffany drives her yellow Bug into him. Rex watches Peter being ran into by Tiffany. Peter makes

45

a very loud, sick sounding splat sound as he is hurled into the almost dark night. As Tiffany goes by she screams to Rex, "I'm going to kill you Rex."

Due to rage, Tiffany must not be able to see what is front of her twenty feet down the side of the road, because she pulls into the road and straight into a coming up the road semi. Tiffany's Bug is destroyed as the semi screeches its brakes like a chorus from Hell. Its high piercing sound snaps Rex out of what just happened in front of his can't believe this is happening eyes.

On his feet Rex runs off the side of the road and into the ditch and beyond it. Rex turns around to watch the semi come to a ugly sliding down both lanes stop. Rex looks at his Dart, it is untouched and so is its path past the semi.

Rex jumps up for joy as he runs to his car. He gets in, starts it up, puts it in drive and stomps on the gas. Fast doing sixty, Rex's sweaty head and body still feel like they are on fire. Rex shakes his head no as he takes his foot off the throttle and places it on the brake. Rex turns on his stereo and turns it up loud. Head banging metal blasts as Rex screams out, "Fuck you world. I'm alive. I'm alive and I'm staying this way."

Rex slows down even more, then he pulls over and stops his car. Rex gets out, he takes ten steps away from his car and bends over to the ground and pukes on it. With a burning throat and watery eyes Rex says to himself, "I can't believe that. A killer cop and Tiffany the wacko lady I fucked once and has made my life a living Hell since, both die in front of me one after the other."

Rex gets back into his Dart and takes off down the road doing the speed limit. Four miles down the road he pulls into Jim's Rock And Roll Shop as police cars and ambulances speed with sirens blazing past him. Rex gets out of his Dart and walks into Jim's Rock And Roll Shop.

Jim is behind the counter as Katie is talking to some customers. Rex looks around at all the vinyl records and feels at home. His heart is still thumping and his brain is still ticking but he's slowly starting to calm down a little bit.

"Hey Rex, come over here man," Jim calls out to Rex as he notices him standing there.

Rex walks over to Jim without responding back or barely looking at him. "What's up Jim?"

"Check it out man, see that fine lady over there?"

Rex looks over at a built brunette lady, shifting through some classic rock albums. "Yeah, what about her man?"

"Man about a year ago or so me and her, man we had a few wild nights together. I thought about her from time to time and here she is, looking so fine."

Rex smiles and says, "Well go talk to her, you're not shy."

"Yeah but man I forgot her name. I only remember how she liked me to have sex with her."

"She liked it on top, huh?"

"No man, she liked it doggy style. Well I guess that is going to have to do. How do I look?"

"Like a burnt out Rock and Roller, with bloodshot eyes and a happy man bulging in your pants."

"Can't get no better than that, I'm perfect."

Jim walks away to flirt with doggy style lady as Rex giggles a bit then he starts to laugh out so loud that everyone in the shop stops what they're doing to check him out. Katie looks over at Rex, she knows somethings up, he looks like he's been hanging around crazy people all day. Katie excuses herself and walks over to a laughing Rex. "Hey Rex, what are you doing? You sound kinda whacked. Are you all right man?"

Rex stops laughing looks over at Katie and says, "I need a drink and to smoke a fat one. Want to join me?"

"Yeah. Maybe we can make out a little bit after that. If you're nice and turn me on, I'll kiss you between your legs."

Rex looks at Katie and sees a maybe future Tiffany coming up in his life. "No Katie I need a break, just friends?"

"All right you sexy burnout, just friends. But I gotta say you're stupid for passing up what I was willing to do for you, all the way to the end. When you can't stand anymore I'll make you hold it just a little bit longer just to punish you for being a dog."

"What? Man Katie, be cool. Less words and slower talking. I have a new date tonight, I have to save my loving. Let's go to the storage room."

Katie jealous and mad, clinches her fists. "You mean one of you're paying sluts don't you?"

"Damn Katie, why don't you say that a little louder? The people in the parking lot didn't hear you."

"Smart ass. Let's go get a buzz going on."

"Yes let's. I'll go tell Jim what we're doing."

"Cool, I'll get the bong out and grab us a couple of beers."

"You know Katie, one day you're going to make a great wife for one lucky man."

"A man and not you?"

48

"No Katie, I love you as a friend. A friend that I like to have hot sex with once in awhile."

"You're stupid. Hurry your ass up."

Rex walks over to Jim, who looks like he is having a nice conversation with doggy style lady. "Hey Jim, Katie and I are going into the storage room to do a little bit of stock checking, We'll only be a few minutes."

Jim looks bummed at Rex, "Okay, I guess man."

"Who is this Jim?" Asks doggy style lady about Rex.

"This is Rex. Rex this is Katie, a good friend of mine."

Rex looks confused and smiling at Jim and Katie, "Your name is Katie?"

"Yes it is. When you said you and Katie were going into the storage room all alone, part of me wanted for you to be talking about me. Sorry Jim, your friend is hot."

"Well Katie, I'm sorry, I'm all booked up for the night." Rex says laughing, like he's kidding her.

"Oh Jim, he's bad, make him join us."

Rex and Jim look at the other. Both of them shake their head no at the same time.

Jim says, "No way, I don't want to see this fucker naked."

"Well I don't want to see your old ass naked either man."

"Well you two are stupid. I want what I want, if I can't have it, I'm out of here."

Jim looks at Rex, like come on man do this for me. Rex shakes his head, no way man.

49

The former doggy style lady, now older Katie, walks away with a great looking ass shaking.

Jim to Rex, "I was going to bite that ass tonight. Damn it Rex why did you have to come over and talk to us? You fucked it all up, you asshole."

"Man Jim, it's not my fault. How was I to know that your date for tonight was an extra horny woman. Not that there's anything wrong with that, I'm just saying."

"I don't care Rex, fix this. If I don't get to fuck my Katie, I'll fuck your Katie instead."

Rex laughs, "I don't have a Katie to fuck."

"The Hell you don't. That is what the two of you are getting ready to do aren't you?"

"No Jim. We're just going to drink some beers and smoke a joint. You want to join us?"

"That sounds great. Wait a minute, all three of us can't be back there at one time. Forget that go bring my Katie back to me. Come on man Rex, I really want her."

"Damn it! This night is really starting to suck." Rex takes off after Katie with the fine ass.

With some quick talking and a promise to fuck her later, Rex talks Katie into going back to Jim for the night.

Rex and Katie walk back over to a smiling Jim. "Here you go Jim, here is your Katie back. We cool?"

"Very cool. You and Katie hurry up, I'm closing the shop early tonight."

Jim says out loud to his customers as Rex is walking away

that he is sorry the shop has to close early due to an emergency.

Rex and Katie are drinking and smoking as Jim and Katie walk into the storage room to join them.

"Got anymore?" Jim asks.

"Always Jim. Here toke this," Rex says while holding out the half gone already joint. (Katie got the bong ready to go but Rex wanted to smoke a joint instead.)

Katie and Katie say hi to each other before long they are talking like they're friends. Jim tells Rex that he would like to fuck both Katie's at the same time. Rex agrees.

Rex rolls another joint, this time it's twice as big. The four partiers smoke it down to a roach while putting away a twelve pack of beer.

Rex tells Katie, Jim and Katie so long and drives his buzzed self home to grab a quick shower. One hour later and twenty minutes late, Rex pulls into the back of Big Mike's Furniture Store.

Rex feels good and ready to make some money enjoying the fresh Dawn. Rex knows this by the way she talked about her husband that she barely puts out for him. Rex makes it to the back door that is next to the delivery area.

Rex is about to knock when Dawn opens up the door fast, starting already on Rex before it is half way opened up. "You're late. Why are you late?" Dawn demands to know.

Rex says calmly as he walks into the door, "Doesn't matter, I'm here now. Let me take a look at you."

Dawn starts to say something, then she decides to show off herself instead.

Rex whistles at Dawn, "You look so fine tonight Dawn, I mean Boss."

"I like that. Yes call me Boss, Rex."

"Take my hand Boss, let me lead you to a spot where I will lay you down and take off your clothes."

Dawn licks her lips and gives her left hand to Rex. Rex takes it firmly and leads Dawn to where he wants to take her in full control. Rex takes his time making Dawn pant and ready to purr.

Rex smiles at how easy it is for him as he is ready to bring Dawn to reality. "Before we go any further Boss, I need to be paid first."

Dawn so happy and turned on looks at Rex like he just turned her sexy dream into a nightmare. "What? No, don't make me pay you Rex. Please don't ruin this for me."

"Dawn my sweet and lonely boss, I do not work for free. Pay me, give yourself to me. Enjoy a night of passion like you have never had. Remember I'm giving you the half off special. If you wait too long I'll increase my price."

Dawn opens up her mouth wide without saying anything for a moment. "Don't you dare try to charge me more." Dawn walks away from Rex to her purse. When she reaches it she pulls out her wallet and takes two fifty dollar bills from it in a flushed mad hurry. Rex knows what Dawn will do before she does it. Dawn crumbles them up and throws them on the floor next to Rex. "Here take your money Stud. You better be worth it."

Rex laughs on the inside getting ready to enjoy putting Dawn in her place. The place she wants to be in but won't admit it, not even to herself. Dawn looks at Rex like she can't believe he won't pick up his precious money.

"No, no, that won't do Boss. I want you to pick up my money and bring it to me and stick it in my front pocket."

Dawn shakes her head no and looks away from Rex. When she looks back at him he is zipping up his pants. Panic rises in her, "Stop Rex, don't be hasty." Dawn puts her purse down and walks over to Rex. She bends down keeping her sexy eyes on Rex at all times to pick up the money. Staying on her knees in front of Rex, Dawn puts Rex's hundred dollars deeply into his right front pocket of his pants.

Dawn looks up at Rex, waiting for her next command. "That's much better Boss. Let's finish what we started." Rex takes Dawn by her hands and helps her up slowly. When Dawn is on her feet she tries to kiss Rex and Rex stops her. "Not yet Boss, take off your dress first."

Dawn takes off her dress sexy, fast. When she is standing there with only her sexy panties on, Rex leads her away from her dress that is on the floor to another part of the room. Rex lays Dawn down on the floor on top of some furniture blankets and takes off his clothes. Dawn keeps on trying to touch Rex but he stops her gently every time. Dawn is turned on and aggravated at the same time, when Rex tells her, "Now baby, I'm all yours to enjoy."

Dawn tells Rex that he's in charge. Rex takes charge like a loving man that wants to please a beautiful woman like she's wanted to be pleased her entire life.

Rex is buzzed and turned on as Dawn begs him not to stop making love to her. Rex relaxes himself to go the distance that Dawn needs so very bad. Dawn is shaking in lust and love as Rex asks her if she ready for him to finish.

After they are done and dressed Dawn reaches into her wallet and pulls out two more fifty dollar bills and hands them to Rex and says, "Here baby, you've earned it. We're going to have to do this a lot more."

53

Rex and Dawn get dressed, they kiss the other goodnight. Rex is about to leave when he looks out the door and sees headlights. "Dawn someone's has pulled up and now they're stopping."

"Great, who can it be?" Dawn says nervously as she walks to the door to look out it. "Damn it, it's my husband."

Rex stays cool for this has happened to him a few times in the past and takes charge once again. "Okay Dawn, here is the deal. You've been showing me the inner workings of the furniture store, nothing else. So get that satisfied look off your face and act like nothing's going on but that."

Dawn looks at Rex, like are you sure? Then she says to Rex, "You're right, I can do this."

About an hour ago Edna called her son George. During their conversation she found out that Dawn was not home so she got an idea how to get back at her real good.

Edna to her son, "George would you please be a dear and go to the store to make sure I mailed out the bills today? You know how forgettable I am sometimes."

"Aw mom, I don't want to go back to the store. Dawn should be home any minute so we can go out to dinner."

"Dinner can wait George, I need you to this for me first."

"All right mom, I'll leave in a few minutes."

"No leave now George, that way you can get back home sooner and go to dinner with Dawn."

"Okay Mom, you're right. I'll leave in just a couple of minutes. I need a coffee first."

"That's fine dear. Remember I love you."

George comes into the back door of the store. When he walks in, he see Dawn telling and showing a man he does not know things about the store. Dawn to George like she is happy to see him, "George come here dear, this is Rex the man I told you about. The man who I and your mother hired earlier today to work in the store."

George walks up to the much better looking Rex like a limp beaten man. "Hello I am George, the owner's son."

"Hello George, I'm Rex, I'm glad to be working in your store. Your lovely wife has been showing the in's and out's of the store. Don't worry George, I'm a fast learner. Thanks to Dawn's help I know where things are suppose to be put. Well if that is all for tonight Dawn, I think I better be going."

George and Dawn say good night to Rex. Rex takes off and leaves a very sexually satisfied Dawn to handle her husband on her own.

This was how the first day and night went between Rex and Dawn. They have had many nights alone together from the beginning of summer to now the middle of it. Rex likes counting his money that he has made by making love to Dawn. Rex tries his best to keep the memory of Tiffany and the Cop out of his mind. Rex worried for awhile but no other cops came to question or arrest him, so Rex thinks he is free and clear from the whole ordeal.

Katie, Jim and Katie all shared that night together making love to each other. The three of them like it so much that the three of them have moved in together. This relationship was a surprise to Rex. Rex wondered to himself what would have happen if he would have stayed at the party and not went to Big Mike's Furniture Store to have sex with Dawn that first night. After each time Rex counts the money he has made, he knows he got the better of the deal.

Chapter Two:

One month later. Katie (The one with the fine ass.) "Rex you promised."

"No I didn't. I just told you I would."

"Well then, what's the hold up? You said you would have sex with me, if I agreed to have my date with Jim first."

"Sorry I lied. But think of the positive. Your life with Jim and Katie. If you wouldn't have said yes to my lie, you wouldn't have the chance to say yes to Jim and Katie."

"We didn't say yes to each other, we just went with it."

"That's hot Katie. I've been where Jim is many times, not as long but I've had it enough times to know how special it is. When two sexy ladies like you and Katie decide to please a man and each other to the point that love and lust become total euphoria. That's beautiful."

Katie looks at Rex like he is free for her to do anything she wants to him. Rex sees in Katie's eyes that he is lunch to her and tries to step back but Katie is fast for loving and is upon him quicker than a moan of pleasure.

"No you don't Rex. After talking to me like that we're going in the storage room."

"What about Jim?"

"What about him? If Jim wants to watch, hey man it's cool with me."

Rex laughs, "Well it ain't cool with me. Katie he's my boss and a friend. It just wouldn't be right."

"Well you've had sex with Katie before."

"Yes I did, but that was before she hooked up with Jim."

"Don't lie to me Rex. Katie told me that you and her have hooked up a few times since the three of us got together."

"Okay a few times. It's like this to me Katie, you are Jim's lady and Katie is the something extra in your relationship that both of you want. How long will this last? I see Katie the one stepping away to find a singular love for herself, while you and Jim soar high in the sky together or fall flat on the ground broken and no longer in love.'

"You did it Rex, you've turned me off. I was all ready for it. It was suppose to be my turn but no you had to turn me off instead."

"It? I'm not a it Katie. Free records and a cool place to be is why I work here. Yes I'm a stud but I am my own stud. I don't like it when someone tries to push me to say yes when I'm wanting to say no. I've said it so be cool and we can be friends."

"Yes friends that's all nice and fine Rex. But please just one time. After that I'll leave you alone I promise."

"Just like I promised you?"

"No Rex, when I make a promise I follow it through. Look Rex you got to help me out here."

"Help you out, like how?"

"Like have sex with me so I can know for myself how great you are. Katie brags to me and Jim how great you are. Then she tells us if she doesn't get more money from the both of us she's going to leave us both to be your one and only, because your loving is almost better than money."

Rex looks at Katie like she's fried out of her mind.

57

"Man the three of you have gone way off course. No wonder Jim keeps telling me to come over and party with you three. I guess that would make it your turn?"

"Yes that is the way it was to go down but I changed things up. I don't really want Jim and Katie to watch us have sex. Do you Rex?"

"No I don't Katie. Right now I say fuck this whole situation. It's out of control, I feel like I'm sinking. I want out of this so tell Jim I quit. Never mind, I'll do it myself."

Rex is pissed as he walks away from Katie, he takes twelve steps and stops walking and starts laughing. Rex looks back over at Katie and reaches out his hand to her. Katie smiles and runs to him. With Katie in tow Rex leads her and himself to where Jim is standing oblivious to what's going on.

"Hey Jim what's going on man? Katie and I are going to the storage room to have a great fucking time. You and the other Katie, that I'm going to have a great fucking time after this great fucking time I'm going to have with this Katie, can both watch the store, we're going to be awhile."

Jim stands there with his mouth hanging wide open enough to stuff his foot into it. Katie with the fine ass looks at Rex like he is king of the world.

"I love you," Katie tells Rex.

"Yeah I know Baby and the great thing about it is, I don't love you. Now let's go screw our brains out."

Katie looks hurt for a moment, then she says as she turns pissed off, "Yeah well I was lying when I told you that I love you. You're just a fuck. And the great thing is, I don't even want that any more."

"Well good for you Katie. Now why don't you and Jim go fuck yourselves. I quit!"

Rex walks away from Katie and Jim to the storage room to grab his stuff out of his locker. Katie looks and Jim like she hates him, then she smacks him hard across his face.

"What the Hell Katie?" A shocked Jim barely gets out.

"'Shut up Jim, I've had enough of you and your slut Katie. You stay here, I'm going to make that pretty bastard pay for how he treated me," Katie screams out in rage that boils her blood even hotter.

Jim takes his hand away from his throbbing face and says to Katie, "Katie my love, please calm down We'll find another stud for you to screw."

Katie smacks Jim across his face again and replies, "You screw him Jim." Then she runs after Rex.

Katie is almost to the storage room when she remembers the knife that is hidden behind the counter for protection and opening mail. Katie turns around and runs back over to the back of the counter and pulls out the knife for all to see. With knife in hand Katie runs while screaming at the top of her voice, "I'm going to kill you Rex!"

Katie running in a blind rage does not see a box of used records sticking out from the bottom of the shelves where they are stored. Katie's expression of rage and hate turns into fear as she trips and stumbles over the box of sticking out used records. Katie does not know how it happened or came to be that she stabbed herself in her heart when she fell to the floor.

Katie rolled herself over after the shock and pain of being stabbed slated within her a bit and pulled the knife out of her heart.

As blood poured out of Katie's wounded heart, Jim ran to her screaming her name out in a panic. "Katie, Katie are you all right? Oh my God look at all the blood! What did you do Katie? How did this happen?"

Katie says nothing as Jim pulls her close to him. Her blood soaks his shirt and pants. Katie uses Jim to pull herself up a bit. Katie looks at Jim, like look at the mistake I've made and plunges the bloody knife into his heart.

A still kneeling on the floor Jim backs away from Katie with a look of surprise and betrayal in his eyes. "Why Katie? Why? I love you."

A dying from loss of blood Katie laughs and says to Jim while gurgling blood out of her mouth, "Yes I know you love me but I never loved you. See you in Hell Jim."

Jim gurgles blood out of his mouth as he pulls the knife out of his heart. He holds it in his hand and watches the blood drip down from it onto the floor of his record shop that he has owned for past fifteen years. Sorrow turns to rage inside Jim as he screams to Katie, "You bitch you killed me for no reason."

Katie dies with a smile on her face as Jim falls down face first on the floor a few moments later, where no one can see if he's smiling or not.

The only Katie still alive walks into Jim's Rock And Roll Shop with bags of burgers and fries in hand. In panic and shock Katie drops her bags of burgers and fries on the floor and screams out, "What the fuck is going on? Who did this? Who killed Jim and Katie with a knife in the middle of the record shop?"

A watching this almost happen Rex says to a jumping up and down Katie, "No one killed them, Katie killed herself then she killed Jim."

"What? Are you crazy? How could Katie Kill Jim after she killed herself? That doesn't make any sense," Katie yells at Rex in confusion.

Rex shakes his head no to Katie, "Okay Katie snapped and ran around the shop with a knife in her hand. She tripped and stabbed herself and before she died she pulled the knife out of herself and stabbed Jim to his death."

Katie not knowing how to respond laughs out loud instead and finally replies jokingly back to Rex, "Well that explains that I Guess." Then Katie stumbles around a bit until she becomes so dizzy that she falls fainting down to the floor about four feet away from a dead Jim.

Rex looks down at Katie, he walks over to where she is laying on the floor and pulls her passed out body away from dead Jim. Rex looks around at all the costumers in the shop and says to them, "Well that is that folks. I have to close up the shop now please come back tomorrow."

Rex walks towards the door and opens it up. Customers with records, tapes, posters and shirts in their hands walk past him and out the door without paying for what they have in their hands. Rex says nothing to them about this as he says so long to the last one to walk out the door.

Katie wakes up on the floor, she looks at Jim then she looks at Katie, she starts to cry as she hears Rex lock the door to the shop.

"You stay there and cry Katie, while I calls the cops."

Katie does this as Rex calmly calls the police. Katie listens to Rex explain what happened to the person on the other end of the line in between sobs. Rex hangs up with a goodbye.

"Everything's going to be fine now Katie, the police are on their way. Do you want a beer while we wait?"

"What is wrong with you Rex? How can you think about drinking a beer right now?"

"Well Katie I'm sad that they are dead. But right before they died I found out that the three of you wanted me to come over to your place and perform sexual acts in front of you. Then Katie snapped for no apparent reason other than she wanted to have lots of sex with me and I said no. And now comes the most fucked up part. You ready? Katie grabbed a knife to stab me with. She ran with it, she tripped, she stab herself. Finally poor dumb ass Jim, Katie stabbed him as well."

Katie stands up and starts laughing hard, while wiping away her tears. "Rex you funny bastard. I just love to fuck you so much." Katie starts laughing again like she has lost a hold on reality.

"Katie stop laughing and acting crazy there are dead people on the floor and the cops are on their way. Go back to crying on the floor, that might help our situation."

"What situation is that Rex?" Katie asks while she starts to dance with her eyes closed to the horror of it all.

"Are you serious? The situation is this Katie. No matter what, the cops are going to bust our balls over this. They might even come in here with pistols out."

Katie keeps on dancing, now even faster, "Well that is great for me because I don't have balls. I know what I'll do, I'll just blame the whole thing on you. I'll become famous and they'll barbecue your pretty ass."

"That's not funny and that's fucked up Katie. Snap out of your mental shit. You mess around, the cops will bust us for something just to lock us up on the account that they feel it would be better for all if we were behind bars."

"Not me, I'm safe. It's all your fault."

Katie's response back to Rex as she opens up her eyes and stops dancing. Then Katie quietly says, "Mess around."

"What?"

"You mentioned mess around Rex. That sounds great. I think if we'd mess around it would help me focus. Here's what we will do, we will go in the storage room and mess around until the cops get here. You better go unlock the door, we don't want them to bust it down."

"No we don't, that would suck." Rex can't help himself he starts to laugh and sound like Katie did a few minutes ago.

"That's it baby, laugh it all away. After that dance around, dance in their blood stains. Then we'll have dirty sex in the storage room."

"Yes Katie that's what I'll do. I'll just have so much fun getting Jim's and Katie's blood all over my shoes," Rex says after he stops feeling like laughing.

"Okay then just skip the dancing and take me to the storage room and take away my pain."

Rex starts laughing again. He puts his hands up to his faces and laughs behind them. He pulls them away fast and says quickly, startling Katie, "Can you imagine the two of us getting busted for fucking at a murder scene. Katie I have to say after today I have seen and heard it all."

"What kind of answer is that? Are we going to the storage room or not?"

"The answer is No," Rex says as he nods his head yes to mess with Katie.

"Stop it Rex. You say no while nodding your head yes. I'm in need of your love, and you make fun of me?"

63

Rex has had enough, "Stop it Katie. Stop before the cops get here. I tell you what if you calm down and act normal after all this is over I'll fuck you any way you want me to."

"You promise? Your not just saying this to me to get me to calm down are you Rex?"

"No Katie. Trust me, I speak the truth."

"Trust you?" Katie looks at Rex with eyes of rage.

"What the Hell's your problem now Katie? Damn woman you are mental. I think I better tell the cops that's it all your fault. They'll take one look at you and think you went murderess mad."

"Oh Really? Is that so? Well Rex do you know what I'm going to do before the cops get here?"

"No Katie. Tell me what you're going to do."

"I'm going to walk over to Jim and grab the knife that is in his hand and stab you in your balls with it. Doesn't that sound like fun to you Rex?"

"Okay that's it Katie. You get no more Rex junior. How does that sound to you crazy Katie?"

"How dare you? Who do you think you are? You're nothing that's what you are Rex. Ladies like me, we only want you for a night of fun because that is all you are good for. Like I said Rex you are a nothing. When you get old and your body gets fat, you'll become less than nothing."

"Well this nothing's, everything is closed to you. So wish and want forever and a day while all those other ladies you mentioned enjoy me night after night."

"I hate you Rex."

64

"And that is all your fault Katie. You want me to be who you want me to be instead of letting me be who I am."

"Maybe so Rex. But I can't help to feel all your ladies even the paying ones are just there for you to enjoy. Until you get tired of them and come to the realization that I have already, that I am the one for you."

"I don't think so Katie. You're hot but what I got going on with a list of fine lonely and wealthy daughters of people with money, I just can't do any better."

"Oh yeah Rex. Well I say your ladies are nothing but sluts that have nothing over me."

"Enough of this crazy shit Katie, the cops are here. Are you going to be cool?"

"Yes Rex, I'll be cool, so cool you won't even know me."

"What is that suppose to mean? Never mind. Damn your making me more nervous than the dead bodies of Jim and Katie lying over there all bloody and ugly."

"I noticed that as well. I haven't seen dead bodies before but I have to say that there has to be a better looking pair of dead bodies out there right now than these two."

"Okay Katie you stare at the dead bodies like you can't believe they are dead and I'll do the talking. Understand this, you're whacked out of your mind right now and I am a little bit as well. For your own sake right now you better do nothing more than answer yes and no."

"Yes King Long Dong Rex. Answer the door, let the cops come in and see all the blood on the floor. I have a feeling that they are not going to like it very much. Then again if there is no blood on the floor anywhere that would make a reason for less cops, which they would hate even more."

65

Rex laughs and tries to stop as he walks to the door, "Stop it Katie, your making me feel crazy."

"Don't worry about it Rex, you've always been crazy. It's just now you're understanding that. Rex is crazy, oh yes he is. Most of the time in his life he is naked and all alone thinking the ladies he is having sex with are real. But unfortunately for Rex they are all in his twisted mind."

Rex looks at Katie and she becomes blurry to his eyes. Behind him the police are knocking on the door. Rex thinks to himself, "Snap out of it, Katie's mind is gone."

Rex walks to the door with eyes that can hardly focus. He unlocks and opens it up to four men and one woman in blue. "Welcome to the bloodbath in Jim's Rock And Roll Shop. Please watch where you step there is blood all over the place. Now if you don't mind I'm going outside to breathe in some air without the scent of dead bodies in it."

The police officer in charge tells one of the other police officers to escort Rex outside and watch him. Four police officers walk in and see Katie dancing around in the blood stains like she is out of her mind.

"Quick grab her and take her outside before she taints the crime scene anymore." The head officer yells out to the rest of the officers that are watching Katie in amazement.

After a few minutes Rex is being questioned. Rex decides to tell the police what happen without all the sex. That did not add up, there was too many questions. Why did Katie want to stab him? So Rex gathered himself as he went into full details with the police officers. About two minutes into it everybody was kicked back and making jokes while listening to the fantastic story that Rex was telling them. There were many more questions, like one very big one. Why the Hell did he make everybody leave the shop? After a bit the police believed Rex a bit more but enough for him to leave on his own.

Katie on the other hand, well Katie received a nice and safe ride to the hospital. Where she spent two weeks before her mind came back to her fully.

When Katie was back home she received some great news. Jim left his shop to both Katies. Since she is the only Katie still alive Jim's Rock And Roll Shop belongs souly to her.

Rex got Jim's two cars and any hundred albums of his choice from the shop.

Katie went back and forth from keeping the shop to selling it many times until she decided to keep it, and make the changes she wanted to make with it.

During these two weeks Rex enjoyed selling off his two new cars and making a few thousand dollars by having hot expensive sex with Dawn and her favorite rich lady friends.

A very big change Katie made to Jim's Rock And Roll Shop about a month after she got out of the hospital was to change the name of the shop to Katie's Bloodstain Record Shop. The new home for great music and mad macabre.

Katie's new shop was an instant hit due to the fact that some of Jim's and Katie's bloodstains still remained for the human eyes to see so horrifically brilliant.

Katie made Rex her partner so the shop's day to day would not be so demanding on her. This way Katie could spend more time talking to and taking pictures with customers that come to the shop to see the bloodstain for themselves.

Katie and Rex have hired a few good people to help them out in the shop. Business is going great, sales are up. The wild thing before all this happened, when Katie and Rex were in Jim's before the name change, Rex jokingly told Katie to do something.

Which Katie did and followed through with great success.

This is what Rex told Katie to do, "Why don't you put that shirt on the floor next to the bloodstain and take a picture of it. Then pin the picture to the shirt and sell it as a combo of Rock and Roll and Mad Macabre."

This is where the theme came from and the same day Katie came up with the new name for her record shop. On that same day Katie reminded Rex about his promise to her and Katie expected him to follow through with it. In the storage room they made love. Rex started in on having sex and Katie would have none of that.

"Make love to me Rex, I need to be made love to. What I been through, my time in the hospital. I need some loving, I need it so bad, I feel it all the way to my soul."

Rex said no because he didn't want Katie to fall in love with him more than she has already. Katie said please so sexy as she rubbed her naked body against Rex's naked body. Rex could only take so much as Katie reminded him how long it's been since she's been touched. Together Rex and Katie made love in the storage room twice.

It is now the end of summer of 1988. Rex has come to the realization that Katie has flipped a switch in her brain that tells her that her and him are in love and a couple. She acts like he's going to hang out with some of his friends when he parties with Dawn or one of the hot ladies that has made it on his list of ladies he agrees to have sex with for lots of cash.

Chapter Three:

The hot August wind blows hard from a storm that is on the horizon outside Rex's small house that he rents. Things have changed for Rex and Dawn. George caught Dawn and Rex in the act of having sex standing outside and looking through the window of Rex's house. Edna has tried many times to make George catch Dawn and Rex in the act but every time there is an explanation of non-guilt.

Enough of enough Edna called George earlier this same night and told him to go to Rex's house. After Edna hung up the phone she rubbed her hands together in a gesture of finally it's over. He will find his wife cheating on him with some good looking, young punk. And that will be that. George will divorce the cheating bitch and finally Edna will make George marry a woman more like her. A woman that Edna will like to call daughter-in-law.

Edna waited almost all night for George's call to her about his cheating wife that was caught in the act of having sex, but the call never came and Edna finally fell asleep sitting in chair next to the phone.

The reason George didn't call his mom in pain and anger was for the fact that what he could not take his eyes off of, turned him on. George watched as Dawn and a friend of hers named Becky took turns with Rex. Clumsy while enjoying himself watching the three lovers, makes George fall and bang himself into Rex's house loud enough for the three lovers on the inside to hear it.

Rex lifted Brenda off him and placed her down on the couch next to him. He got up and put on his pants and shoes. Rex turned on his outside light and walked outside his house and spotted some guy with his pants down to his feet laying on the ground next to Rex's house trying his best to get back up. Rex walked over to him and kicked him in his naked ass that was hanging out.

69

"Please Rex it's me George. Please don't kick me in my ass again, I'll leave you three alone," George pleaded out to Rex, which freaked Rex out big time.

In Rex's mind, "I just kicked one of my bosses in his naked ass after he caught me fucking his wife. I'm going to be fired. Wait a minute the freak was whacking off, while he was watching us!" This re-pissed Rex off.

"Damn George you freak what the fuck is wrong with you? Get off your ass and come with me, I'm taking you to your wife." Rex waited for George to get up and pull back up his pants.

"Okay George get your ass in my house, I bet your wife has a lot to say to you."

George walks with his head down into Rex's house. Inside the doorway of Rex's closed door Dawn and Brenda wait naked and holding on to the other for protection. The door comes swinging open as Dawn and Brenda brace themselves for what is to about to happen. In walks George first and Dawn goes off on him.

"I can't believe you George following me to Rex's house. I bet it was your nasty mother that told you to come here, wasn't it?"

"Yes Mom told me to come here but she didn't tell me why. I can't believe you Dawn, I love you." Rex shakes away Deja-Vu as Dawn continues her berating of George.

"Of course you love me you fool, look at me, I'm fine. This may come to you as a big surprise George but I don't love you, I just love your money. Hey George, what are you going to do now?"

George red and embarrassed says softly, "I don't know. I love you, I want to stay married to you Dawn."

Dawn laughs as she flaunts her naked shapely fine body around, "You make me sick George, you are so weak. It's all because of your mother, she turned her son into a weakling. Okay George I feel for you I tell you what, I'm going to let you have your chance at keeping me George. All you have to do is sit down in that chair right there. After that you are to keep your mouth shut and your eyes wide open, as the three of us finish something so special between us that you will wish you could have but will never get from me."

George walks over to the chair and sets down in it without saying a word. "That's very good George."

Dawn turns away from George and looks at Rex. "I'm so sorry Rex for my husband. What was he doing out there?"

Rex looks away from Dawn not wanting to give her, her answer. Rex looks over at George and says, "He was just looking into the window at us."

"Really? Ha,ha,ha." Dawn turns back around to look at George. "Did it turn you on? Did you learn anything George?" Dawn laughs again, "And what good would it do you George? You probably just forget what you learned."

Rex can't keep quiet anymore, "Come on Dawn give George a break. I think we better call it a night."

Before Dawn can say anything a very quiet until now Brenda shouts out, "Bullshit! I want to finish. It's not fair, it's not my husband that caught me. Rex I don't know why you and I can't finish. Let's just send these two packing, we don't need them."

"You damn bitch Brenda, how dare you try to take over. I am Rex's number one, don't you forget that." Dawn screams at Brenda in a sudden rage. Two naked ladies square off for the battle of Rex's body.

71

Rex steps in between Dawn and Brenda, "That's enough ladies. This whole thing is getting out of hand."

Dawn and Brenda look at each other with faces of fury and then little by little they calm down enough to give the other a hug of forgiveness.

"I'm sorry Dawn. You can understand where I'm coming from? I have to finish."

"I understand Brenda, I can't blame you. It's just George showing up like this and messing everything up."

"Yeah I know, what's his problem?"

"He's a loser, that's what his problem is."

"Well I wouldn't stand for it if I were you."

"Yeah you are right. He needs to be punished for his unforgivable actions tonight. Let me see."

Dawn steps away from Brenda and closer to Rex, "Do you have a pad of paper and a pen Rex?"

"Yeah why?"

"Don't worry about it sexy lover just get them for me."

Rex takes off to get a pad of paper and a pen for Dawn. Dawn and Brenda stand next to the other staring at a wanting to get out of here very badly now George.

"Look at me George, watch what I can do." Dawn says to George as she leans over to Brenda and gives her a kiss. Brenda kisses Dawn back happily. Two sexy ladies stand naked kissing as Rex walks back over to them. Dawn and Brenda stop kissing but it takes a while for them to stop completely due to them restarting.

Dawn to Rex, "Good you got them. Brenda you go ahead and finish with Rex while I punish my bad husband." Dawn commands as she takes the pad of paper and pen from Rex. Dawn does not wait for a response as she walks towards George with a look of anger in her eyes.

Brenda grabs Rex's arm for him to come with her over to the couch. Rex looks at Brenda and says to himself, "If I finish Brenda off she'll take off after and then all I have to worry about is Dawn and George.

Rex and Brenda have sex on the couch as they hear Dawn giving it again to George. "For your punishment George I want you to take this pad of paper and pen and write one hundred times on it, I will not follow my beautiful wife when she goes out to have sex for the night with her sexy stud."

"No Dawn I won't do this for you, you ask too much from me. Put your clothes on we're leaving right now." George yells out at Dawn getting up from the chair.

Rex tells Brenda to stop and Brenda replies, "Forget them they're fine. We can't stop now, I'm almost there." Rex does not know what to do as Brenda starts to moan loudly in his ears. Rex looks at Brenda after she is finished and she looks so hot to him that she makes him finish as well.

Dawn and George stop yelling at the other to watch Brenda and Rex finish. "You see that George that is a real man right there. Now if you want to keep me as your wife you better sit down and right one hundred times what I told you to write or we are through."

George stomps over to the chair and sits down angrily into it. "That is better George now start writing and don't stop until you are finished." Dawn walks away from George to join Rex on the couch. Dawn makes Rex make love to her. He doesn't want to until Dawn offers him one thousand dollars to make her moan like crazy in front of her husband.

Brenda split while Rex and Dawn were going at it. Rex and Brenda looked eye to eye as she was heading for the door and they both knew right then that this was going to be the last time they spent together.

After Rex and Dawn were through having sex, Rex walked to the bathroom to be alone, while Dawn made George finish writing the thirty or forty times he missed writing down. Looking into the mirror after Rex took a piss he sees a man that has gone too far making money from having sex. The fun and the excitement of it all has left awhile ago and now it's been replaced with frustration.

Rex looks deeper at himself in the mirror and says to his reflection, "No more."

Rex walks back out of his bathroom naked and scarred. He walks into his living room and picks up his clothes and puts them on. Dawn will not let up, she is beginning to get evil with George. After Rex is dressed he listens to Dawn for about a minute more before he is ready to end their fling fast, cold and hard.

"Dawn stop. It's time to give your husband back his balls. It's now over between us. Keep your money that last fuck I gave you is on the house. You are fine and a beautiful woman with kindness in your heart. So sad Dawn you just don't seem to be able to get to it unless you are betraying your husband and his family."

Rex grabs Dawn's clothes off the floor and hands them to her. "Love your man or leave him. Take a step back and look at what you have done to your husband. It's warped and cruel and I don't want any part of it. I am glad of the time we had together but like I said that time is now over."

Dawn looks at Rex like he is dead meat and then she starts to put her clothes back on. When Dawn is fully dressed she walks over and picks up her shoes and puts them on.

74

Dawn looks at Rex with dead looking eyes, "Yes it is over Rex, not because you said so but because I said so. You see Rex you have become boring. You sided with my husband over me. I cannot forgive this. We are through and you are fired. And all used up. Rex two more things. First do not try to have sex with any of my friends that are on your list. And throw that list away, you're only embarrassing yourself. The second thing Rex and this is important so you might want to write this down so you don't forget. And that is Rex, don't fuck with me. Just keep your pretty mouth shut about me, you got it?"

"Damn after all that Dawn, I have to say to you this, no fucking way. My silence will cost you ten thousand dollars. No make that twenty. After you pay me, don't worry I won't even remember your name."

Dawn is about to say something when she is cut off by the sound of George laughing his head off from behind her. Dawn turns around in amazement to look at her husband. "What the Hell you laughing about George?"

George stands up and throws the pad of paper and pen on the floor. Rex smiles at this, George notices this, which makes George nod his head yes to Rex for the approval. "I'm laughing at you horrible wife. You're so high and mighty and Rex put you in your place without even trying. Grab your purse, I'm taking your sorry ass home so you can pack your bags and get the Hell out of my life forever."

George walks past a can't believe what is going on Dawn and right to Rex. "I hate you Rex but I'd also like to thank you. Yeah you fucked my wife but so fucking what asshole, in the long run you did me a big favor. Believe me my next woman is going to put my ex-bitch to shame. Don't worry about your ten thousand dollars, I'll pay it to you. After that I never want to see or hear about you again."

"That's cool with me George," Rex says very coolly.

75

George looks at Dawn and says, "Well you coming or are you going to walk your ass home, since Brenda left you?"

Dawn says nothing as her world crumbles in her mind. She walks to the door, looking at Rex, like help me. Rex shakes his head no to her and waves goodbye.

Rex stares at his closed door and takes in a deep breath and sighs it back out slowly. "What a fucking night. What will come at me tomorrow?" Rex says out loud. The rest of the night Rex drinks a couple of beers and smokes a joint. Rex knows that he is buzzed but he can't feel it. So Rex goes to bed with a clouded mind and barely sleeps.

On the way home from Rex's house, George and Dawn ride home in silence at first. Lightning strikes the sky followed by heavy thunder. George turns on his windshield wipers as the rain comes pouring down hard on them.

Dawn looks out her window at the rain, then over at George. She pauses herself and then she starts to speak with a much clearer mind, "Yes you are right George it is over between us. I don't love you anymore, it's been a long time since I have. Tomorrow we will go to see an attorney and start our divorce. If you don't give me any shit, I'll only take half of what you have. If you give me any shit, I'll demand more. Now when we get home you're spending the night in the guest bedroom..."

George screams out, "Shut the Hell up Dawn, you're not my mother." He looks over at Dawn and says to her with eyes on fire, "But you're just as bad as that bitch."

Dawn looks at George without knowing what to say, "George calm down and watch the road, it's beginning to get dangerous out there."

George laughs out loud harshly, "Dangerous? I'll show you dangerous." Then George stomps on the gas pedal.

George's car slides out of control and into the other lane, where a car happens to be coming up the road at them. Some how George pulls their car back to their lane just in time saving them from a head on collision.

Dawn scared out of her mind yells at George to slow down. George looks over at Dawn and tells her, "I don't love you anymore Dawn." Then George stomps back down on his gas pedal even harder.

"Stop! Slow down! Stop!" Dawn continues to scream at George as he drives faster and faster down the road. Dawn is crying as George steers their car off the road and straight into a huge tree that is standing all alone.

The sound of George and Dawn's car hitting the tree is as loud as the thunder in the sky. When the smoke clears George and Dawn are dead and their car is totaled beyond repair. The last words George and Dawn said to the other was, I hate you.

The next morning, the storm is over and the sky is sunny as Rex makes his way to work at Katie's Bloodstain Record Shop. Rex has his window rolled down all the way with his car stereo jamming Heavy Metal for the world to hear and hate.

Rex's and Katie's day goes on without any drama and Rex is very glad for it. Rex hears a couple of costumers talk about a fatal car crash that happened last night during the storm but Rex does not ask who or where.

That same day the lives of two other people are going much differently. Edna cries in Mike's arms as they are told the horrible news about the car crash that happened last night, that took the lives of their only son George and his wife and their daughter-in-law Dawn.

After the police leave Edna tells her husband of many years what she did the night before.

How the accident of George and Dawn was all her fault. Mike listens to every crying word Edna tells him with ice flowing in his veins. After Edna is through with her story, she takes a pill and goes to their bedroom to lay down, her pounding head. Mike on the other hand pours himself a scotch and drinks it down fast not paying any attention to the burning it causes his dry throat.

The next day Rex and Katie are all alone in the shop, talking about the great future they see the shop will bring them in the near future.

The door opens up and the bell rings as Mike of Big Mike's Furniture Store comes walking into Katie's Bloodstained Record Shop with shotgun in hand.

Katie looks at Mike with his big shotgun and says to him that they are closed for the day. Rex turns around to see who Katie is talking to and sees Mike and his shotgun.

Rex stands up and begins to talk to Mike calmly, "Mike you don't want to do this, it is all over between me and Dawn."

Mike clears his dry throat and says in response to Rex, "Fuck that bitch, this about my son."

"What about George?" Rex demands to know.

"Don't you dare say my son's name you sorry bastard. He's dead, my son is dead and it is all your fault."

Rex says to Mike, "George is dead? How? What happened to him?"

Mike looks at Rex like he is dead already and says to him, "You Rex, you are what happened to George. George must have went crazy about the fact that you were fucking his horrible wife. He drove off the road and straight into a tree killing himself and that slut Dawn, after leaving your house two days ago."

Rex clears his now very dry throat and says, "I'm sorry Mike, I did not know..."

Big Mike cuts off Rex with, "Save your sorry you piece of shit for it will do you no good. Rex you are a dead man."

Rex tries to run to the storage room to hide but Mike is too fast with his shotgun as he pulls the trigger of it without a second thought.

Katie watches as Rex starts to run away from her to being shot to death ten feet away from where she is standing. Katie looks over at a smiling big time Mike and watches as he lowers his shotgun to where it's pointing towards the floor and away from her general direction.

Mike turns around and heads for the door as Katie calls out to him, "Wait a minute Mike. Can you do me a favor before you leave and go to jail for killing Rex?"

Mike turns around and looks at Katie like she is out of her mind, "What the Hell kinda of favor could you possibly want from me young lady?"

Katie asks Mike, "Can you sign Rex's shirt before you leave. I could probably get ten thousand dollars for it."

Mike still full of anger tells Katie to go fuck herself and walks out the door and out of Katie's life forever.

Katie walks over to Rex and starts dancing around his dead body with her eyes fully opened up wide. Katie waits an hour and then she calls the police.

One month later Katie has a grand reopening sale, with two different bloodstains dried on her floor for her customers to see and take pictures of

Mr. Death And Mr. Rancy

Knock, Knock. "Yeah, what do you want?"

"Hello Mr. Rancy, I am Death. I am here to talk to you for awhile, you know kick back, have some beers, perhaps some laughs, who knows, anything is possible. Save for one thing. No need to ask me Mr. Rancy, I am willing to tell you, this one thing is a deal not for your life. No, Mr. Rancy. This deal concerns your Soul!"

"Mr. Death is it, yeah I'd like to talk and all but I don't have any beers to offer you. And even if I did you Freak! I would not drink them with you. So fuck off. And have a great freaking day, Mr. Death."

"Wish I could Mr. Rancy. I am Death, well one of them anyway. So sad, Mr. Rancy, I no longer get to fuck, even myself."

Mr. Rancy, who is a real fuck up, tries to close the door. In reality, he did close the door with Death on the other side, but doors do not stop Deaths, they can walk through Mountains and on Water. Death has no boundaries, only the certainty of time. Mr. Rancy closed the door and went to go sit back on his crappy couch, in his even crappier apartment.

Just six steps behind him, Death followed, walking straight through the closed and lock door, in all its Death. Death was fully dressed out in a large black cloak, with a ten foot tall sickle in its hand, and best of all, the blade was covered thick with the blood of those that were marked for death.

Rancy screams, "Please, please, no I don't want to Die!"

Death says, "You don't want to die tonight?"

"No, I don't. I want to live. I have so many things I want to do. I'm too young. I'm too..."

"Mr Rancy. Shut the Hell up, you sniveling, waste of my time. I am Death, your death, no way around that Mr Rancy."

"Excuse me Mr. Death. I would like to accept your offer to drink some beers with you. Yes, that sounds like the best thing ever right now. I tell you what Mr. Death. Just have a seat and I'll go grab some beers, I won't be longer than ten minutes or so...

Just relax, put your feet up, read a magazine. Under the couch is some hot and wild sexy magazines, if you're interested? Oh Shit! I didn't mean to bring up that you can't have sex. I wasn't thinking. You're a eunuch. Mr. Death, Man, I am sorry, please forgive me. I'll be right back."

Death says, "Sit your stupid ass down on that couch, you babbling twit. I am not a eunuch, you moron. Here I'll prove it, look at my dead prick. Well never mind, but I tell you what and that's for damn sure. I am hung like a God, if you know what I mean. Now sit your dumb ass down and shut up..."

"I am your Death. However Mr. Rancy, your death day is not on this day. No, your death day is thirty days from this day."

"Thirty days?"

"Yes Mr. Rancy, in thirty days."

"Why are you here tonight then? Is this some kind of warning I'm getting? If I change my life, I'll get to go to Heaven?"

81

"You are dumber than you look, aren't you Mr Rancy? Hang on a second."

Death laughs his ass off while a confused Mr. Rancy looks at Death in horror.

Death says with tears in his eyes, "Heaven is out of your reach. Hell will be your home. Unless you listen very carefully to what I have to say and do exactly as I say. Then Mr. Rancy, you might just save your soul from going to Hell and straight to Heaven."

"I'll do whatever you say Mr. Death, just save my soul from burning. Wait a minute. Man this ain't right. Death? I've been drugged. You're not real, just an Hallucination from whatever drugs are in my brain telling my mind that you are real because, because, I am a half bad person. That's right, but at the same time I am a half good person...

I got it! It's that way deep down in the cobwebs of my mind, I feel that Hell is one step away from my soul, with Heaven two or three steps away from that same soul that is scared to be tortured for all eternity in Hell. I won my mind battle, you are purged from my mind, I am now free to enjoy my buzz. Now 1-2-3, fuck off Mr. Death."

"Mr. Rancy, damn man, what a theory you have thought up. Have to say I like the ending with myself being purged from your mind. 1-2-3, living dumb ass. Can't you see? I'm still here for your wanting red eyes to see. Red due to drugs. Mr. Rancy, your eyes are blood shot, your brain feels like it is being squeezed tightly by your skull. Your blood has turned to ice while your muscles are tightening up making you feel that if you stretched them out fully they would snap, due to deterioration...

It may feel like a drug is going through your brain to you. For anything I know, you wish this to be true. Druggish as it may seem to you, I am happy to say to you.

I am Death, your Death, I will take your soul when you die in thirty days...

Listen very clearly, fool. I am to take your soul to Hell. But if you do what I say I will take your soul to Heaven instead. I am tired of telling you this, it's getting boring. Maybe I made a mistake in choosing you. There are so many men that are going to die the same day you will be dying all over Earth to choose from. I think it is for the best to say goodbye, and watch you die it thirty days."

"No! Please Mr. Death! I believe you now, you are Death. Just tell me what you want me to do and I'll get right on it."

"That easy, just like that? All the babbling I've had to endure. Mr Rancy you are a pain in my afterlife. No, you are too much trouble."

"Mr. Death, what do you want? What will it take, to make you change your mind?"

"I don't know? Well maybe? Alright, Mr. Rancy. Stand up, walk over to me, then stop when you are within arms' length of me."

Mr. Rancy, gets up shaking like a leaf, Death scares the life out of him. In his mind, Mr. Rancy is saying to himself, "I don't want to go to Hell."

"Stop. That's perfect, right where you are standing. Anything, Mr Rancy?"

"Anything, Mr. Death!"

"Okay then, this is for myself as well for you Mr. Rancy. I want you to truly believe that I am Death and my words are as true as your forth coming death day. This is going to be great. I've been wanting to do this to you ever since you answered your door to me the way you did.

What a prick you are Mr Rancy. And it's mostly why you are going to Hell. There are no pricks in Heaven."

Mr. Rancy is looking at Death, when Death says, "Take this you prick," and punches Mr. Rancy in his nose and mouth at the same time. Without warning blood bursts from Mr. Rancy's nose like an explosion. At the same time Mr. Rancy's four front teeth are knocked out by their roots and go flying down his throat.

Pain and darkness is what Mr. Rancy feels and sees, as he hears the words that Death is saying to him like they are coming to his ears from a mile away.

"Damn that felt good! Would you like another? It has been awhile since I've had blood on my hands, Mr. Rancy. And not dead blood but living blood, man does it look so for real on my hand. Compared to living blood, dead blood is almost lifeless in color and brilliance. Dead Blood? What is dead blood? You ask me with your eyes, for your mouth can not speak, for it looks like a bloody mush of tremendous pain and agony...

Remember this pain, remember this fear of I. For if you fuck with me or fuck up, I'll leave some of your soul in your dead body, there it will stay away from you, rotting for eternity. While the rest of your soul will be in Hell, wishing that the part of your soul that was ripped away from the whole was there to help you endure the constant, never ending pain, that will be your afterlife." Death stops speaking and looks at Mr. Rancy, like he is nothing to him, but a tool. This makes Death feel good.

"If anything else happens except exactly as I command from you... Mr. Rancy, look here on my sickle. Look at the blood stains. That is dead blood in all its dead glory. Are you curious, Mr. Rancy as to how my sickle has gotten so thickly covered in dead blood?"

"No Mr. Death. I think I know."

Mr. Rancy puts his hand towards Death's sickle, wanting to touch the dead blood that is stained on it. Death with a quick slap to Mr. Rancy's hand sends it flying back away from harm to the touch.

"Dead blood is not to be touched by the living, nor for living human eyes. It really messes with their minds."

"My eyes are living human eyes."

"Don't worry about your mind, you have only thirty more days to live until you die. Compared to death what is some dead blood to you, Mr. Rancy? Still don't touch it."

"I have no desire to touch dead blood, Mr. Death. Thirty days? This cannot be. I don't want to die. Why do I have to die? Why can't I live forever?"

"It is so simple, it is so beautiful, Mr. Rancy. Death, when it happens I am there or another just like me. When a person dies, human eyes see only a dead body. What they don't see is me ripping open that same dead body from throat to crotch to free the soul from its human body so it can be lead by myself to its final destination...

One slice from my sickle and all the dead blood that occupies that dead body comes pouring out like a river of dull redness, that stains heavily all that it touches. That stain is forever. Whoever has been close to someone that has died has the permanent stain of dead blood on their body, face or both. That is why the living must never know about dead blood, Mr. Rancy, for if it ever came to life to their eyes. Dead blood soaking the Earth is all their terror stricken eyes will see everywhere."

Death walks over to a corner and places his sickle against the wall. "Mr. Rancy I will tell you a tale of betrayal, of my wife and best friend, that landed me this job of being death until time served.

85

Only then will I be able to feel the light and warmth of Heaven on my soul. So yes, just like life, afterlife is not fair as well."

Death pauses with a sad look on his face as he repeats, "Afterlife is not fair."

"Fifty years ago I married the girl of my dreams. We were both so young, in love with each other and ready for what life had to offer us. Well at least we thought we were ready. Life can give you shelter on a rainy day or it can make you get stuck out in it with no chance of escape from the flooding waters that will drown you as soon as they catch up with you, no matter how high you climb up to try to reach safety."

"Our first years of marriage, we both worked hard at two jobs each just to get by. I went back to college after dropping out to get married. We both knew deep in our hearts that if we wanted the better life we dreamed about, education was that answer to it. I studied real hard, graduating with honors. After graduation, I searched for the perfect job to start my sky rocket to success for the career I was destined to have.

I met old man Smiley who owned a marketing firm. The only thing that Mr. Smiley wanted was for his son to take over and run his business after he retired. The only problem was, his son Peter was an Idiot. So with time and hard work, I put myself right in the position to take the reigns away from idiot Peter and right into my deserving hands," Death rubs his hands together slowly.

"At first it was a dream come true, I took to the workings of marketing, like second nature. Old man Smiley loved me, bless his trusting soul."

"When I started, the most important thing I felt I needed to do was to learn and learn even more.

Become the one that even the highest in the company came to for whatever they needed. I was the man, my mind a sponge and my wallet was getting thicker with lovely bills of green."

"I admit it. I changed. How could I not? My wife Emily told me more than once that evil had made contact with my eyes and soul. Women. Like I would not remember her saying that to me, for her to repeat it more than once. Emily was so beautiful, making love to her a most every night was what I looked forward to most of every day. She was hot, I mean hot. Emily had this philosophy, as long as it was with her, never with anyone else, she would let me do whatever I wanted.

I enjoyed myself. When Emily left me, the first thing I thought to myself was, How the Hell am I going to find a woman willing to come over and screw me every night? Yes, I was addicted to sex. When she left, I thought I was going to explode from not having sex.

I even called her a few times for some very needed sexual release, hoping she would be the friend I also married and not just the woman that I loved with all my heart. Third time was a charm. I called her, she said enough. If I promised to never ask her again, she would grant me a favor by letting me get off properly."

"That was the last time I saw and laid Emily. Her and ass face took off a little bit after that, to go live in the woods somewhere, like woods people. I know the reason, the real reason that is, why she left our town after already being divorced from me for three months.

When she came over to my place for that last time, Emily felt like she was untouched for awhile. After three hours of doing whatever I wanted with her, she knew no matter how evil she thought I had become, no one would ever get her going and going like I could.

87

She did call me two days after our encounter, blaming me for the feelings that were going through her mind. I loved my power when I told her that I did not want her back as a lover and that the last night of sex we shared together told me that sex was the only thing that I would be interested in from her again.

I tried not to laugh my ass off when I asked her how that sounded. Emily got pissed off at me, hung up on me, then took off with her little prick lover, running away as far as possible from my manhood. She feared it making her willing to become my 'when I have the time for her plaything'."

"One day out of nowhere, Emily told me that she had fallen out of love with me, all because my best friend came around one night looking for me. I was not there, they talked. Then he came back again and again."

"This I never knew. I came home, I had my dinner, I had my sex, I went to sleep, woke up and repeated every day the same way with the love of my life, my wife, who in a little while would be the wife of the owner of the company, as soon as Mr. Smiley died. This she did not know. For me at least, this was a good thing. Because she divorced me before this plan of mine came to life."

"She told me that the money I craved did not mean anything to her anymore, she wanted freedom and love. The love that I did not show her anymore. Emily said she did not want money but that did not stop her from wanting more than a cheating whore like her deserved. In the end, Mr. Smiley was getting sicker and I felt it best to get it over with, so we talked things through.

She got more than I wanted her to have but it was worth it to have her out of my life. The way I see it Mr. Rancy. Karma had a play in things. She screwed up my life, divorced me, then we screwed one more time.

88

And by doing so I screwed up her perfect life full of love and freedom, with the return of wanting to have perfect sex with the man that use to love her and was now only interested in screwing her." Death is silent for a moment.

"Where was I? Yes I was the man. Mr. Smiley was almost like the father I never had. It became all too clear to me, when Mr. Smiley asked me for a favor, his words, and he would be so very grateful, that I would want for nothing, being second in charge after his son, the idiot. I saw my life flash in my mind, his idiot son would bring the company down, while I drank and smoked myself to death, trying my best to hold on to any of the life the company still had.

I said fuck that. Fifteen minutes after the meeting between the three of us, I must have said beep it in my mind about fifty times. In my mind I had no choice at all. I owed Mr. Smiley for my chance. It would be better if the company was owned by me, the son he perhaps deep down wished was his true son and that the son that was his could have been me, coming to him for a job. A job that he would have never given to him."

"Okay I was stretching, giving myself the answer I wanted. If nothing else, I felt that from the grave, Mr. Smiley would smile, knowing that his company was alive and doing fine. Even better. May-hap in death he would get the closure that he never had in life, that his son was a fuck up and it was not his fault. Three days after Mr. Smiley's funeral. I set my plan into action. Well phase two of it."

"In my favor at the end, I persuaded Mr. Smiley to sign some papers, giving me the power I needed, so that idiot son would not have the all the power he thought he would be gaining after the reading of the will. Idiot son flipped his lid after hearing that he was not in total control. That we were fifty/fifty partners. Idiot son had to be restrained and heavily medicated. My plan was ready to start to take effect with the slow down fall of idiot son's part of the company coming slowly into my waiting hands.

89

Then I found out that idiot son loved doing drugs and gambling, he owed a lot of money to some really bad people. With the great big heart in my chest, I had idiot son released from the hospital. I told him that I would pay off his debt, give him some spending money for some more drugs and gambling, if and only if he would sign his half of the company over to me. Six months later stocks in my company doubled, while idiot son's body was laid to rest beside his father's."

"Some years later I found out where my ex was living, I hired some men to burn down their cabin in the woods. Dumb asses burned it down but with Emily inside it. What a horrible mistake I made. They got caught and turned on me. I went to jail and got shanked in the shower and died. This is how I got my gig as Death. Lucky for me, in Heaven and to God, pointing at someone and telling someone else to shoot them is different than pulling the trigger yourself."

"I am getting to the end of my tale and where you will come into the story Mr. Rancy. Ass face is still alive, he is old as shit and dying. I know you are not intelligent enough Mr. Rancy to guess when his death day is coming up for yourself. So I will help you out with the answer. That's correct Mr. Rancy in thirty days the same as with you. Ass face, can you believe it he is scheduled to go to Heaven? If anyone should go to Hell it is ass face. That way him and Emily can be together forever."

"It is so simple of a plan, Mr. Rancy. All you have to do is be at the time of death of ass face, holding on to dear life with the help of yours truly. When ass face dies I'll slice his soul out of his dead body and hide it really quick in my cloak. And then I will let go of the power I am giving you. You then will die, I will then slice your soul out of your dead body and switch the places of your souls in my cloak. His soul will be placed on the side that is for souls that are destined for Hell.

While your soul that is meant for Hell, I will put it in the side of my cloak that is for souls that are destined for Heaven."

"There will be so much dead blood everywhere. I don't think even if God is watching me, he would be able to tell what I am doing until it is too late to change things. For I will take ass face's soul to Hell before I take yours to Heaven. Is that a plan or what Mr. Rancy? Don't answer me just nod your head if your in." Mr. Rancy nods his head yes. Death gives him the time and the address of when and where he needs to be to make this happen. Death then takes his leave, while Mr. Rancy tends to his bleeding and hurting face.

The last 29 Days of Mr. Rancy's life and his life history:
Mr. Rancy the fuck up's last twenty nine days were not as grand as he hoped they would be. Mr. Rancy drank a lot of whiskey and he smoked a lot of weed, which cost him almost all his money. Money he would need if he stood any chance of getting laid. Mr. Rancy had to pay for it because when the ladies looked past his mushed up face to his body, they stopped him and told him, before he could get an erection, that they demanded more money up front first because of his ickyness.

Damn what a beeped up life Mr. Rancy lived. He's the kinda guy you look at and would not be surprised if told, that he liked to put his hand down his pants, then smell his finger tips. You know a real nasty looking man, that was hardly ever treated nice, life kicked him in his ass and face. The time of his life portrays to the world that he does not wear time well.

When he was five, Mr. Rancy heard his father say to his mother that she was a dirty whore, because no boy that looked like him could ever be the son from his loins. His mother got mad, threw everything that was in the kitchen at his father, whacking him a few good times making his forehead bleed pretty damn good.

When his mother ran out of things to throw, she looked at his father with rage in her eyes. His father wiped some blood off his forehead and said, "Fuck you, you crazy cheating whore, I'm out of here. Raise your ugly as fucking Hell bastard on your own."

This, not a surprise to anyone, really messed with Mr. Rancy's mind. He grew up believing he was ugly as Hell and he was a bastard. He believed every word his gone and not his father, said to his mother. When Mr. Rancy was thirteen he demanded to know the name of his real father from his mother. His mother looked at him and for the first time really saw what everyone else had seen since his birth. His mother cursed his birth, saying that the son of a bitch that had left them without any money was his true father.

Then went on to say that his father must have laid with some whore the night before they created him together, for the Devil must have been inside his flesh that horrible night. There could be no other answer, because her eyes could see now what the Devil had hidden from them since his birth, that he is as ugly as sin.

Mr. Rancy's mother then like a half good mother, went upstairs to his bedroom and packed his backpack with clothes, added a couple of books then went into the bathroom and added his toiletries to the backpack. She came back downstairs with it all nicely zipped up in her hands. Mr. Rancy's emotionless mother handed him his backpack and told him to go sit on the couch.

She then proceeded to walk into the kitchen and fix a meal like it was a lunch for school, paper bag and all. Still emotionless, Mr. Rancy's mother walked him to their car, made him get in and buckle up. Then his mother got in and started the car, backed out of their driveway, put the car in drive, then pressed on the gas pedal and started their car ride that would last until dawn.

"Wake up, wake up, Wilbert. You are made from sin, Wilbert. You are evil created by the Devil himself. For God, Heaven and Earth, I should smite you dead and bury you face down in a hole so your father Satan can look at your rotting face. You are so lucky, Wilbert that I am too faithful towards God to let your tainted by evil blood get on my hands. I can no longer love you.

Right now, I think I never did. That is one more thing Satan must have put inside my mind. A false love of you to make me feel like you deserve to be loved. Look at that bench over there, a bus will be by to pick you up sooner or later. Give the bus driver half of this money, tell them to take you as far as that will take you...

When your bus ride is over, get out and live the rest of your evil life alone until you die and go to Hell to be returned to your father Satan. Now get the Hell out of my car. Maybe since I've finally gotten rid of you my husband will come back to me and we can restart our lives together the way God wanted our lives to be. Peaceful, loving and without evil in them to turn our souls towards Hell."

Wilbert Rancy got out of his mother's car at the age of thirteen. He never saw her again or looked for her. The first night by himself he crouched next to the back of a diner's wall crying himself to sleep, trying to stay dry from the pouring down rain.

He stuck around the diner a couple of days until he ran out of money. He then put his best foot forward, walked to the roadside and stuck out his thumb. Hours went by, some cars stopped but as soon as the drivers looked at Wilbert's face they stomped on the gas pedal before Wilbert could ask them for a ride.

With tired feet, a thirsty mouth, an empty stomach and a shaking hand, Wilbert put out his thumb one more time, knowing that if this truck coming towards him did not stop to give him a ride he was going to be in serious trouble.

93

Mr. and Mrs. Whitestone were driving down the road towards their home in silence with tears and dry tears in their eyes. They were just making their way back from the graveyard. Today was the funeral of their son Johnny, he was thirteen years old, he died three days ago.

Johnny scratched his leg while playing in the woods, he left it alone and it got infected. Four days later the Whitestones were driving to the doctor's office, singing along to the songs playing on the radio. Sunny, happy day, happy family, everything was perfect except for one small scratch that had gotten infected.

The car was parked and the family got out of the car, Johnny walked away not paying attention, complaining about the painful scratch on his leg. He stopped and bent over, rubbing the painful scratch, right in the middle of the rear end of a parked car's parking spot. The driver of this car was in shock, he had just been told by the same doctor that Johnny would have seen, that he had maybe a year to live before the cancer he had would take his life.

A fit of anger made this dying driver scream out with rage, "Why me? Why me? Why me?", while he started his car, he put it in reverse and stomped on its gas pedal like he was cursing God for the news of his death. Johnny heard the car start up, said, "Oh Shit." Too dead late. The speeding in reverse car, in a instant smashed into Johnny's head, face and body knocking him to the ground.

The car kept going in reverse faster and faster, then turned towards the left, dragging a dying Johnny along with it. The car finally stopped, the Whitestones screamed together in horror. Horror had paused, horror was about to restart its final act in the play of life. A play that has been around since life began on Earth. With a revved up engine the car flew straight forward towards the main road.

There was a dip in the parking lot where the road matched up with it, the speeding car slammed down on that dip hard, hard enough to smash Johnny flat. Johnny was left lying in that dip, while the car sped away and with his blood squirting out of the deep wounds in his almost dead body. Too many wounds to count, and without enough time for help due to the shear bloody number of them all. The driver of the car was eventually stopped and arrested. He lived another eight years in prison for manslaughter, then three months later he died from his returning cancer.

So sad this tale's ending, Death sliced out Johnny's soul allowing his dead blood to flow free. It mixed with his life's blood, to make a stain that was so horrific and beautiful at the same time, shining so brightly in the early summer morning's sunlight. Death even noticed this and told his fellow Deaths when he caught up with some of them and had the time for a chat.

This Death's description of the mixed together blood stains did not match the brilliance of its effect on the eye and mind.

When the Whitestone's truck passed by a very disappointed Wilbert, Mrs. Whitestone shouted for Mr. Whitestone to stop their truck. Mrs. Whitestone got out of their truck where it stopped, with hopeful tears in her eyes she ran towards Wilbert, hoping with all her heart that he was her son Johnny and today was just some big mistake. Wilbert was so exhausted from standing there for hours that all he could do was watch as Mrs. Whitestone came running up to him shouting the name Johnny.

"You're not my Johnny, how could I think you were? Out of the corner of my eye I saw my Johnny standing here as you. But my Johnny is dead and I know that to be painfully true now." Mrs. Whitestone fell to her knees and cried a river on top of Wilbert's shoes.

Mr. Whitestone walked up slowly with tears in his eyes and said to Wilbert, "Sorry son my wife's mind is full of sorrow, we just came from the funeral of our son Johnny, he was only thirteen years old, so young and so full of life."

Wilbert with tears in his eyes said, "That's okay, I don't mind. It is nice to see parents that love their son, I am sorry for your loss. I tell you what, I'll just walk along so you can have time alone with your wife." Wilbert starts walking away, when Mrs. Whitestone tells Mr. Whitestone to stop Wilbert from walking away from them.

"Son stop a minute. What is your name?"

"I am Wilbert."

"Where are you going? Are you traveling home to your family?"

"No, I have no family, I have no home. I am all alone."

"I am sorry to hear that son. How old are you?"

"I am thirteen years old going on well, hopefully fourteen."

"Oh Charles, did you hear that? Can you believe it? This is a miracle come to life for us. We no longer have a son and this lost lonely boy has no family or home. He is the same height with the same eye and hair color as our Johnny. God has given us a gift Charles. Wilbert, God has given all three of us a gift. Please Wilbert, would you like to come home with us? We want you to be our new son. Everything you could possibly need or want will be in your new bedroom. Please say yes Wilbert? If it's alright with you Wilbert can I call you Johnny?"

Wilbert's mind is going a million miles an hour, wondering to himself if he can do this. Then says to himself jokingly - At least they lost a son and not a daughter.

"Yes, Mrs. Whitestone, I would love to come home with you to live with you like a family. And I would be honored if you would call me Johnny."

"Call me mom, Johnny and Charles here, call him dad."

Charles looks back and forth between his wife and Wilbert. Wondering to himself if he should stop this now because of what the torment of losing another son would do to his wife.

He is about to do just that when Tiffany looks at him and says, "Charles can you believe it? Now we don't have to pack all of Johnny's room away in boxes, because our new Johnny will be there to enjoy and use everything. Charles we are so blessed. Come on you two let's get in the truck and go home, I have a giant dinner to cook us. Oh rats I have nothing laid out to cook. Well I tell you both what, let's go inside this diner and have some lunch together as one new and happy family. What do you like to eat Johnny?"

"I like to eat everything, mom. I am so hungry now mom, I could eat a horse."

"Oh Johnny, I never get tired of you saying that. Remember Johnny how you have said that same thing to me so many times over the years? Charles the two of us are going to grab a table, you go park the truck and then join us. This is going to be the best lunch ever, I just know it. Do you believe that Johnny?"

"Yes I do mom."

"I love you Johnny."

"I love you too mom. Let's go eat, I want a rare steak, some fries and skip the salad."

97

"No, no, no, young man, you will eat your salad and you will eat it first or you have no dessert, it's all up to you."

"Mom?" / "Yes Johnny?"

"I love you mom, thank you for caring about me, it feels like years since I've felt any kind of love."

"I know what you are saying is true in my mind, but in my heart, I feel like I've loved you for years. Johnny you are such a handsome young man. I guess I will have to do my best to keep all the girls away from you. Lord does my work ever end? I just buried you and now I have to make sure you don't sin anymore."

"Mom are you alright?" Wilbert reaches out and grabs a hold of Tiffany's arm with concern.

"Am I losing my mind? Every look at you, I see Johnny more and more. Are you my Johnny reincarnated in this other young man's flesh? Do I ask too much? Or just enough?"

Wilbert, older in mind than body, thinks very fast, on the perfect thing to say to Mrs. Whitestone. "Mom, you are my mom. Well in fact you are mother to one of the many reincarnated, young men of this earth. All of them live within me in unity...

No sorrow, no pain, just another way of life to live, where they are never alone and loved for who they are, not how they died. All souls that live within me are souls of the young men who have died, like your son Johnny, in an accident. Or by no accident at all, souls of those that have been murdered. Mrs. Whitestone, I am a Soul-Carrier, I absorb and keep safe souls that are tainted by fear until Heaven tells me to bring them home."

"On my face and body are their death wounds that they carry with them to their afterlife.

I heal their wounds by providing love and security. When their wounds have turned to faded scars, their time for Heaven is upon them like a long dream finally becoming true."

"Mrs. Whitestone, I am tired, I need a vacation away from all the pain I feel. I will go away for awhile, leaving your son Johnny in lead place over my body. Lead place, Mrs. Whitestone, is not in total control. Johnny will still have thousands of other souls to be in charge of.

Time has no meaning for me, not so for you. You have to believe in your heart and soul that who you see and feel to be real to you is your dead son Johnny. If you don't believe that always, Mrs. Whitestone, I will have no choice but to take back over and leave you all alone without your son, to go find somebody else to take your place. Can you do that Mrs. Whitestone? Can you always believe, even if what you see and feel sometimes is not your son?"

"Yes I can. Please give me back my son, Soul-Carrier."

"Swear to me then, that this gift I give to you, is worth more to you than your very own soul. Even the soul of your husband."

"Yes, yes, I swear to you, Soul-Carrier, Johnny is the only thing in this world that means anything to me."

"Enjoy your extra time with your son Mrs. Whitestone, you are truly blessed this day."

"Yes, I know and thank you Soul-Carrier."

"One more thing Mrs. Whitestone. Never say a word of this to Charles, his heart and soul are not as pure as yours. By being this way, Charles will try his best to convince you that what you see and feel are nothing but lies.

If you let Charles get in your mind, then he will win and your heart and soul will turn away from believing that I am your son. Let that happen, Mrs. Whitestone and I will take your son away from you."

Five years later, due to a random burglary, Mr. and Mrs. Whitestone are killed and Wilbert who was not their son, inherited everything. A few years later due to gambling and drugs, Wilbert lost everything. Wilbert went on to cheat, steal, lie and kill his way through life, which is the reason that his soul is destined for Hell.

During the same twenty nine day period, Death did his job. Like a reaper he sliced open dead body after body from throat to crotch taking those souls to Heaven or Hell. His demeanor did not change. No other Death knew of his plan. As far as the universe was concerned everything was above board just as usual. Death counted the days off in his mind with great resolve, feeling deep in his soul that this same universe owed him this much.

Day thirty, ass face, whose real name is Paul Winder, feels like today is going to be the last day of his long and almost happy life. He is ready for death so his soul can fly free to Heaven. He is ready for this constant pain of being old to end. Not knowing if it is for real or in his mind, Mr. Winder has seen a dark shadow out of the corner of his eyes since he woke up for his morning medication.

As the day grows longer, certainty comes to his mind that Death is going to call on him today, probably when it turns to night and when he is all alone.

Wilbert Rancy wakes up on his last day to live, feeling like there is nothing wrong with him enough to make him die today. He thinks to himself that Death is fucking with him. Maybe Death just told him that he was going to die today so he could have someone in the waiting who is fresh and ready, that is going to Hell after they die anyway, so Death can finally have his revenge on ass face.

100

Then again, he thinks, maybe Death is messing with me but since he wants revenge on ass face, I get to go to Heaven instead of Hell. If Death didn't want revenge, Death would not be giving me this chance at Heaven.

Wilbert out loud to himself, "What should I do? I don't want to die. Maybe if I don't show up I don't have to die. But if I don't die today and die another day, well then my soul goes to Hell. This is not fair. So I did things I'm not proud of but it's not like I had any choice in what I had to do.

The world has shit on me since day one. My mother and father, what a couple of fucked up people they were. I don't feel like I was born from them, but rather that I was shit out of them, because life that is how they treated me. The Whitestones, wherever you are, I am sorry. If I could go back in time, I would have hugged you, let you take me in with the understanding that I was not your dead son come back to life...

I would have stayed maybe a week or two, then I would have taken off, leaving you alone to live your lives without me and my greed for a better life. Maybe if that would have happened, my whole life would have changed and I would not need Death to sneak me into Heaven instead of throwing me head first into Hell."

"Don't count on that thought, Mr Rancy. You are just one of those souls that was born evil. Hell was always to be your home. That is why I chose you. Your hell bound soul is my middle finger to Heaven and God for letting Ass face walk into Heaven just like that after what he did to me.

He was my friend and he betrayed me by calling on my wife many times. And me, I have to be Death for five hundred years. That Mr. Rancy, is not fair. I was made for Heaven until ass face and my so called wife, fucked with my life and made me become a soul that has to wait five hundred years before I get to go to Heaven."

"So yes you are correct, Mr. Rancy, I lied to you. You don't have to die today, you can wait three more days and be shot in your stupid head for trying to rob a liquor store with a gun that has no bullets in it. And then of course your soul goes to Hell!"

"So what's it going to be, Mr. Rancy? Today or in three days? Like I said, don't let those thoughts you were thinking out loud make you change your mind. Do the right thing for your soul."

"Okay Mr. Death you got me, today it is, the day I die."

"Don't be so melodramatic, Mr. Rancy, your life is not that big of a deal, as far as Heaven and God is concerned you're just a mistake that has finally gotten erased. So your answer is yes. Mr. Rancy, you're not going to back out at the last minute like a coward, are you?"

"No I will not back out, Mr. Death. And as far as I am concerned, I cannot wait to be away from you and this shitty life I was forced to live."

"Make sure your answer stays yes, Mr. Rancy. If you fuck with me, remember what I said about leaving a piece of your soul in your dead body? Well if you change your mind, I will now leave an even bigger part of your soul behind in your dead body. Got it?"

"I got it Mr. Death, I'll be there, now fuck off you asshole, I want some time to myself. I deserve at least that don't I, Mr. Death?"

"You deserve nothing, Mr. Rancy, but have your needed time, it matters to me not."

Death leaves by walking through the wall. When he is gone, Wilbert gives his absence the middle finger in defiance.

102

Wilbert heads to his kitchen to crack the seal on the last quart of whiskey he has left to his name. Bottle opened very fast and drank even faster. Bam! "What the Hell? Who's there? Mr. Death is that you coming back to check on me? Don't worry this bottle of whiskey don't mean a thing, just think of it as medicine. Mr. Death?" Wilbert walks back into his living room, sees someone and says, "Who the Hell are you? You're not my Death!"

Death waits outside of Paul Winder's nursing home for a running late Mr. Rancy. Death is pissed. "Mr. Rancy you ass head, I will rip your soul into shreds for your betrayal. I will torture your soul so much, after I am done with you Hell will feel like Heaven to you. You, you, ass head you!

Damn it to Hell, please no! I don't want to take ass face to Heaven, I hate him so very damn much. Well if nothing else, for me, just for spite, I'm going to cut off ass face's prick with my sickle before I slice out his soul.

Damn it, damn it, Mr. Rancy, you better get your ass here right now! My plan was perfect. What a dumb ass you are Mr. Rancy, I hope you enjoy Hell. No I don't, I want you to hate it" Out of the dark fog walks Wilbert Rancy.

"Here I am Mr. Death. (hiccup) kiss my ass, you sorry bastard (hiccup)."

"Are you drunk, you dumb ass?"

"No I am not drunk, Mr. Death-Ass-Hole, I'm just fine, I'll do my part. Just don't get on my case, for if you do Mr. Death, you can go fuck yourself (hiccup). You cheating whore. Ha, ha,ha. (hiccup)"

"What? What the fuck, did you just call me?"

"Never mind, it's an inside joke."

103

"Ass head, don't you ever call me a cheating whore again. I am a man damn it, what the fuck's wrong with you?"

"Alright Mr. Death, get off my ass and let's do this damn thing (hiccup). Are you going to give me your help now, Mr Death?"

"What help?"

"The help you said you would give me, that would keep me alive long enough for you to reap ass face (hiccup)."

"You drunk dumb ass. Remember I told you I was lying about you dying today?"

"So I don't need your help staying alive (hiccup)?"

"No, no, no, you dumb ass! Look no more questions, just shut up and follow me. And just in case your drunk mind thinks this over, which I doubt, yes you can see me, but no one else can. So keep your mouth shut or people will think that you are talking to yourself. You understand me you drunk dumb ass."

"I got it Mr. Death. I stay here and shut up while you go to ass face's room and reap him. Correct? (hiccup)"

"No! That is not correct. What? What? I cannot believe this. How many times do I have to tell you, you drunken buffoon? You are to shut up and follow me!"

"Right now?"

"Yes right now! If you don't start walking right now Mr. Rancy, I'm going to stick my sickle up your drunk ass, you got that?!"

"Damn Mr. Death, why don't you go change your panties already? Ha,ha,ha. (hiccup)"

"That's it Mr. Rancy, I'm going to reap you right now!"

"I'm going! I'm going! Damn, Mr. Death you have no sense of humor." Wilbert Rancy takes off like he is on fire, then Death tells him to slow his drunk ass down and wait for him to catch up with him before he enters the nursing home on his own without him.

Fast forward a few, close to almost being caught, minutes later. Death and Mr. Rancy enter Paul Winder's room. Death stops walking and Mr. Rancy walks right into him making Death drop his sickle on the floor, waking up a dying Mr. Winder.

Mr. Winder turns on his light and loudly says, "Who is there? Oh, it's you Mr. Death. I am ready to go to Heaven.

And who it is that you brought along with you? Is he a Mr. Death in training?"

Death says, "What? Just shut up you dying fool. I am not here to take you to Heaven, I am here to take you to Hell. This piece of drunk crap you see here is the one that is going to take your place in Heaven."

Mr. Winder says, "That is not fair. Just look at his face. He looks like he has already been in Hell."

"Kiss my ass, ass face, I get to go to Heaven so eat my shit you old dying bastard."

"Oh yeah?"

"Yeah!"

"Well you can eat my shit and go to Hell because if I'm not going to Heaven, well then, I just won't go. How's that sound to you? You two assholes."

Death picks up his sickle and waves it around the room causing wind forces that blow everything in the room around in the air. "That is enough from both of you! I am Death, both of your Deaths. You both will listen to me. Now shut up and get ready to be reaped very bloodily."

Mr. Winder says to a pissed off Death, "What about God?"

Mr. Rancy says, "What about the Devil?"

"What about them? I'll tell you what about them. They both can go fuck themselves, that's what!" Death raises his sickle into the air and tries to reap Mr. Winder but nothing happens. Death's sickle just bounces off Mr. Winder's body without doing any harm. In shock Death turns around to look at a laughing Mr. Rancy, who no longer looks like Mr. Rancy anymore.

Death takes his sickle and tries to reap whoever is laughing at him and the same thing happens, which is nothing at all.

The stranger stops laughing and says, "How about it God, do you think that he has had enough?" Death turns around and sees the Voice of God standing there all tall and Heavenly.

Then out of the silence the Voice of God speaks God's words out loud, "Mr. Death you have abused your power. You have forfeited your right to go to Heaven. I gave you a chance, a chance you did not deserve. Your former wife Emily begged me to give you one more chance. Now that chance is over with, now you go to Hell. Hand your sickle to my Voice, Mr. Death. You are fired!"

Death hands his sickle and cloak to the Voice of God, looks over at the stranger and says, "I guess you are Satan, the lousy, stinking Devil of Hell, then?"

106

The stranger says to a fired Death, "Yes dumb ass, I'm the Devil of Hell. I am Satan. Don't worry dumb ass you don't have to wait to get to Hell to know your punishment. I am going to stick you head first in the burning pit of shit. There you will stay forevermore. Oh yeah and don't start just shut up, your begging will do you no good. See you later God, glad I could help you out with your death problem."

"Silence Devil and go back to Hell taking your new damned soul with you."

And thus now ends the story of Mr. Death and Mr. Rancy. Where there lies no reason for a sequel. Or is there?

Two Cans Of Peaches

Kevin is walking to a nearby grocery store, named The Store And More, to pick up two cans of peaches. The reason Kevin is footing it to the store is because his car is out of gas. Kevin wishes this to be the truth. In his mind this is what Kevin is telling himself to be as the truth. He wants to calm his mind to the fact that his transmission is shot. This real fact really pisses Kevin off and tonight for at least a few hours of it anyway, Kevin wants to have nothing heavy on his mind when he goes over to one of his girlfriends' house for some hot loving and wild sex.

Becky is built and fine and so is her twin Gloria, who needs two cans of peaches. Kevin on the way to see her and her twin Gloria, said no problem baby. Kevin loves when it's Becky's night, which is Friday night. He gets a two for one, every time. As can be told, Kevin is a man that has sex almost every night. Kevin has four girlfriends that do not like the fact that Kevin has three other girlfriends. They all call the other sluts. Sometimes they even add other words before or after slut. Kevin hears their complaining with only one ear. That way it's a lot easier for him to forget.

Kevin laughs on the inside, when one of his girlfriends tells him that she doesn't know how much more she can stand on how the ways things are. They always sound so serious, while their taking off their clothes. They complain, Kevin pleases them for a little bit, then Kevin gives them what it takes for them to remember why they put up with all of his shit.

Kevin is about to head in the direction of The Store And More, when he spots Willy. The very same Willy who owes him a hundred bucks for the sack of weed he fronted him a week ago. Willy didn't want to pay, Kevin told him that he would kick him in his ass and face. Willy a man that likes his face and ass gave Kevin all he had and that was seventy three dollars.

Poor Willy, he's twenty seven dollars short, "This is not a hundred Willy."

"I know man, I'm short..."

"And don't forget stupid Willy. One week goes by, I don't hear from you. You smoke up my weed and don't come back over to pay me in full. I did you a favor Willy. Now it's time to do yourself a favor."

"What kind of favor Kevin?"

"You see this seventy three dollars I'm holding in my hand Willy?"

"Yes I do. I just gave it to you."

"Don't be a smart ass, stupid Willy. Now like magic Willy I want you to make this seventy three dollars turn into the full one hundred dollars you owe me."

"How can I do that Kevin?"

"By thinking really hard how you can come up with it really fast. I haven't much time. In a little bit I need to be someplace for a night full of hot sex."

"Kevin, man I'm tapped out. You have to wait until next week. I promise, you'll get the rest of your money."

"Nope stupid Willy. I want my money now. Tell you what Willy, go grab something from your place you can pawn at a pawn shop. See how great it is when you're not stupid. Now get going. No fuck that I want my twenty seven dollars plus fifty more."

Willy starts to walk away and Kevin stops him, "What? Like I'm just going to wait here for you to get back. Damn your stupid is showing Willy."

"Kevin, man you don't have to be so mean."

"Mean? Mean would be me kicking you're ass all the way to your place. You ripped me off. Your lucky I choose to think that you forgot to pay me, instead of thinking you just said fuck it, I ain't paying him."

"It's not like that."

"Which way?"

"Neither. No both."

"Well that's really good for you Willy. Still get your stupid ass moving, I want my money."

Inside Willy's place on his kitchen table is fifty dollars doing nothing but just lying there, "What the fuck Willy?" Kevin says to Willy as he picks up the fifty dollars off of Willy's kitchen table.

"That's for my rent."

"Well too bad for you Willy... Look on the bright side."

"What bright side Kevin?"

"Out of the kindness of my heart Willy, I'm calling this fifty dollars your giving me as your debt to me paid in full. The bright side, stupid Willy, is that your saving twenty seven dollars by paying me off now."

"Well Kevin, it doesn't feel so bright to me."

"That is because you are a negative person Willy. Be thankful for your health. You can always make more money Willy."

"No Kevin... I want my fifty dollars back. I need it man."

110

"Too damn bad Willy. This money belongs to me now. Save yourself an ass whipping and let it go."

"Come on Kevin. I'll give you my toaster. Look at it, it's like brand new."

"I don't want your toaster stupid Willy. I think it's for the best if you just shut up about it now. I'm tired of hearing you. You just go on and on. Life lesson, don't buy what you can't pay for. Now roll a joint, messing with you has made me lose my buzz."

"I'm out Man."

"Bull shit. I know you Willy, you have a stash somewhere."

"Alright. Damn Kevin you owe me for this."

"I don't owe you shit Willy. Now go on and be a good pot head. Roll up that joint man."

Kevin and Willy smoke a joint, they are about half way done when a knocking comes at Willy's door.

"Who is it man?"

"It's me Willy. Open up the fucking door." An angry lady's voice yells out from the other side of the door.

To Kevin, "Damn it's Pam. What am I going to do?"

"How am I to know that? I don't even know who Pam is."

"Pam is crazy man. Like really crazy. She went out on a date with me. Man she told me that I wasn't good looking enough to have sex with her."

"That's fucked up. Ha,ha,ha."

"Yeah man but there's more fucked up.

She keeps coming back over... Man she's crazy. She says I'm not her boyfriend but she bitches at me like a girlfriend that hates me."

"What? You're telling me that this lady comes over and bitches at you and doesn't give you any ass?"

"Yes. Like I said man, she's crazy."

"What the fuck is wrong with you? Damn man act like a man. Tell Pam to put out or stay away."

"I did. In my own way... But it didn't work. She just got more mad at me. Then she made me take her out to dinner, where she bitched at me more."

"Man I should smack the dumb fuck out of you. But I ain't got all day."

"Come on Kevin man, help me out."

"Help you out like how? What's Pam look like anyway?"

"She's hot and innocent looking with a soul that was dipped in Hell before it entered her body. I can't take her anymore. Man I feel like running away but I don't have anywhere to run to."

"You're pathetic Willy...

Pam beats on the door again, "What are you doing in there Willy, playing with your little bitty dick again?"

Willy has had enough, "Shut up you crazy lady. Get away from my door. Go away and never come back. I'm breaking up with you."

"Willy you stupid little dick man. You can't break up with me. We aren't going out, now open up this door or I swear Willy, I'll stomp on your balls as soon as I can get to you."

"No you won't. Besides I'm not alone. I have company. Now go away and come back never."

"Company? I know what kind of company you keep Willy. Hey lady whatever he's paying you it's not enough."

"Shut up you crazy bitch and go away. I don't have a lady in here with me."

"You know how much I like it when you call me a bitch. That's right little dick Willy, I am your bitch. I will stay your bitch until I make you my bitch. You should thank me for wasting my time on you. You know you are not worth it. Now open up the door and lay on the floor so I can walk all over you. Whoever you are in there stranger, you can watch me belittle your friend, then maybe I might just do the same thing to you."

Kevin smiles, "Not me Pam, not my way of getting turned on. I like ordinary type of fucking better."

"You're as stupid as Willy Stranger. I don't fuck Willy. And if he's your friend you are probably just as bad as little dick Willy. Now stranger what is your name?"

"I'm the big dick man known as Kevin."

"Kevin? Is that you? It can't be you?"

"You know me Pam?"

"No dumb ass, I'm only fucking with you. Like saying your name to me would make me all horny. Oh Kevin you're the man. Come on baby don't stop. Dream on loser."

Kevin to Willy, "Man you are right, that is one crazy bitch."

Pam still from the outside of the door, "I heard that Kevin. You just made my shit list. When I get done with you, you're going to beg me to stop, like every man does.

113

When you beg, and you will beg me Kevin, I will turn my bitch up higher, all the way to maxim and burn you up alive."

Kevin and Willy look at each other, "Open up this damn door now, you two little dick bastards."

Willy nervously walks over to his door and opens it up very slowly. Before he can get it barely opened up Pam pushes it fast and hard making the door smack Willy on his forehead, "Don't you ever not unlock your door to me again Willy. You're going to pay for this very badly. Now out of my way, I want to see this friend of yours."

Pam stomps her way through Willy's entrance to his apartment, straight to Kevin, who is standing up waiting on her in Willy's living room, "I'm not a friend of Willy's."

Pam with rage in her eyes looks at Kevin and in an instant her eyes soften up to come on and get me big fella, "Hello Kevin I'm Pam. It's so nice to meet you."

Kevin takes a closer look at Pam and likes what he sees, "Damn Pam! Come over here and give me a kiss."

Pam smiles from ear to ear, "Is that all you want from me?"

"For starters. Let's see how it goes."

Pam runs to Kevin and jumps into his arms like she is acting out a scene in a movie, "Take me stranger. Make me feel like a real woman."

With Pam's little five foot body in his arms, Kevin looks into her blue eyes as Pam shakes her long blond hair out of the way for their upcoming kiss. Kevin squeezes Pam and then he gives her a little kiss followed by a larger one until they both have their tongues in the other's mouth.

Willy watches as Kevin and Pam kiss longer and longer.

Then Pam on her feet now takes off her clothes as Kevin is joining her by taking off his. Willy watches Kevin make love to the most beautiful naked woman he has ever seen in his life and wishes that he was Kevin.

After sex there is talking, mostly by Pam. "Well Stranger big dick, how was I? Did I do it for you?"

"Yeah you were great Pam. Damn I'm late, I gotta get going."

"Typical. You had time to fuck me but no time to get to know me afterwards."

"Pam you know how it is. We had our moment. You're fine and a hell of a lay but you are crazy trouble."

"Like how Stranger?"

"Well let's see darling? Well the way you come over here and bust Willy's balls like it gets you off for one."

"Oh that. Well a lady has to have her fun after all. Willy is a little bitty man that will never turn me on. You Stranger, you are different. I could get use to having sex with you."

"Not going to happen Pam. I already have four girlfriends, I don't need another at this time."

"You're a pig! You're a damn sex pig. I hope you fuck so much, your dick falls off. I can't believe this, I'm number five for you?"

"No Pam. You were a sex moment."

"That's all. You don't want me again?"

"Of course I do Pam. You felt better than all my girlfriends. Still you are trouble waiting to happen. You like it when a man suffers."

115

"So the Hell what Kevin. That is what men like Willy are for. I wouldn't treat you the same way. You're my hunk, that I want to fuck. What do you say?"

"I don't know Pam... I tell you what, Sunday we can get together and talk about it more. Sunday is usually my day off from having sex. But for you Pam, I'll make an exception."

"Lucky me."

"Wrong answer Pam. Damn, you were so close."

"I'll show you close!" Pam picks up a half full can of beer and throws it at Willy, hitting him in the face with it.

"See how close that was Kevin? Any closer and it would have took Willy's head off."

"I see what you mean Pam."

Willy, all wet and pissed off, looks back and forth at Pam and Kevin, "You crazy bitch, you hit me not him."

"No shit dumb ass. I don't want to hurt Kevin. Just think of yourself as his proxy for the punishment that he deserves from now on."

"No fucking way Pam."

"Shut up Willy, like you have a choice. You know you love it when I punish you."

Kevin tired of it all, "Hang on you two. I have to be going. We still on for Sunday Pam?"

"Yes Kevin. You can come over to my place and fuck me all over my apartment."

"Sounds great. Let me have your number."

Kevin gets the number and leaves. Pam stays naked as she makes Willy lay on the floor, fully dressed.

Kevin to himself as he is walking over to Becky's, "Figures. Always the crazy ones are the best lays. Oh well, I guess I can fuck her a few more times. Too bad she knows my real name. I think I could fall in love with her. Damn man not very smart, I can see trouble on the horizon. I just hope I can steer myself to calmer waters before her storm makes me sink."

About an hour late to Becky's so Kevin skipped going to the store. When he knocked on the door, Becky was not there, only Gloria waited it out. Becky went to get the two cans of peaches. Kevin asked Gloria if they were to wait for Becky to get back. Gloria laughed as she started to take Kevin clothes off for him.

One hour of having great sex goes by and Becky does not come back home yet.

"I wonder what's taking Becky so long?"

"She probably met up with some guy she knows and went back to his place. You know Becky. She's my twin but she's a slut. Unlike me. I'm fresh and sweet. That's why you like me better. You know what I was thinking Kevin?"

"I do not Gloria."

"Well having Becky around is great and all but I have to be honest. I had a much better time tonight with her not around, taking up time with you. My time."

"Your time?"

"Yes my time. We don't need her. Drop her and make me your only for Fridays."

"Damn that's cold Gloria. Becky's my girlfriend."

117

"I am also your girlfriend."

"No you're not. Your my girlfriend's sister, that she likes for you to join in with us while having sex."

"It was my idea."

"It was? That's hot. That makes me like you and understand you more."

"Is that a good thing Kevin?"

"If you want to be my only Friday night it does."

"It does? That's great. Let's get out of here and go over to my place. You can spend the night, I'll make breakfast."

"Sounds great. First, I have a weird feeling about Becky. I think I'm going to head to the store to see if she is still there. Yes that's what I'll do first. That way I can tell her about me and you. Unless you want that honor?"

"Hell yes I want it. I'm going to be a total bitch to her when I do it to. I can't wait. Finally, I get the better for once. I'm better than she is. She's going to hate it, I just know it."

"I imagine. I think I better be the one to tell her. Then again, no I think it's for the better if we just keep things the way they are. That way both of you can be the better together at the same time. I'll go even better than that Gloria. From this time until I decide to drop you, you are now my fifth girlfriend."

"Fifth? Like Hell I am! I'm number one."

"No you are number five. Becky is number four, you come after her so you are number five. It's the best I can do Gloria.

"I want my own night."

"Your own night? I don't know about that."

"Why the Hell not?"

"I'm all man and all that but still I need a break now and again. You know, give my dick a rest."

"That's not fair. Rest your dick on another girlfriend's night. Better yet just dump the bitch."

"No Gloria. If I do any dumping, I do it when I want to. I have it made, all my girlfriends are great."

"Yes lucky you. What about me? I'm number five."

"I say to you lovingly Gloria, share me or lose me."

"I kind of hate you right now Kevin."

"I understand. Still I have to know if you're cool with being number five. Because I just met this hot thing and I'm thinking about adding her to my list of girlfriends."

"What? You did what?"

"Yes, I'm blessed. If she becomes a girlfriend that would make her number six. Now that you are number five."

"You bastard."

"Yes that is all good and all but you see my concern. If I gave you your own night that would be six times a week I would be fucking. Yes, you and Becky will have to keep on sharing me. That way in case I need a night off during the week, I have an extra day to let that girlfriend that missed her turn have it."

"Oh you just think of everything, don't you Kevin?"

"Well what can I say Gloria, I do my best.
119

A well prepared man is a man that gets laid the best."

"Is that a fact?" A very mad Gloria asks as she steps closer to Kevin.

"That is a fact Gloria. I think I better go check and see what's keeping Becky."

"Yeah that's a good idea Kevin. Try not to forget what you're doing on the way and try to fuck another woman you damn slut you."

"What? What's wrong with you? Don't call me a slut."

"Oh you don't like that?"

"No I don't."

"Well too damn bad. Every time from now on when we fuck, I'm going to call you my man slut."

"The Hell you are."

"Yes I am. Listen. Slut, slut. You are my man slut."

"Fuck this, I'm out of here."

"Wait don't forget your personality, I mean your dick on the way out you sorry horny bastard."

"I have to say you have changed Gloria and not for the better. Yes I'm out of here and we're through."

Gloria thinks to herself good. She is about to say something really mean, when she stops herself, "What am I doing? This is not what I had in mind. I had him right where I wanted him, what happened? I got to tell him I'm sorry before he leaves. Then again he is the biggest asshole I have ever met. But still he has the biggest..."

Kevin is just about at the door, "Baby I'm sorry. I just got a little angry. Will you forgive me?"

Kevin turns around and looks calmly at Gloria, "Yes I will forgive you. Still I think it's for the best to call it quits. The lady I just met is kind of high strung enough. I do not need two of you making my life all crazy. I just want to get laid and not deal with any complicated shit."

"Yes boo hoo to life Kevin. You're a hell of a lay."

"And what?"

"Nothing. That's all you're good for."

"Says a woman that is going to go out and settle for nice and boring."

"Sounds great to me right now."

"Yes everything will be great until this limp man doesn't get you off when you need it the most. Then you will fall back to your horny ways and I will not be here for you."

"Well then, I'll just go and find a man just like you baby. You and every man like you are a dime a dozen. It won't be hard to find something hard to please me."

"Well good luck to you Gloria. It was nice fucking you."

Gloria rushes past Kevin and opens up the door, "Get the hell out of here you slut and take your superior nothingness with you."

Kevin says nothing else as he walks out the door of Becky's apartment. A door that was slammed very hard behind him by, a hating him even more now, Gloria. Kevin turns around and looks at the closed door and thinks to himself, "Just think a few moments ago I had her screaming my name out of lust.

121

If she didn't want love from me I would have made her scream my name again. Women, who will ever understand them? Not me for sure."

Kevin walks down a cold, dirty, dark alley underneath the moon in New York City. It's a shortcut that Kevin doesn't sweat too much. In the distance Kevin hears some sirens sounding off together very close to where the store resides. Kevin walks faster, wondering what is going on. When he reaches the store there are six police cars and a few ambulances parked outside and down the road from it. Kevin walks over to a crowd of people who are watching to see what is happening. Kevin is told about some men with guns who shot at least ten people or more dead.

Kevin feels the hairs on his neck stand up. He looks around trying his best to spot Becky. She is nowhere to be found. So Kevin takes a big breath and walks up closer to the store. At first no one notices him or says anything to him. Closer Kevin walks up to the carnage. On the ground ten feet away in front of him is a man that has been shot in his face. Kevin looks past him and sees bodies more than ten in number laying on the ground, all dead.

Kevin with a freaked out mind has to know so he walks up closer. Four bodies past the first dead man is Becky's dead body. She was shot in her chest a few times. Beside her is a bag with a can of peaches sticking out from it. Kevin does not know why but he has to have the bag with two cans of peaches in it. He would like to close his eyes as he walks to pick up the bag from off the ground but instead he looks at all the blood and death with eyes fully opened.

No one says anything to Kevin as he bends down to pick up the bag with two cans of peaches in it. Kevin looks at Becky's dead body and her short skirt is pulled up exposing her panties to the world. Kevin very softly pulls Becky's skirt down. It gets stuck from the way she is laying on it.

122

So Kevin pulls harder until Becky's panties are fully covered up, "Hey you what are you doing over there to that body?" A police officer asks Kevin with anger in his voice.

"Her name is Becky. She's my girlfriend." Kevin says back with tears falling from his eyes.

"I'm sorry about your loss. Please you can't be here. Walk over to a clearing and wait there someone will be there to talk to you when time is allowed."

Kevin stands up and walks away with the bag with two cans of peaches in it.

Kevin just keeps on walking not paying attention to the pickup truck that is coming his way and not stopping. Kevin has walked into the middle of the street and into coming traffic. The driver of the pickup truck was looking at what was happening up ahead and before he spotted Kevin it was too late.

A couple of police officers walk away from a murder scene to a man that has been ran over by a truck.

"What happened sir?"

"I don't know? One minute he was not there and the next moment he was. I didn't see him until it was too late. I'm so sorry, I can't believe this happened."

"Try to calm down sir. From the way things look it was not your fault. It was an accident."

An hour goes by and the man is allowed to leave. Before he walks away he bends down for some reason and picks up the bag the man he ran over was carrying. He looks in it and sees two cans of peaches. The man closes the bag back up and takes it with him to his truck. Then he drives away and out of sight.

Monsters

{Special Bulletin}

"In the bowels of New York City there is a flesh eating, killing machine, monster, that uses metal teeth to rip, tear and chew up its victim's meat. We here at News Channel Thirteen are very sad to inform you, our public of this monster. We, the people, not only have to protect ourselves from all the horrors on our city streets, but now we have a living, human eating Monster to contend with.

We here at News Channel Thirteen along with other news channels, have questioned the police and the mayor. At this time no comment is all that has been said. We are here for you. When we here at News Channel Thirteen find out anything, no matter how small, we will inform you. We also here at News Channel Thirteen, would like to ask you, our audience, if you see this monster, to call the police first then call us or email us and we will inform everyone about your sighting. Send us pictures and maybe we will mention your name on air.

On a personal level, I say a line needs to be drawn here. If we are to be killed... Well at least, we the people, should be able to keep the flesh on our bones, so that way we can be buried in respect, fully intact."

"Turn that shit off!"

"Yes Captain Fork."

"Who turned on that crap in my office, Lieutenant Maple?"

"I have no idea Captain Fork." (It was me.)

"Well Lieutenant, I want you to remind everybody here that we do not watch News Channel Thirteen, we watch News Channel Seven."

"Yes Sir, Captain Fork, I'll get on it right away."

Lieutenant Maple, turns around and starts to walk out of Captain Fork's office, "Hang on Lieutenant Maple, you can get to that later. First we need to talk about this damn wacko that keeps on eating people."

"Captain, I have a thought. His metal teeth cannot be his real teeth. He must have had metal bonded to his teeth."

"No shit Lieutenant, tell me something I don't know."

Lieutenant Maple looks through the folder of the Monster in a hurry, trying to find something, "I've got nothing Captain."

"Well don't brag about it, especially on dates."

"Captain?"

"Never mind, it doesn't matter. How many police officers on the case Lieutenant.?"

"All of them just like you ordered Captain."

"That is what I wanted to hear. Damn it to Hell. I've got the Mayor on my back. Like tearing me a new one is going to help things. I tell you Lieutenant the only thing that happens is that the Mayor pisses me off. I'm glad I didn't vote for that sorry bastard."

"Me too Captain."

"Lieutenant, I need more police officers in my office like now. The brainstorming between the two of us has not panned out very well."

"Yes Captain. Who should I bring in here?"

"Anyone with a badge Lieutenant. Tell you what Lieutenant pick me a variety of Police Officers.

I want male and female, all skin colors. Together maybe one of us can come with an idea how to catch this lunatic."

The Police's brainstorming comes up with some sound and not so sound ideas. The Monster eats everybody, his taste of choice in prey is humanity. The people of New York City go about their lives knowing they're safe from the Monster during the day. This monster is nocturnal, when the night comes down, people hold their breaths a little longer.

Two months have gone by until now. The Monster is a creature of habit, every night he eats bloody raw only one victim. Two months should mean that the Police should have found at least sixty eaten on dead bodies by now. The number of bodies the police have found does not add up. Fifty two bodies have been found. By the date this all started, the figure is to be believed that eight or more eaten on dead bodies have not been found as of yet.

The Mayor called the Governor, who has already sent the Mayor twenty extra officers to help him, has now sent fifty more officers to help the Mayor. The Mayor thanked the Governor many times, glad for the help. In the late hours of the night, when the Mayor is suppose to be sleeping, he stares at the ceiling and wonders if more officers well do any good.

Nothing is always the answer. No traces of stable DNA. Everything they find is some how tainted with unknown DNA. Not one person who has seen it is a reliable source. There are crude drawings in papers, depicting the Monster as a Man Beast with long fangs and a very hairy body. The fact that unknown DNA was found at more than one crime scene was leaked to the press. The Press went crazy with their interpretations of New York City's number one sought after serial killer, who also happens to be a Cannibal as well.

The people of NYC have had enough, they want this Monster found. They want it dead.

There are reports that some people have asked the Mayor if they could buy the dead body of the Monster after the police kills him first. There are also reports that the Mayor cursed at them loudly.

Four months have gone by. Ninety eight eaten on dead bodies have been found. It is figured that twenty two eaten on dead bodies have not been found. The mayor has lost thirty pounds and spends most of his free time in the bathroom, hiding the whiskey he drinks down like water. Mixed with all the pills he's swallowing the Mayor is just about ready for a long stay in rehab.

Those closest to the Mayor tried their best to hide the Mayor's decline but the bad news got out yesterday and now the Mayor has stepped down, leaving the Lieutenant Mayor in charge. The Mayor's last act as Mayor was the firing of Captain Fork and Lieutenant Maple.

Two weeks ago the Monster hit an all time low when he ate a woman and her six month old baby boy. The sickness gets worse for it seems the Monster has now gotten the taste for children meat. Where is God? A lot of people ask and receive no answers.

Six months have gone by. The body count of eaten bodies found so far is up to one hundred and thirty one. That means for now forty nine eaten on dead bodies have not been found. Out of good taste no one has counted the nineteen children's bodies that have been found eaten on and dead.

Strangers have taken it upon themselves to crowd together when they go out at night alone. People will tell other people to come stand over by them for safety in numbers. This is nice and it brings people closer together no matter how different they are from another, but in the end this human eating Monster always hunts down and feasts on someone new every night.

The new Captain, Captain Stern, assures the people of New York City that the Monster one day soon will make a mistake and they will catch him. Until then they are to do their best to protect themselves.

One year has gone by, Monster still has not be captured, found or even identified properly yet. Way over three hundred and sixty four people have been eaten to death. Monster, during a few periods ate more than one person a night. Monster's record to date is six people in one night. It is believed Monster ran into a house where a door must have been unlocked and killed the entire family. He must have not been that hungry, for Monster only ate small parts of all the family members.

{Special Bulletin}

"We here at News Channel Thirteen have just found out about some very interesting news about Monster. A body was found earlier in the morning around nine o'clock, three days ago. This body is believed to be the very first person Monster ate to death. Hang on for this folks, this next part will blow your minds...

Are you ready? The day this person is believed to been killed was on April first, April Fool's Day. Can you believe it folks? What does this mean? Does this mean that we, humanity, are nothing but a joke to Monster? I don't know about the rest of you but this reporter, I don't feel like a fool, even though it seems I and all of you have been fooled by Monster...

Monster, I am talking to you. You are a coward. Why don't you come out into the light of day. Quit hiding in the darkness. If you have something to say or want to tell me your story, I am here and waiting for your call. Monster you are a beast but you still are a man. You have to be, no animal could have went this long without being discovered. This entire city wants you dead, Monster if nothing else just a few words. It might be your only chance."

128

Three months later.

{Special Bulletin}

"We here at News Channel Thirteen have just found out
that it is believed that just a few hours ago the Police
arrested Monster. I hope this to be true. The Mayor is
rumored to be hinting at giving a speech later today or
perhaps tomorrow. We will let you know as soon any word
of this becomes official at anytime."

Six months later.

{Special Bulletin}

"We here at News Channel Thirteen have just found out
that Randy Ford, Monster was given a life sentence
without the chance of parole. Yes folks it's finally over with.
New York City, it's time to party. The trial was crazy.
Randy Ford still says he's innocent. All I know is that every
since Randy Ford has been behind bars not one person
has been found eaten to death. Folks, to me it cannot be
truer that Randy Ford is Monster and I say good riddance
to him."

Two days later.

{Special Bulletin}

"We here at News Channel Thirteen have just found out
that a body was discovered this morning. It is believed
that Monster, killed and ate this unfortunate man last night.
I cannot believe this folks... The first full day Randy Ford is
in prison is the same day Monster decides to eat and kill a
human being once again. What is going on? Randy Ford
is suppose to be Monster. If he is not, who is Monster?
We here at News Channel Thirteen do not know if Monster
is back on his murdering rampage or if this was just for one
more time."

Inside an old man's apartment in NYC. "Come here Ranger." Ranger, a German Shepard walks over to his friend, wagging his tail, "That's a good boy Ranger."

The old man pets his Friend and drinks his cup of hot tea, "You know Ranger I have no idea why they call you Monster. A good boy like you Ranger, you are never a monster. So what if you have to eat people to survive. There are too many people on Earth anyway. What's one person a night?"

Ranger looks at his friend, "I know what you mean Cliff. I being a Alien to this planet, can't help to say that your world of people one day might just kill all life on it."

"Yes this is true Ranger. I pray every night that God takes away all the wicked from this planet."

"Until then Cliff, I guess I have to thin the herd one human at a time."

"Show me Ranger, Transform into your other form."

"I don't feel like it Cliff, I like being a dog, it's so simple of a life. I'm going out to hunt down a human and eat them in a few minutes. You can take me for a walk and watch me change into my Alien form."

"I would like that Ranger. I'll carry your metal teeth for you, that way you can stay as a dog until you find someone tasty to eat. Ha,ha,ha."

"That was funny Cliff. I think I'm getting hungry just thinking about it. Let's go and head out for our walk."

"Okay, but please Ranger not too far of a walk. You know how tired I get. Let me grab my sweater, I feel there's a chill in the air tonight."

"Go ahead Cliff, I'll get a drink of water while I'm waiting."

Outside their apartment, Cliff is walking Ranger down the sidewalk. The air is crisp as a few people ask if they can pet Ranger. Ranger like the lovable dog he is, wags his tail and licks their faces. Further down the sidewalk Cliff and Ranger are alone beside a few homeless people, "You know Cliff you still surprise me."

"How's that Ranger?"

"How you are not only hiding me from your planet's people but you are also on my people's side when they arrive and go to war against your people."

"Like I told you Ranger, I feel no love for my people. The love I use to feel inside my heart for humanity has been gone from inside me for a very long time."

"I understand Cliff. Don't worry, when my people get here we will take over Earth and make it a beautiful again."

"I get to watch this happen, right Ranger?"

"Yes of course Cliff, I owe you my life. When you found me after my ship crash landed on Earth, I was sick and dying and you fed me someone to eat. I tell you what, Earth people are sure full of protein, that I need to survive. That is why I built my metal teeth. It makes tearing the flesh off of a human so much faster and easier."

"Have you decided who you want to eat tonight Ranger?"

"Yes, I think I'll eat that couple over there. Look at them they look so much in love. Okay take off my leash, it's time for me to transform into my Alien form."

"Here's your metal teeth, sic 'em, Bon Appetit Ranger."

"Watch this Cliff, it's going to be a b oody great time."

Cliff watches Ranger transform into an eight foot Alien. The size of his mouth is over sized compared to any human. When Ranger snaps his metal teeth into place no human stands a chance. Cliff wishes he was still young enough to hunt humans. The kill is the best thing next to feasting on human meat but Cliff always enjoyed the hunting of humans and he misses it so much. Wiping tears away from his eyes, Cliff thinks to himself at least I have Ranger to hunt for me now. He is so generous, he always gives me the most tender parts of the humans he kills.

Ranger, his real name is not Ranger, runs towards the couple at forty miles an hour. Ranger is lean and muscular and is upon the couple before they can scream for help. Ranger's blood lust is full this night as he knocks the man down to the sidewalk and grabs the woman who is in shock in a death grip and rips open her throat with one bite. Ranger pulls his razor, sharp metal teeth away from the woman's throat with a thick chunk of her meat hanging out of his mouth.

Ranger drops the dead woman to the ground as he slurps down his throat her chunk of meat. Ranger then stomps on the man's back, breaking it in two very fast with a loud snap at the end. Squatting down Ranger lifts up the man and turns him around so he can bite out his throat.

The couple are dead as Ranger picks them up, one in each arm and carries them towards a hungry for human meat Cliff. Cliff is smiling from ear to ear starring up at Ranger as Ranger looks down at Cliff, who would not stand a chance if Ranger ever decided to attack him and says to him, "You feel like male's meat or female's meat tonight Cliff?"

"How about a little of both?"

Cliff and Ranger walk into a alley and down it about half way. They stop next to a dumpster and Ranger sets the dead couple on the ground.

Ranger rips open the chest of the man and pulls out a big chunk of his meat and hands it to Cliff, "Here you go Cliff, start with the male and finish with female."

"Sounds great to me. Thank you Ranger, you're the best friend a man could ever have."

"You too Cliff. Next to my family and friends, you are the best friend, I've ever had."

"Isn't life great Ranger. The two of us, we're never lonely and we always have so much human meat to eat. I'm going to stuff myself."

"Go for it Cliff, I think I'll join you and stuff myself full tonight as well. Besides I have nothing better to do."

Cliff looks at Ranger and starts laughing, making himself spit out some of the male's meat and blood on the ground, "Damn Ranger, I tell you, you're a riot."

Ranger laughs along with Cliff for a few moments then he is all business as he starts eating the male like he is starving to death for human meat.

Five minutes later there is no more meat of the male that Ranger wants to eat. Ranger wipes the blood away from his mouth before he rips a big chunk out of the woman's chest and hands it to Cliff, who still hasn't finished his male's meat.

Cliff has a chunk of human meat in both hands as he looks back and forth at them, "Here let me help you out Cliff." Ranger says as he takes what is left of the male's meat out of Cliff's hand and swallows it whole in one giant gulp.

"Thanks Ranger, I guess my eyes are bigger than my stomach tonight."

"Not a problem Cliff, enjoy your female's meat."

133

"I can't finish Ranger. For some reason, I feel kind of sick to my stomach."

"Cliff, I'm a flesh eating Alien from another planet. Human meat is perfect for my digestive system and absolutely delicious tasting on my tongue."

"Yes I know Ranger, you've told me this before."

"Yes I know Cliff. Now here is the rest of it... You Cliff, you are not a Alien from another planet... You're not suppose to eat human meat. It's not good for you. I'm saying this to you as a friend and confidante... Maybe you should stop eating human meat for awhile."

"No way. I'm seventy now and for forty years I have eaten human meat. I messed a few days here and there. I am a man and I needed to get laid once in awhile."

"Did you eat, who you had sex with?"

"No. It just wouldn't have been right. And if you think about it, it's sick. I mean I couldn't just finish inside her and then chop her into pieces."

"Well maybe this will make you feel better? Before this couple we just ate was on their way to wherever they were going, they had sex just a few minutes before that."

"That's disgusting. Why would you think telling me this would make me feel better Ranger?"

"I didn't. I was just messing with you. Give you a little laugh that will make your stomach bubble."

"Thanks Ranger, but I think I've had enough laughs for the night. It's time to go home, I'm cold."

"One more thing first Cliff."

"What is that Ranger?"

"You had to think about it before you hunted and killed one of your fellow humans."

"Think about what?"

"How many humans you hunted had sex right before you killed and ate them?"

"I didn't think about it. That's just nasty as can be. Damn humans, all they do is have sex all the time."

"Well Cliff, old man, I have no complaints about humans having sex. The more sex, the more births, the more I have to eat."

"I guess that's true Ranger."

"More than true Cliff, it's a fact. A fact that I have to hammer into the brains of my people when they get here."

"Why is that Ranger?"

"I am a conservative Cliff. I like to thin the herd not deplete it to extinction. There are many like me on my planet that are conservatives. Then Cliff there are many more on my planet that will kill two humans when one would be enough, just so they can stuff themselves full."

"I can understand that. Just like you sometimes, when you eat more than one human a night."

"What can I say Cliff? Sometimes I have to splurge. I deserve it once in awhile to be completely full."

"Yes you do Ranger. You're my best friend I want you to be happy here on Earth. Especially since you are so far away from your planet."

135

"I know you do Cliff. That is why I'm going to take such special care of you when my people get here."

"When is that going to be Ranger?"

"Very soon Cliff. Sooner than you think."

"Ranger can you tell me again the story about how your people had cyborg technology added to their DNA, on the walk home?"

"Sure Cliff, let me turn myself back into a dog first."

"Don't forget to toss the humans into the trash before you do Ranger. "

"Yes Boss." Ranger laughs as he picks up the dead couple and places them into the dumpster. "Stand back Cliff, I'm going to piss all over the feasting scene."

"I hate when you do that Ranger, it stinks so bad."

"Of course it does Cliff, it's piss. It's suppose to stink."

Ranger takes his piss as Cliff walks far enough away not to get pissed on again. Ranger then takes his metal teeth out of his mouth and hands them to Cliff and then he turns himself back into a dog, "You ready Cliff?"

"Yes I am Ranger. Come over here and I'll put your leash back on you. Does it bother you to act like a dog, when other humans are around?"

"Not really Cliff, it's easy being a dog. All I have to do is lick, scratch and bark."

Ranger lets Cliff put his leash on him and then they both start walking out of the alley. Ranger notices that Cliff is walking slow, so he slows himself down not to hurry him.

Cliff is slowing down more, the further he and Ranger walk. Ranger has Cliff sit down on a bench to take a needed break, "You starting to feel better Cliff?"

"Yes I am Ranger, thank you."

"You just relax Cliff and I'll tell you your favorite story."

"That would be nice Ranger."

"Over a thousand years ago on my planet, a few scientist made a discovery about our planet. Cliff, our climate was changing faster than we as a people could handle it psychically. It was believed to be true that we as a species would not survive longer than another two hundred years or so. My people panicked and they started killing each other faster out of fear of up coming death."

"That's terrible Ranger."

"So many of my people died Cliff. All hope was lost until some more scientist discovered what happened when cyborg technology was added to our DNA. The effect was amazing and sad. We as a people lived on but we lost what you would call on this world, our humanity."

"How did your people survive this big change Ranger?"

"Very slowly at first Cliff. But time went on and so did we. After that we built our first spaceships and flew them faster than light to the stars..."

"After that Ranger?"

"After that we as a people made another discovery."

"What was that Ranger?"

"That we as a people would rather eat the new people we encountered than live in harmony with them."

137

"That must have been hard on the mind Ranger?"

"Yes it was Cliff. In the end it was said it is better that we eat them, than they eat us. After that things just became easier on us. As of right now my people have nine planets that we harvest the people on for our food. Earth is to be the tenth."

"I can't wait. Every human on Earth is to be used as food for your people besides me. Ain't that right Ranger?"

"That is right Cliff. You are the only human on this planet that will not be used as my people's food."

"Thank you for that Ranger. I'd hate to be eaten."

"No problem Cliff. You feel like you can make it the rest of the way home now?"

"Yes I do, let's go."

Cliff and Ranger go home together without incident. The next few weeks Ranger goes out hunting for humans by himself. Leaving Cliff sitting in his chair covered up with a blanket and drinking tea.

Three weeks later, Ranger insists that Cliff goes hunting for humans with him this night. Cliff is tired and grouchy but Ranger will have none of it. So Cliff finally says yes to get Ranger off his back.

Out they go into the night, friend and friend, human and Alien. On the way Cliff has to tell Ranger not to talk so loud because people can hear him. Ranger ignores Cliff's concerns and keeps on talking without a care in the world.

Cliff tired from being pulled faster than he wants to be by Ranger, gives up telling him to be quiet and does his best to keep up the pace that Ranger is providing him.

Still out in the cold night air Cliff tells Ranger that he needs to sit down. Ranger tells him to walk into a alley, "You stay here Cliff, I'll be back in a few minutes with someone very tasty for you to eat."

"Okay Ranger, please try to hurry. I'd like to go home early tonight. I'm so tired and in a lot of pain."

"Don't worry Cliff, I'll hurry. Think about this when I'm gone. Tonight will be the last night you will go out hunting with me."

"You don't mean... Your people are finally here?"

"Yes Cliff, My people will be here tomorrow, bright and early and on time."

"On time?"

"Yes they are secluded to be here in the morning exactly at 9:18."

"9:18? Well we better get a lot of sleep tonight for our big day tomorrow. I can't wait."

Cliff turns from dog into giant size Alien and runs off, like he is trying to out run the wind. Fifteen minutes later Ranger comes back with no dead human in hand.

"What's going on Ranger?"

"Can you believe it Cliff, I couldn't find one human for us to share to eat?"

"Really? Why? What's going on out there? We better go home. I'm scared."

"You should be human!"

"What do you mean by Human, Ranger?"

139

"You just like every other human are nothing more than food for myself and my people to eat."

"You don't mean that Ranger?"

"Yes I do Human."

"But I saved your life? Without me you would have died."

"No Human, I wouldn't have. I let you believe that. But no Human, I would have been fine in a few minutes if you didn't find me. I am strong just like all my people. How do you think I have lived to be over one thousand years old?"

"That would mean... You was there when your people implanted cyborg technology into your DNA?"

"That is correct Human. Just like all my people, when we added cyborg technology to our DNA, it was like drinking from the fountain of youth. There's a drawback, I didn't tell you about Human."

"What, it made you lose your humanity?"

"No stupid Human! The cyborg technology made it impossible for us to create life anymore. But the big trade off is that we can possibly live forever. Think about it Human, it took my people only a thousand years to enslave ten planets peoples for our food. How many planets will we own in another thousand years?"

"Hopefully none."

"None Human?"

"Yes Ranger. Hopefully all your people will choke to death on me and my fellow humans."

"Don't hold your breath Human."

"What's next Ranger?"

"Do you even have to ask Human?"

"I guess not. Can I say one more thing before you kill and eat me?"

"Yes Human, it is true I'm going to kill you but I'm not going to eat you."

"Why not?"

"You're just too damn old Cliff. Your meat will be tough as leather and you'll probably taste like shit as well. No matter though, go ahead and say your final words Human."

"Thank you. All I have to say to you Ranger is that you can go fuck yourself, you sorry ass, Alien bastard."

"Damn you hurt my feelings Cliff.. Take this." Ranger swings his massive hand in Cliff's direction so hard and fast that its strike knocks Cliff's head off his shoulders. Ranger laughs as he watches Cliff's head roll down the Alley and straight into a wall.

The next morning at 9:18 AM sharp Ranger's people came down to Earth. Unlike in the movies we did not see their spaceships arrive in our skies. No Ranger's people all transformed themselves to look like the people of Earth.

Day by day Ranger's people ate humans and took over their lives afterwards. This took place until the time came when it didn't matter anymore. Ranger and his people killed and ate enough humans to make sure the resistance they met by the humans would be minimal, when they finally introduced themselves to humanity.

Ten years later all there is on Earth are Aliens from outer space and breeding camps for worthless, tasty Humans for the Aliens to eat.

The Creation Of God On Planet Futick
Chapter One:

This tale takes place on a planet in another galaxy. The time of the season we on Earth would refer to as the end of Fall. On this planet known as Futick, there are Kings and Queens. There are Knights and Soldiers. There are poor people. Just like here on Earth when Knights roamed the planet the people on Futick tried to live their lives without being killed in the process. Not a surprise on Futick people liked to have sex just like the people on Earth. We the people of Earth are different looking as the people on Futick. This is the truth but sadly, as on Earth, the poor people of Futick are treated like common, worthless poor people. All Kings say repeatedly that the poor never pay their fair share of taxes.

Kings around Futick have a summit and decide that the time is now for them to pass a law that prevents poor people from having sex more than one time a month unless they are married. The time for people collecting money from having sex with whomever is over with from now until forever. The Kings laughed at the thought of poor people. Then with lots of ale thrown down the Kings throats the thought of poor people existing at all made them all want to puke out that same ale.

One King puked on another King. The puked on King pulled out his sword and cut the left arm off of the puking King. The bleeding King ran around in a panic squirting his blood out of the hole where his left arm was a attached a moment ago on every King he ran by in this panic. Drunk and fearless Kings covered in blood stood up and pulled out their swords. Three hundred and eight two Kings were the number of Kings that shared their lands next to other Kings' lands before this battle of Kings took place. One hundred and sixty nine Kings survived and stood tall with blood soaked swords pointing in the air, as two hundred and thirteen Kings laid dead on the floor, many who had been decapitated.

The remaining one hundred and sixty nine Kings looked around at the Kings that survived this death battle because of ale and puke and cheered. For so many years, many of the surviving Kings tried their best to kill the Kings that lay dead on the floor. Law of Futick states when a King kills another King with sword or during battle, the surviving King inherits all the dead King's lands and properties. Including all wives and consorts. The people of Futick had no idea of the pain and misery that was coming at their lives like a plague of hate filled destruction.

Victorious Kings had not the time nor the will to have the time for all their people in their kingdoms before. Now with the joy of owning another kingdom came the joylessness of all the extra not needed poor people that filled it with filth. The one hundred and sixty nine Kings made an oath that they all would follow through no matter how much blood stained their swords and minds. They would decrease in haste half the population of the poor people on Futick.

With the freezing of Winter on the loom, the Kings decided to wait until Spring to implement their bloody plan. This plan had to be the greatest plan that there ever was. The strongest of the Kings, King Thicklog placed himself as the Grand King of all Kings. A second battle almost started between the Kings but more ale was poured instead.

King Thicklog made his way home with his party of fifty men and four consorts. He smiled as he rode his horse looking creature. His first Queen would be standing in the front of the line as was her right and privilege. The reason that King Thicklog is smiling is the thought of the look on Queen number one's face when he walks past her and Queen number two through Queen number twelve, to get to his newest Queen of only three months Queen number thirteen. She is so fresh and fine, King Thicklog cannot wait to lay down upon her. When the party of fifty five enter the castle, King Thicklog and Queen number thirteen head up to the King's chambers until the light of dawn.

143

The reason that Queen number thirteen and all other twelve Queens are referred to in number instead of name is on the account of King Thicklog. King Thicklog is a hard man that feels that it is a show of weakness inside him to say any of his Queens' names out loud.

All the Queens feel this as great. For none of them truly want their names called out by a King that never gets them to blush. King Thicklog is not very thick at all. In fact his name should be King Thinlog. Historians in the future will blame King Thicklog's short comings on his need and will to carry out so much bloody, bloodshed.

King Thicklog enjoyed the foreplay he demanded from all of his Queens. Let's checkout what turns him from blood thirsty King mode to I want to mate all night with you King mode. Queen number thirteen whose real name is Lady Fineness reaches into the chest of sexual props, while King Thicklog drinks a large mug of ale and tells her of all the dead Kings.

Queen number thirteen to King Thicklog, "On your knees you unworthy King, it is time you take your punishment."

"Yes my Queen..."

"Did I say that you could speak? No, I did not. For speaking out of turn, you are to crawl to me and kiss my feet, like a good unworthy King."

"Yes my Queen."

"Stop talking and crawl now!"

King Thicklog does as he is commanded to. While he is kissing Queen thirteen's feet across his back a whip is smacked from lightly to hard many times. This is Queen thirteen's favorite part. Everything after this unfortunately just doesn't have the same sexual appeal to her. Poor Queen thirteen.

144

Let's skip past the whipping and the quick first moaning and to some pillow talk.

"Wife thirteen, it is like something never to be conceived. Two hundred and thirteen Kings dead and rotting. May the animals eat their flesh from off their bones before their bodies turn to gray."

"That is so poetic my King."

"Yes so true."

"Tell me more my mighty and strong King."

"More there is my Queen number thirteen. All the Kings that lay dead are those that needed to become dead. They were the reason for so many wars. Without these Kings living, Futick will finally be ruled correctly. They caused all the problems. Now maybe for the first time there can be peace on Futick. Peace by my command."

"It is just like you my King. You are so grand. Only you my King could bring not only the hope of peace out peace itself here on Futick. I am truly a lucky Queen. This I can feel inside my heart. I love you my King. No man on Futick is mightier than you. Especially the way you make love to a woman. I tell you my King you should show off your manhood. And for great sport my King. You should show your kingdom the proper way to make love to a woman. All my King will be jealous of you. Then out of a great silence they will all cheer you."

"You don't say. Well, why not. Maybe someday I will do just that. But remember this my Queen. Only making love will I show. Never will it be known but to my Queens how I like to be turned on before I make love. Is that not correct my Queen number thirteen?"

"Yes my King. After it is over, I am not even to speak of it. I know this and respect this.

145

My King trust in my love for you, that I will never betray your trust in me. I am your Queen. I am also your servant. To my grave it will go."

"That is why I love all my Queens. I ask so little, I give so much more back and all my Queens have a place in my heart. I love you all. You Queen thirteen, you are my favorite lover. I think tomorrow, I will have you watch as I give my loving to Queens, ten, eleven and twelve. Would you like this my favorite Queen?"

"Yes my King. If you grow bored, I will chase them away and please you myself."

"That is very kind of you my Queen. That is why I have not searched yet for Queen number fourteen."

"Yet my King?"

"Yes as of yet. This will stay yet as long as you stay my favorite. In you I must feel the most love and trust. If there ever came a day when I needed to have only one Queen instead of thirteen. In my heart as of now you would be that Queen. Never betray me, always stay true and you will remain my favorite."

"Yes my King. I wish this day would come true tomorrow."

"Ha, ha my Queen. I bet you do. Tomorrow could not be the day for I would have to have one more night alone with all twelve of my other Queens. Since they gave me all of their hearts and love, this is the least I could do for them."

"Yes my King. You are so kind. Your unwanted Queens receive one last night with the greatest lover on Futick and then the next day it's off with their heads."

"No my Queen. Off with their heads, could not come after their night with me until I have all twelve in a row.

146

On the safe side, I'll give them a few extra days just in case I want another last night with one or more of my Queens."

"You surprise my mind even more my King. How much kindness can you have in your great heart? I and every one else on Futick will always stand in your grand sized shadow. We are so small compared to you."

"Yes how true the words you speak. I am as grand as Futick. Am I not my Queen?"

"Yes my King. Well in truth, you are grander."

"Come to me my Queen. I shall have you again."

"Yes my King make me feel like a real woman. Do you want me to beat you a few times with the whip first?"

"No thank you my Queen. I am still able as of now. But keep the whip close my Queen, for you might need to whip me before our third time of love making."

"Yes my King. I promise to keep on whipping you so great, until you want me to stop."

"That is all I ask of you my Queen."

King Thicklog and Queen thirteen make love again. King Thicklog looks down at his Queen, in his mind he is the greatest man to her. In her mind she thinks of her plans for tomorrow as she moans in delight out of practice.

King, tired as can be, Thicklog lays flat on the bed panting, trying to catch his breath as Queen Fineness sits on her knees looking down on her conquered enemy. A King looks up at his satisfied Queen and smiles at her.

A Queen's thoughts of her King's blood flowing out of multiple deadly wounds upon his less than a man's body,

147

stays in her mind as she smiles at him with love on her lips and a wicked sparkle in her eyes.

"My King, tell me more of your thoughts. Tell me of your grand plan."

"Let me rest a moment my Queen."

"Rest my King. I'll pour you another ale."

King Thicklog takes his fifteen minutes, while Queen thirteen rubs all over his tired body. "Where was I, my Queen? Yes my plan."

King Thicklog sits up on the bed and has his Queen thirteen sit down on the bed so he can rest his tired head on her lap.

"My Queen, the poor."

"The poor, my King?"

"Yes the poor, my Queen. Half of them on Futick must die. There are too many of them to control with all Kings alive. Now with only one hundred and sixty nine of us alive the poor in our new larger kingdoms are even more massive."

"When is this to take place my King?"

"This coming spring. Make it easier on our solders."

"I do not want to talk out of turn my King."

"You have my ears. Let your words come forth without fear my Queen."

"Thank you my King. Maybe you should have another plan besides killing so many poor."

"Why should I, my Queen?"

148

"The poor out number us nobles thousands to one. If word gets around of your plan. The poor will revolt my King."

"They would not dare! However maybe you are right my Queen. The poor are like savages. All they want is food, shelter and sex. Who are they to ask for so much, when they barely have any gold to pay their fair share of taxes?"

"If I understand this correctly my King, the poor fear most of all that there is not hope in their lives. They have nothing to rally behind and to love more than their very lives themselves. So they eat, drink and have as much sex as they can."

"Yes my Queen, your words are the truth. The poor need something to make them aspire to be more. I'm glad I thought of this my Queen."

"Yes my King. You are so wise."

"Let me think more..."

"I have it my Queen. Tomorrow I will summon all my wise men and scholars together in my throne room. There they will all stay until they create this something for me."

"That is brilliant my King. How do you have such grand thought after grand thought?"

"Because my Queen, I am the greatest and mightiest man that lives on Futick."

"Yes you are my King. Every man pales to you in comparison. This is why you will never see the smile on my face fade away. I am truly lucky."

"So true, my love. Now pick up the whip, I need help becoming turned on."

King Thicklog lifts his head up as Queen Thirteen gets off the bed. She grabs the whip with controlled, until now, anger boiling inside her for her pitiful, murdering King. Queen number thirteen no longer, turns around dancing and singing an ancient song of hope and victory. Queen Fineness looks at her King, "Watch me dance my King. See the body that you cannot have enough of."

King Thicklog grins his lustful grin of wanting and controlled passion. "Dance Queen Thirteen. Shake your curves. Your body I love the most of all my Queens"

Queen Fineness stops dancing, "Why even mention them? They are unworthy. I'm the Queen. All others are just bodies for your lust. Look into my eyes if you can my King, see your forever. Let's be as one, I see it in my mind. You and I will rule the world. It is time for a child my King. You need a son to rule your world after you're nothing but dust. Do you not my King?"

"Yes my Queen. I need a powerful son. One who likes to slay thy enemy and have their woman when there are no more enemies to slay down dead. This my Queen, will come to be soon. It better. I've waited long enough. I have thirteen Queens. Not one of you as of yet is worthy to carry my seed. It is my Queens' faults, I have no question in that. I am full of seeds. They have just not found the right time to explode into life."

"Yes my King. This changes tonight. Your seed will create life. I will carry this life to birth. To you my King, I will give you a son."

"Let the King's foreplay commence, my Queen."

"Yes my King. On your knees, unworthy King. I will whip you until passion rises within you." Queen Fineness brings her whip lovingly hard down upon her King's back, which makes him grown in painful pleasure. Queen Fineness is about to strike down again when she stops suddenly.

150

"Whip me my wife. Make me feel passion." King Thicklog looks up at his Queen. In her eyes he see the rebirth of herself coming to life, with sexiness mixed with rebellion. "My Queen, your eyes?"

Queen Fineness starts dancing away from her king, turning her back to him. King Thicklog stands up to take control over his misguided Queen, "Queen Thirteen, never turn thy back to me. Face me now."

Queen Fineness shakes her body faster and harder as she takes no heed to her King's words. Air rushes towards Queen Fineness's back as she turns around with no more of this in her sexy presence. No words are spoken as Queen Fineness strikes her whip gently across a surprised King Thicklog's face, "Down on your knees my King. Down on the floor, like the sick, twisted man that you are. No more my King. I am your Queen. I am Queen Fineness. No longer will you refer to me as a number."

"My Queen, stop this..."

"Silence your words my King. Slay me dead if you have murder in your blood instead of passion. I will be your only Queen in thirteen nights from this night. All your Queens will be dead by your command or by my very own hands."

"My Queen, how dare you..."

"Silence! In our bedroom I rule supreme. On your knees King. Take the first whipping of your new life. I will make you bleed, I will make you beg for more. After you have your lust with my precious body, I will punish you. I will make you beg me to stop whipping you. I will laugh at you as I whip you more. On your knees now my King, or I will whip you down to the floor with extreme pleasure."

"Yes Queen Thirteen!" King Thicklog falls down on his knees, hating the dark lust that burns within in his blood.

151

Queen Fineness looks down at her halfway broken enough useless King as rage engulfs her eyes, "I am Queen Fineness. Say it my King. Say my name." Queen Fineness does not wait for an answer before she strikes her King on top of his head with her whip.

"Ouch, ouch, ouch. Queen Fineness have you lost your mind? Stop this now, I command you!"

Queen Fineness laughs at her helpless, lustful husband and pushes him hard onto the floor with her right foot making his ass make a smacking sound upon contact, "You command me? You fool, I am in total control in our bedroom. Take the worst whipping you can ever imagine and love it. Like the wicked, lustful, all mighty King to everything on Futick, that you are."

King Thicklog wants to stop the whipping he knows he will receive by the look and voice of his thirteenth Queen. He is strong and mighty but at this moment in his life he has never felt weaker than he does right now. Instead King Thicklog raises his hand for his Queen to pause, "Strike me my Queen. Turn me on like I've never been before."

Queen Fineness grinds her teeth together has she whips her King unmercifully. Her eyes see the lashes on her Kings body start to bleed. Her bleeding King looks so beautiful to her that Queen Fineness drops her whip and pounces herself down on top of her King. Balled up fist punches her King in his face. Her King makes no sound, nor even a whimper as he bleeds more and more.

With a throbbing fist Queen Fineness wipes the blood away from her King's lips. She lays herself down upon his hard body and kisses him madly as she begins to cry. She stops and has only one thing to say to her King, "I love you and I hate you my King."

King Thicklog tries to move Queen Fineness off of him but she stops him with a kiss.

"I have felt your lust two times this evening my King, this third time you will fulfill my lust. This third time is all about me. I'll let you finish when I have had enough of you."

Queen Fineness on top of her King makes love to him, her way for the very first time. She repeats many times to him, "I love you, I hate you."

With both of her hands choking her King, Queen Fineness gives herself a moment of pleasure that she has never experienced before. This pleasure is not from her King's manhood, it is from knowing that her mighty and strong King is now going to be her loyal servant from now until the day he dies. With her tongue rubbing against her teeth she hopes his death day comes sooner than later.

"Say my name my King. Say to me that in our bedroom you are my servant. Say this to me and I will let you finish. Hurry my King, I feel your love sinking away. You could not stand the pain if I stopped right now and left you lying here begging me to come back to you. Which my servant I will not. I will laugh off your agony before I fall asleep. Hurry my King, I am through with you for the night. Hurry before my body sits no more upon yours."

"I love you Queen Fineness. I am your servant in our bedroom. Please let me have my release, I beg you."

"Have your finish my King. Know this as you feel the best of your life that it means nothing to me."

"You damn Queen, love what I give you. Love my seed, that will make our child."

King Thicklog finishes and screams out loud in pleasure for all of the castle to hear. After this Queen Fineness licks the almost dried blood away from his face, "That's enough for you my King. I'm thirsty bring me an ale, then call for our bathing ladies. I feel dirty. You make me feel dirty my King. How lucky for you, I love this for now."

After Queen Fineness and King Thicklog have their baths, they are laying down in bed ready for sleep. The sun will rise in six hours as King Thicklog feels like he is in control now tells his perfect Queen before she falls asleep in his arms, "I tell you, my fine Queen Fineness, I will have all the power. All other Kings and their kingdoms will bow to my power. This world will bow to my great power. I can see it now. My life will be one grand festival. Every day will be as if it's my birthday."

"Yes my King. I can see this becoming true as clearly as you my love. It is so great to be your Queen. Now that you are the King I need you to be. Together my King, we out shine the stars themselves."

"Yes my Queen Fineness, you are my one and only."

"I like that my King. Now let's go to sleep."

Let's settle into the next day after King Thicklog's and Queen Fineness' new type of loving together. With mixed emotions digging at his brain, King Thicklog summons his wise men and scholars. Sitting upon his throne drinking ale and eating meat, King Thicklog commands that his wise men and scholars create something that is grander than the planet of Futick itself.

King Thicklog is short of patience as he speaks, at the same time he is unwilling to tell his wise men and scholars, that he wants them to create something for the poor to have hope in. He knows from battle how to spot weakness. If he gives his passive assembly his full thoughts, they would make it weak to mirror the poor. King Thicklog feels power within himself as he orders his wise men and scholars to create something strong and almighty. Something that he and he alone will be able to stand next to and not be consumed by its massive power.

Not knowing or caring to know, King Thicklog was halting progress, making the first day start off very slow.

It was Queen Fineness' idea/command for King Thicklog to stay close to all the discussions that would take place. King Thicklog grew so bored that he had his first wife summoned to him. Queen number one is mad underneath her skin that she was not last night's victory Queen as she enters her King's throne room.

"My King."

"Queen number one, after all these years you are still such a pleasure to set eyes upon."

"Thank you my King. As always you look great. May I come closer so our conversation can be private?"

"Of course my Queen. But first take off your dress and sit yourself on top of me. We will make love until noon as we talk in private."

"In front of all these eyes, my King?"

"Yes my Queen. You are my Queen One, you receive day one. The next twelve days in a row I will have you and Queen number two through Queen number twelve. I miss you twelve. None of you have what my Queen Fineness possesses. Still beauty shines in all of you. Faster my Queen, there is no time today for foreplay. Our way of foreplay no longer applies to us. From this day forth just lust and sexual pleasure from all my Queens besides my Queen Fineness. Only she now gets to please me before we make love until dawn."

"I get the day she gets the night, my King?"

"No my Queen. All day and all night is all for you. Am I not a generous King?"

Queen One is undressed as she sits on top of a not ready to make love King Thicklog, "Yes my King generous you are. I am so lucky to be your first Queen."

155

"Too true my Queen. Now say what you want to me."

Queen One feels nothing happening so she bites her tongue so she won't relax her King anymore than he already is, "I just wanted to tell you how much my heart misses you my King."

"I know my Queen. I have missed you as well. Now do something to turn me on."

"What can I do my King? The whip is in your bedroom."

"Forget the whip. Bite my neck. Taste my blood."

"Is this what turns you on now my King? So sad it is, that you have let your Queen number thirteen fill you with such dark love inside your blood."

"My Queen, that is enough. You will show respect to my Queen Fineness. She is so special that I have decided to call her by name. Look at me my Queen number one as I have what I need to go forth with our love making. Only Queen Fineness will I call by her name. You my Queen and all my Queens are to answer to your number."

Queen One wants to bite King Thicklog's eyes out, instead with pleasure on the outside and none at all on the inside of herself she replies, "Yes my King. I am so happy for you. I am glad you finally have your perfect Queen."

"Enjoy your special day my Queen. No more speaking of my Queen Fineness. Today is your day, make every moment count like it is your last one with me."

"Yes my King. Show off to your wise men and scholars how powerful at love making you are. Show them how great it is to be King Thicklog."

"You are great my Queen. That is why I married you first."

Quiet laughs and remarks between wise man and scholars on how bored and beautiful looking Queen number one looks making love to King Thicklog. One said it, "King Thinlog", and all who heard it laughed out too loud not to be noticed by their King and Queen.

King Thicklog stops his motion with his first Queen and is about to yell out fury as his Queen number one bites down on his neck. King Thicklog gets a burst of quick pleasure that makes him restart his love making, "Make love to me my King. I've missed you so much."

"Yes my Queen number one, I know you missed me. I can feel how fresh you are. I always make your day."

"You make my life, my King. Please make me cry out in hot love from your love making, my King."

The first Queen looks into the eyes of her lustful King. In his eyes she sees that she is nothing to him but for love making. Tears fall from her eyes as the realization that after today that good for only one thing, whore Queen number thirteen will be in charge of her King's heart and bedroom. Tears fall faster as she says to herself, "Who will love me from now until the day I die?"

King Thicklog finishes making love with his first Queen. "You were as great as always my Queen."

Queen number one wipes the tears from her eyes and says to her King, "I love you my King. I have to say to you that your Queen Fineness will be your downfall. My King, she will break your heart and bury your dead body."

"My Queen number one, no more of my Queen Fineness, today is your day. Enjoy your King, leave nothing left for tomorrow."

"Yes my King. Today is my Day?"

Chapter Two:

As King Thicklog had his day, Queen Fineness made her way to the inner city, where the poor live and roam. She laughs on the inside how weak her King is for not being able to give her a living seed. Deep in the city Queen Fineness will find a man that looks close enough to her King and make him make love to her. After that the poor fool has to die. Now Queen Fineness laughs out loud and says, "What a way to die."

Queen Fineness chooses a young man of nineteen. The young man begs Queen Fineness not to make him do this for her, for fear of what King Thicklog will do to him. With threats to the poor young man Queen Fineness gets her way. The feel of Queen Fineness' body to the young man makes him finish before five minutes of time.

The young man tries to leave but Queen Fineness will have none of it. She wants to feel more love making with a man that has a full size manhood. The young man gives Queen Fineness thirty minutes of his hung, poor man's manhood. Queen Fineness scratched the young man's back for giving her such painful pleasures she had never felt before.

After the second loving, Queen Fineness crosses her legs to hold in what she needs. With a soft hand she rubs the face of her young lover. He closes his eyes and never sees the blade that slices his throat. Queen Fineness moves away from all the blood the young man is squirting out from his wound. All this is watched by a man (Knight Trustworthy) that was sent to follow Queen Fineness around and report back her doings and sayings to his King.

Dressing, in front of a man that she does not know is watching her with his sword in his hand, Queen Fineness takes her time and sings aloud her ancient song of hope and victory.

The Knight full of rage for his Queen of her betrayal to his King hears her sing and calmness flows inside his heart for a person whom has endured wars.

Total fear coming forth from his Queen is what Knight Trustworthy had in mind. Now that he is calm, he is simply going to arrest his Queen and take her back to her King for punishment. He feels comfort inside himself that the thought of a quick deadly strike to his Queen's heart is gone from his mind.

"Stand still my Queen. Give me none of your lies. I've seen with my very own eyes your betrayal. The poor young man had no chance of survival. Maybe your King might show lenience to you for killing your lover. Though I doubt it. Put your hands behind your back and stand still. Do not make me strike you down and I will not."

"No lies then. Yes I made love with this poor young man and killed him after. I have a great reason for having to do this. Listen to my words before you cast judgment on me. I am your Queen, I deserve at least this."

"My Queen, make your words fast. I have no time to waste on your attempt to make me set you free. You have shamed yourself my Queen, do not shame yourself any further."

"Thank you, Knight?"

"I am Knight Trustworthy, my Queen.'

"You have such a noble name. Knight Trustworthy, I like the sound of your name. I feel there is still hope that you will do the right thing for your kingdom and set me free."

"I cannot imagine any words you have to say to me that will make me change my mind, my Queen."

"Alright Knight Trustworthy, this is the truth. I had no choice, I had to make love with someone else."

Knight Trustworthy laughs and shakes his head, "My Queen that was the worst attempt to sway my decision, I have ever accounted. Put your hands behind your back, this is over with."

Knight Trustworthy reaches over and grabs a hold of his Queen's shoulder and she pulls away from him, telling him to let her explain her reason better.

"No more words, my Queen. You make my heart hurt, for you show no remorse at all."

Queen Fineness, turns from frightened Queen to how dare you speak to your Queen in such a manner, "I have no remorse, for I had to do what I did!"

"Why my Queen? Tell me why now!"

Queen Fineness, hides her face in shame as she yells out in frustration to Knight Trustworthy, "I had to make love to someone that looks close to the King so he could give me his seed... For King Thicklog's seeds are lifeless as death itself."

In shock Knight Trustworthy responds back, "My Queen... Your words must be lies. Thy King is mighty and strong."

"In battle Knight Trustworthy, my King is mighty and strong. In bed he is weak as an infant."

Knight Trustworthy in deeper shock, "My Queen your words have to be lies. I cannot believe this as truth."

"Look at me Knight Trustworthy. Why else would I do this? If I had lust in my heart, I would find a fine man like you to lay down with. Would I not?

Look at me, reached deep into your heart, please believe what I say to you to be the truth. The cold hard truth."

"I do not know my Queen... I'd like to but I cannot."

"Well then how about this Knight Trustworthy?"

"What else could you say my Queen?"

"Brace yourself Knight Trustworthy, the truth will send you backwards in shock... King Thicklog has thirteen Queens and not one of us has ever carried a child. King Thicklog is full of passion. All of us Queens are bedded from time to time. Think about it Knight Trustworthy. What other answer is there? There is not one. King Thicklog will never have a son unless someone else fathers it for him."

Knight Trustworthy looks away from his Queen. "I... My Queen go back to the castle. Speak of this to no one. I have sorrow in my heart for my King. You have to be right my Queen. Any man would have fathered a flock by now."

"Yes Knight Trustworthy." Queen Fineness says as she reaches out and touches his back gently, "For my King and my kingdom, I will carry this burden alone. What choice do I have? Our kingdom needs a Prince."

"Yes but a Prince from a poor man's seed? What would the dead think of our betrayal? It is our betrayal now my Queen. I will carry your secret to my grave."

Queen Fineness calms herself as she undresses Knight Trustworthy with her eyes. She knows she has to have complete control over him.

"Not good enough Knight Trustworthy. Unless you die this moment, I will have my doubts."

Knight Trustworthy turns around and looks his Queen in her eyes,

161

"My Queen, what do you need more than my death? If you can think one thing that will make you have trust in me, let me know. If you cannot think of one thing, I will give you my sword to take my life with."

"Knight Trustworthy, you are worthy to your King and Kingdom. If only thy peoples would know why you had to die, your name would forever be remembered. Give me your sword. I'll make your death very quick my wonderful and dear to my heart Knight of compassion."

Knight Trustworthy hands his sword to his Queen and kneels down on the ground, just a few feet from where his Queen had sex two times, like a common woman. He looks over and sees the wetness of what remains on the floor and then he closes his eyes, preparing himself for his unexpected death.

Queen Fineness with sword in hand looks down at her conquered noble Knight Trustworthy. What a waste she thinks, he would be even better at love making than the poor young, dead man. That's it! "Knight Trustworthy I have thought of one thing that you could do, to make me believe you would carry my secret until the day you die."

Knight Trustworthy, looks up at his Queen, "What is it my Queen? Tell me and I will do it."

Queen Fineness drops the sword on the ground and takes off her clothes, "You will make love to me Knight Trustworthy. If you defile me, your Queen. I will believe you."

"I cannot my Queen... I am not worthy."

"This is true Knight Trustworthy...

But neither was the poor young dead man over there. He did his part for our kingdom and you will not?

162

I cannot believe, that you a mighty and strong Knight, would let a poor young man best you at love making. Perhaps you are correct when you say you are not worthy. If you can't make love to a beautiful woman like me, your Queen... Well I feel so sorry for you as a man."

Knight Trustworthy hates when his libido comes into question. Even when it comes from some high and mighty lady like his Queen, "If making love is what you want and need from me, my Queen... Making love I will give to you like you have never had before. I promise you this my Queen."

"Well Knight Trustworthy, are you going to talk to me about making love or are you going to make love to me?"

Knight Trustworthy, leaps off his knees and undresses, "Come to me my foul worded Queen. I like your wicked words. I will have you speak many when I am having my way with you like no other man has before. Not even your less than mighty King Thicklog."

Queen Fineness lays down on the ground in the dirty shack that belongs to the young, dead, poor man. "Take me Knight Trustworthy, make love to me as if I belong to you. With your mighty seed, push the poor man's seed out of the way and claim your son as the new Prince of our kingdom."

Queen Fineness, wants to speak more but the feel of Knight Trustworthy manhood prevents her from doing anything but enjoying herself.

Knight Trustworthy, looks at his Queen and knows in her expression, that he is the grandest she has felt in her life, "Take my love my Queen. Try not to scream too loud, when euphoria engulfs your mind and body."

Queen Fineness, some how in the back of her mind reminds herself that she is the one in control.

163

No matter how much intense lust she feels boiling in her blood for the greatest man that ever lived in Knight Trustworthy.

When Knight Trustworthy finishes making love to his Queen, he gives her a loving kiss out of compassion. His thoughts are of his greatness as Queen Fineness is about to send reality straight to his mind, "Is that it Knight Trustworthy? You have no more love making to give to me? Oh well, you were almost as good as the young, dead, poor man."

"Stop your words my Queen. You are angering me with them."

"So what!? I do not care if I'm angering you or not. What I care about is that I'm naked and beautiful and you gave me a promise that you, as of yet, have not fulfilled."

Knight Trustworthy looks at his Queen in astonishment, "You want more you lustful woman? I will give you more. I'll give it to you tomorrow hiding somewhere in our castle, if you want my Queen. I will best you every time. This I promise to you my Queen as well."

Queen Fineness readies herself for more intense, painful, pleasure. She jokingly says to herself that she hopes she will be able to walk straight after this love making. Queen Fineness holds back her screams as she makes Knight Trustworthy make love to her a third time.

After this love making is over with Knight Trustworthy is panting on the floor unable to stand up.

Queen Fineness with incredible willpower stands up the victor. Her legs shake as her heart is pounding out of her chest, but her mind is clear and free, "That is better my Knight Trustworthy. I will expect many more times of love making like this. Now get on your feet, it's time to go back to the castle."

The few days after this did not go as King Thicklog expected them to. Out of disgust King Thicklog started with daily beatings for his wise men and scholars. As King Thicklog's mood darkens with each passing day, Queen Fineness meets Knight Trustworthy every day in their secret hiding place to make love. The days keep passing until it is now the twelfth day since the wise men and scholars have been imprisoned within the King's throne room.

It is also the last day King Thicklog will enjoy the body of a Queen that does not belong to his Queen Fineness. Even though King Thicklog has made love to a different Queen for the past eleven days. He misses his Queen Fineness, he has not laid eyes upon her since their last night together. He cannot wait until tomorrow to have her once again. It's been so long that her freshness will be so welcoming to his needful lust.

King Thicklog finishes his twelfth day with his Queen number twelve. She was his favorite of all his Queens of the past eleven days. Making love to her made it tolerable for King Thicklog to receive another day of nothing from his wise man and scholars. The King's sated passion is all that keeps his rage from boiling out of control from making their daily beating become more intense.

The morning of the thirteenth day, bright and early Queen Fineness walks into her bedroom and chases away Queen number twelve from her bed with her King. She calls in the bathing ladies to clean the filth off her King. After he is all clean it is time to say hello and do some needed talking.

"My King, after we finish breakfast, you will need to have all twelve of your not needed any more Queens rounded up and expelled from our castle and kingdom forever. I agreed to this out of love for you my King. Please do not make me regret my decision."

"Yes my Queen Fineness...

Let's make love after breakfast before we carry out what needs to be done."

"Yes my King, I have missed your strong touch. Making love to you will put a bigger smile on my face as I watch your unneeded Queens ride out of sight and out of minds and hearts forever. I cannot wait."

King Thicklog and Queen Fineness make love. King Thicklog feels something is different with the feel of his Queen, as Queen Fineness counts the seconds before she has to endure any more of her King's tamed and boring love making.

After breakfast, Twelve Queens are dragged out of their chambers and pushed with hardly any possessions in tow towards the castle's outside walls. They beg their King for mercy as he holds the hand of his Queen Fineness tightly.

"My King stay strong, this is almost over. Look at them down there. None of them ever had what it took to be one of your Queens. In fact we are doing them a favor. Now with no reprisal for them, they are free to live out the rest of their lives in peace..."

"They can remarry whom every they choose to. If they get lucky enough, if any man has pity on their over used bodies and hearts."

"Yes my Queen. Now it is just you and me from now on."

"Yes my King, only you and I forever. Now tell me everything your wise men and scholars have created for you to increase your power on Futick."

"Nothing my Queen, they have provided me with nothing."

"Have you stayed constantly with them? Your great presence surely should have made them have one hundred thoughts to give to you by now.

Something must be halting their progress? Let me think my King..."

"It cannot be your presence. What could it have been?"

"I have no idea my Queen."

"Yes I know. Let me think... I have it It must have been the presence of your twelve former Queens. It was their negativity that halted progress. You didn't have sex with your former Queens in front of your wise men and scholars, did you my King?"

"Yes I did, all twelve of them, twelve days in the row."

"I am sorry my King, they messed up everything for you. Do not blame your wise men and scholars, they are only men. They cannot help their weakness."

"Yes my Queen. You are so wise. Now what are we going to do about my wise men and scholars?"

"For them my King you have to show that you can endure going without what you love in life the most."

"What is that my Queen Fineness?"

"Me my King. From now until you get your creation, we will not make love to the other. In fact for greater luck my King, we will not even lay eyes on each other again until your creation comes to life."

"No way my Queen. I will go crazy, if I don't feel your love everyday. You know how great my passion is?"

"Yes my King. When it comes to your passion, no man on Futick dares compare theirs to yours. But for the greater good you will have to endure without making love to my beautiful body. Take plenty of cold baths my King. This may help you a little bit.

I think it would be for the best if I went on a holiday until this comes to be. I will leave tomorrow. Until our kiss goodbye, I say goodbye to you until then."

"Please my Queen do not leave me alone. What of my lust? I know I will find a few consorts to ease my burning passion."

"No my King. No sex. No sex with any woman until you have your creation made for you. You know I'm right. Feel my words in your heart, my King. No sex. Just think about how great I will feel to you when we finally make love once again."

"Yes my Queen. I hate this but I promise you I will hold back my lust until the day you come back from your holiday."

"Very good my King, until tomorrow."

"Until tomorrow my Queen."

As Queen Fineness has her bags packed for her holiday, the caravan of twelve expelled Queens is attacked by cutthroat outlaws. Outlaws that are led by Queen Fineness's lover, Knight Trustworthy himself.

With all twelve Queens dead, Knight Trustworthy pays off his band of outlaws and rides back to the castle and his missed lover, Queen Fineness. In his mind keeps on playing the way her face will shine in delight when he tells her the great news about the twelve dead Queens.

Later that evening as King Thicklog goes to sleep for the first time alone, since he's been King, without a woman sleeping beside him, his Queen and her lover make love three times. Taking breaks in between making love to make fun of their foolish King and his flawed plan.

One month later, eighteen dead bodies have been carried out of the throne room, that none of these unfortunate men have been allowed to leave, since day one of this mad obsession that King Thicklog started. The wse men and scholars wish they could feel fresh air in their lungs.

Two months later, while taking a piss a wise man gets an idea. In his mind this wise man thought that if he could come up with a word that described the want and need for fresh air that the wise men and scholars wanted so badly, that this word would be the greatness that King Thicklog desired so much to obtain.

One week this wise man stays away from all the other men, so that their desperate constant talking and pleading would not disturb his immense thoughts. On the seventh day as winter has set in with all its glory the wise man says out loud one word. This word is Faith.

The wise man gathers all the men that are still alive together and tells them of the new word he created. He makes them understand that Faith is what they all have to have inside themselves if they are ever to breathe fresh air into their lungs once again. It takes many times of repeating himself before this wise man can carry forth from his creation of Faith.

After Faith had to come something great and grand for all Futicks to give their undying Faith to. The next word this wise man created was God. From God came religion. Out of religion came praying and finally Priests and such. Now the hard and the heavy. God was to be great, vengeful but great. There had to be his opposite. Life and death, good and bad, God and the Devil.

The Devil had to be so bad that a word had to be created to describe his presence. This word became Evil.

Finally a home for God and the Devil. One word created had to be all that is beautiful.

The other word that had to be created and to be filled up with every horrible thing a man or woman could think of. It took a whole day for the wise man to create Heaven and Hell. He told no one that he created Hell before Heaven. The reason was a selfish one. To create Hell this wise man had to have thoughts of total evil. After this he could have all the peaceful thoughts he could think of to place inside Heaven.

The wise man sits by himself. He is calm, it is getting closer to the end of winter. Today is the day he has chosen to give his King some of his thoughts about Heaven and Hell. It took some negotiating by the wise man to convince all the other men to hold their tongues about their discussions for one more week. The wise man knew the King had to wait until all was perfect in Heaven and Hell. The King like a child would scream out in rage if he could not comprehend Heaven and Hell.

This waiting period weighed heavy on the wise man, for every day came more beatings. Beatings so furious that death followed the ones that could not be healed. The total death for this over two month span raised to fifty seven deaths. Blood stained the floor, blood stained the walls. There was even blood on King Thicklog's throne.

The wise man's thoughts are disturbed by the banging open of the doors to the King's throne room. In walks King Thicklog like he does every day. He walks in and heads straight for his throne. There he sits shaking from nerves that never give him any pause. The wise man far away enough from his King for him to notice him, smiles at the irritation the King has placed upon himself.

The wise man is about to walk to his King, when a calling from his mind makes him remember, something he has forgotten. After death a man or woman that lived their mortal lives on Futick, had the immortal something extra that was given to them by God, either fly to Heaven or sink to Hell.

170

The wise man in a panic sits back down and ponders to himself what was the name he created for that something extra from God?

A soldier walks up to him and stops. The wise man is the first to be picked for the starting of the beatings of the day. Grabbed up by two soldiers the wise man says to himself it is now or maybe never. Two thoughts away the wise man is about to be beaten. One thought away the whip is raised. He remembers, Souls, as the whip strikes him.

"Stop my beating. I must have words with the King. I have what he demands to be created."

"If you lie to the King, I will beat you to death. Time is short. King Thicklog has no times for lies. Are you still wanting to have words with the King?"

"Yes I am soldier."

King Thicklog watches as a man from quite a distance is being brought to him. King Thicklog keeps both eyes on this man. Excitement within himself starts to flourish as this stranger looks him in his eyes, "You have it? You have what I need?"

The wise man is let go of and allowed to stand up tall, as he answers his King, "Yes my King. I have the beginning... I have the end. I have Heaven and Hell for you my King."

King Thicklog looks at one of his, unknown to him, wise men and laughs out loud heartily to the two new powerful sounding words he just heard, "Heaven and Hell? Tell me my wise man, what is Heaven and Hell?"

"My King, Heaven is pure as peace, love and ale. Hell is as pure as war, sickness and death."

"I love it! What is your name, wise man?"

171

"My King, my name is Genius. May I tell you more?"

"Yes Genius, I want more. I want it all. But first you must wash your body. Genius, you smell like you shit all over yourself. Quick soldier, bring this man to the bathing room. Have the bathing ladies use lots of extra soap on his stinking ass. One more thing soldier. Genius is to be treated like royalty as of now. I will let you know if or when this changes."

"Yes my King. Please follow me, Sir Genius."

After his bath, food and wine, Genius lays out in full details on how to make the poor crumble to King Thicklog's power. King Thicklog tries his best not to daydream, while hearing all these new powerful words and their meaning for the first time. Then he hears Church and Kingdom.

"No Genius. It is kingdom and church. I, King Thicklog and my kingdom will be all powerful as if God resides within my walls and inside my soul. I have faith in this Genius. Your place from now on is standing beside me. I am very proud of you Genius. You with your small ideas, I will turn into my grand idea. The idea I thought of all by myself. Your job is to remind me of my grand idea. Do you understand what I demand from you Genius?"

"Yes my King. I am to shut up unless you want me to remind you of specifics of your grand idea."

"You learn fast Genius. Maybe you should change your name to Smart One."

"Yes my King."

"And one more thing Genius. Try your very best not to anger me. Do you have a wife?"

"No my King. I have not found, as of yet, a woman that controls my interest longer than it takes to have a drink

172

and a dance on the way to bed them for the night."

"Genius, you are a man of same heart as I. You are right Genius. Pleasure and lust is of most important deep within man. Battle and Victory makes your body and mind stronger. While the bedding of a woman for the night makes you satisfied and weak. To Hell with it, will be my new saying. Tonight, you and I Genius, we will enjoy my consorts. Respect this Genius, for I never share my women be them my Queens or my consorts."

"Yes my King. Thank you."

King Thicklog and Genius spend the late hours of the night being greedy with the King's consorts. Four hours before dawn King Thicklog calls Genius his friend. Both are drunk and spent laying on the floor, as the King's consorts slowly begin putting back on their clothes. Genius calls his drunk King his friend as well, hoping in the morning light his King will remember calling him friend and not servant to the court.

"Genius my friend... Which of my consorts was your favorite?" King Thicklog ask then burbs out loudly.

"My King all your consorts are very special. But my favorite two was that blond with the pretty face and ass..."

"Which other my friend? Call me friend, Genius."

"My King, my friend, I like that brunette with the pretty face and pretty big breast. I had them together at one time while making love. Both so very beautiful and both so different looking than the other."

"You pick women great my friend. I tell you what I am going to do for you my friend. Both..."

King Thicklog stops talking, trying his best not to puke, "Both? My King, my friend."

173

King Thicklog, steadies himself and continues, "Yes both my friend. Both the blond and the brunette now belong to you as your wives. Now it's time for you to leave. Grab your two future wives, find an empty bedroom and fall asleep with them, for the few hours we have left until dawn."

Genius cannot believe his ears, "Are you sure my friend?"

"Yes my friend, they are yours to keep. I've had enough time having sex with them. They are perfect for you now."

Genius insulted deeply, would love to punch his King in his big mouth, instead he thanks his King for his gratitude. Genius gets off the floor, leaving his empty cup behind for the King to deal with. He walks over to his two future wives and introduces himself to them. Hearing what was said by their King, the two consorts no more, jump up for joy at the freedom of being away from their King.

Genius feels like the greatest man on Futick, as his two future wives whisper to him how much larger his manhood is compared to the very small manhood of their King. In the middle, between two beautiful women, Genius falls asleep and dreams only great dreams.

For the next week Genius reminds King Thicklog of the importance of his grand idea.

During this time and the two months before this time, Queen Fineness and Knight Trustworthy made love hours at the time. Queen Fineness loves the power of control she has over her Knight. He is so weak for her now, she probably could will him to assassinate her King husband.

Queen Fineness is starting to show herself with child. She laughs at her King and her Knight, knowing her baby is the bastard that belongs to the young, dead poor man.

Queen Fineness brushes her hair in peace looking out the window at all the snow that has fallen as of late. A servant woman knocks on her bedroom door, telling her she has a message from her King. Queen Fineness walks to the hall and listens to the soldier's words, given to him in letter by his King. The letter is short. "It is time to come home my Queen, all is fine and great. I cannot wait to lay eyes on your beauty."

Three days later Queen Fineness enters her castle showing off her belly to her King. King Thicklog is so happy. If he didn't know better, he would believe he has been blessed by God.

The kingdom survives the freezing cold winds and heavy snows of one more month of winter. Many poor died from lack of food and shelter. King Thicklog and his only Queen now, Queen Fineness, lived life happily. From afar it seemed so romantic how the King doted over his Queen. With a closer look, you would see a Queen daily talking about the death of her King to her lover, Knight Trustworthy. Who believes that his Queen is carrying his child and not the poor man's. Queen Fineness, hates Genius and wants the King to have him put to death quietly. She fills her King's ears with words of doubt and betrayal. Just like this, two weeks ago.

"My King, my love of my life, you cannot trust Genius. He has served his purpose. As soon as he finishes writing down all there is to know about God and the Devil, have his throat sliced. You must do this my King. If you let Genius live after he finishes, he will betray you."

"My Queen, you must get over your obsession of mistrust about Genius. He is my friend and my most valuable wise man. Without him there would be no God or the Devil."

"Yes I know this my King. This is why I say what I say to you about his death it's a must for you and your kingdom."

"No my Queen. I trust Genius. He would never dare betray my trust. I am his King, he fears my power and strength. I am also his friend, he loves me."

"Well my King, I say to you this... After your mind returns back to normal. When you return to being the King that is blood thirsty once again, we will have these words again."

"Fine my Queen. Your wait will be for a long time. Now let me see you. Let me see how beautiful you look carrying my child. Yes, yes, you are prettier than the day is long. My Queen, you must release all this death that infects your mind. Give Genius a Chance."

"Alright my King, for you I will try my best. I have one more thought for you my King."

"Let me hear it my Queen so all this can be over with."

"My King, maybe you are correct. To his dying day Genius never betrays you. Still for his whole life he will be there next to you as a constant reminder, that he knows everything. Your most precious secret will never be truly all yours, while he still lives. You will always have to share this with him."

King Thicklog, takes a step back from the new heavy on his mind that his Queen just gave to him, "Yes my Queen, I will keep this in my mind. Thank you my Queen, you always have my best interest in your mind and heart."

"Very true, my King. There is one more thing. Maybe you should say along with my mind and heart, my soul also has its best interest in you now."

"That is funny my Queen. Your soul."

"What is funny about having a soul, my King?"

King and Queen, look at the other and share a big laugh together. It's been awhile. Too bad for King Thicklog that his laugh is the only true one. His Queen is just playing her role until she doesn't have to anymore.

The seed is planted inside the King's mind. He thinks he is in total control, never suspecting the looming betrayal by his Queen and one of his favorite Knights, Knight Trustworthy.

Away from battle and having his mind filled with Heaven and Hell everyday has changed King Thicklog's idea about the poor. He feels that it's better not to kill half of their population off Futick. With God and the Devil coming after their souls, the poor will be so easy to control now.

The King smiles as he prepares himself for the day he will introduce God and the Devil to his kingdom. The poor like never before will finally have something to love more than their very lives themselves. They will all have brand new souls inside them to protect from Hell. Fear is what will keep the poor in line. The more laws he passes for God, the more faith they will place inside their souls.

King Thicklog, tells his friend Genius about the newer version of his plan for the poor. Not to King Thicklog's surprise, Genius loves this plan more than the original.

So happy, King Thicklog tell his Queen of his newer plan for the poor. He expects happiness from his Queen but instead, she hates it. The idea of her King having all this power at his command makes her blood boil in a rage.

After Queen Fineness leaves her King, she heads straight to her lover, Knight Trustworthy and tells him that the day for their King to die has to come sooner than later now.

177

Chapter Three:

It is the first week of spring. King Thicklog invited the rest of the one hundred and sixty eight Kings to a festival. Not one of the other living Kings did any planning about ending the poor during the past winter. They all happily left that responsibility for King Thicklog. One hundred Kings did make plans on how to kill King Thicklog and take his place as Grand King. Mostly these Kings ate lots of meat, drank a lot of ale and had as much sex as they could.

Queen's of the dead Kings where made to report to another King to become his new Queen or simply a consort. Kingdoms fell and were swallowed up by neighboring kingdoms. Many families were ripped apart as many other families were completely dissolved to nothing but fading memories.

All new larger kingdom armies raised in greater numbers, as men with no more homelands walked many miles to join another kingdom's army. Hope was depleted even more, everyday by the sheer number of poor people who just sat down on the cold winter's ground and gave up waiting for someone Royal to tell them what to do.

Not one King did anything to help the sheer number of poor people that needed help. By doing nothing the Kings made many of the poor give up hope and be ready for anything to replace it with. The one hundred and sixty eight Kings unknowingly helped King Thicklog's future plan for Religion to be started on Futick.

Unknowingly to even Queen Fineness, King Thicklog made haste with another plan this past winter's time. A number came to King Thicklog's mind, one hundred and one. One hundred Kings and himself as the Grand King, the number one King of all of Futick. His greatest Knights he sent to specific kingdoms to have words with the second in charge of these kingdoms. All one hundred gave their pledge and loyalty to King Thicklog.

178

Over this past winter's time, one hundred coups took place across Futick. Now these new one hundred Kings ride into King Thicklog's kingdom full of excitement for this coming day's festival. Unknowingly sixty eight kings ride into King Thicklog's kingdom to greet the last day of their lives.

These out numbered Kings ride up on Kings that they never set eyes upon and demand explanations for them being the new Kings of their kingdoms. No answers are given to them but one, that all one hundred old Kings are dead and replaced with themselves.

No soldiers or Knights are permitted to attend the meeting of the one hundred and sixty nine Kings. It takes only a few moments after King Thicklog's appearance for cries of outrage to start. All by the out numbered sixty eight confused and angered Kings.

King Thicklog tells all the Kings to be silent, that he will explain everything in great detail as soon as they have some ale and calm down their anger. Silence commences as lots of ale is poured into empty cups. After many cups of ale are drank down, King Thicklog starts the meeting with the one hundred non-drinking ale Kings to assassinate the drunk sixty eight Kings.

Blood everywhere stains the meeting room. More ale is drank in celebration that not one of the one hundred and one Kings died. Some of the surviving Kings had bleeding wounds on their bodies but nothing that would be considered life threatening.

The dead sixty eight Kings' bodies are dragged out of the way, as King Thicklog begins telling his one new hundred getting drunk Kings his plan for Religion for all of Futick. All one hundred Kings are awestruck as King Thicklog, with the help from Genius, makes them believe his words so much, that many of his new one hundred Kings start to believe that they have souls of their very own inside their bodies just waiting to fly to Heaven after they die.

The meeting is over, the festival has to wait for one more small matter to be over with, before it can officially begin. The sixty eight dead King's Knights and soldiers, are out numbered as they hear the news of their fallen Kings, from a powerful speaking Grand King Thicklog.

"Look around noble Knights and loyal soldiers. See the force you will have to fight. I am not speaking to the part of you that will die for your kingdoms and King. No I am speaking to good men that have no reason to fight. Your kingdoms no longer exist. Your Kings are dead, your kingdoms now are owned by one of my new one hundred Kings. As of this time there is only one hundred and one kingdoms on Futick..."

Many of the dead Kings' Knights and soldiers attack every body with all the love of their Kings and kingdoms in their hearts. Sadly they are slayed easily and quickly. The ones that surrendered are herded together without arms.

"Kill them all," is spoken out loudly by many Knights and soldiers. King Thicklog waits a little bit before speaking so the surviving men will have higher fear inside their loyal minds, "Wait Knights and soldiers. Give these surviving men some clear space and a pause from your anger."

Knights and soldiers step back from the surviving men. Words of discontent are spoken lightly. The surviving men look at the men who would kill them if ordered to in a heartbeat and hope that they don't die.

"Men, Knights and soldiers, I am your Grand King. In fact all of Futick is mine to command. You surviving men do not have to die. You once again can be referred to as Knights and soldiers. All you have to do is pledge your loyalty to me and my one hundred Kings. What do you say, are you men to die this day or become what you once were just a few moments ago? Pledge or die, it is all up to you men. Be buried or drink some ale? Let me know without haste."

Nineteen men spit on the ground and yell out King Thicklog is a tyrant. Without emotion King Thicklog gives the wave for their deaths. The rest of the men that give their pledge of loyalty to King Thicklog walk away and join ranks in whatever kingdom they choose to join

After the dead bodies are removed from the court yard the festival officially begins. Sitting in the best seats, King Thicklog and Queen Fineness watch all the games and challenges of the days events. Queen Fineness mad from being pregnant, tries her best to be a gracious host for her King. King Thicklog, drinks ale and looks around the crowd for that one special stand out kind of lady. It takes a few hours for King Thicklog to find her This beautiful lady is a servant to an ugly Queen.

King Thicklog, calls over one of his guards and orders him and four more guards of his choosing to bring this lady to the bathing room and have her cleaned up, fed and wined. King Thicklog tells the guard to tell the ugly Queen that he is very pleased with her and she is very welcome to have one of his servant ladies in trade. Laughing now, King Thicklog tells the guard if she refuses, for him to slide his sword into her belly.

One new and fresh lady for the night to enjoy King Thicklog smiles, wondering what other ladies he will pick to join them later for this evening's love making. He looks over at his wife, his Queen and gives her arm a little squeeze.

A brand new type of game is about to start, this game is for women only. This new game is introduced by King Thicklog himself. The woman who wins this game will get to spend the rest of the day with Knight Trustworthy. The game is simple, the first woman who makes it to the finish line in a race of speed wins the game.

Queen Fineness looks at the back of her King while he is giving his introduction to this new game this year and sneers in anger.

181

She knew nothing of this and she cannot believe her Knight Trustworthy is the man chosen for these not worthy of him women to spend a day with. Her King will pay for this, she reassures herself.

The game is over, a slim young woman of moderate looks is the winner. Knight Trustworthy, walks over to her with a single flower and carrying no sword nor weapons on his person. King's orders.

King Thicklog, sits back down and looks at his very angry looking Queen and smiles at her, like she's the punchline of a very funny joke. Queen Fineness does not smile in return to her King.

"Well my Queen, that should keep your lover occupied for the rest of the day."

Queen Fineness, drops the look of anger on her face and replaces it with a very worried look instead, "I do not understand your jest my King."

"You don't my Queen? Well I can't have that. It's like this my Queen number thirteen. Your lover will not be able to be with you for the rest of the day. That woman right there is his responsibility for the rest of the day. I hope he enjoys his day for it is the last day of his life."

"My King, please show mercy."

"Mercy? You cheat on me with one of my Knights. Now I am to show mercy for him. My Queen, your thoughts should not be about a dead man. They should all be about if you are going to keep your head on your shoulders."

"My King, please spare my life. I am carrying your child."

"That is a lie my Queen. Your bastard belongs to the dead man. Does it not?"

"No my King. This child belongs to you. It is our child created out of love."

"I'll think about this my Queen. While I'm doing this, I have a surprise guest for you to meet. Well you already know her, you tried to have her killed after all. I tell you what my Queen, she can't wait to lay eyes on you once again."

King Thicklog, waves his hand in the air and down walks from out of the shadows Queen number one, the beautiful, Queen Best.

Back story: Five days ago Queen Best snuck herself into the castle and into King Thicklog's very own chambers, without getting caught. King Thicklog was very surprised by her entrance into his chambers. He was even more surprised by her looks. Queen Best had cut and colored her hair from brown to blond.

At first King Thicklog did not want to listen to his former Queen but in the end he decided to give her his time of the day. After Queen Best was through speaking, King Thicklog had her fed and cleaned up so she could look and be dressed like the beautiful Queen she still is.

Queen Best always the smartest of all of King Thicklog's Queens, had the foresight to have one of her servant ladies trade places with her. Queen Best and a small trusted group of her servant ladies followed the caravan of Queens a day behind them.

In Horror Queen Best's company found the dead bodies of the eleven expelled Queens and all that accompanied them on their journey as well. With luck one of the Queen's still had a few moments of life left inside herself. It was Queen number seven who told Queen Best about Knight Trustworthy and his band of cut throat bandits. Queen Best took her time and changed her appearance, waiting on the day, she could tell King Thicklog all about what his favorite Queen had done behind his back.

Queen Best, feeling energized for payback, had three of her servant ladies return back to King Thicklog's kingdom to be spies for her. Her former Husband and King, what a weak fool he has become. What Queen Best spies uncovered for her, something that even the King nor his company found out about until she told the King herself, was that his favorite and only Queen as of now, cheated on him with Knight Trustworthy. Not only has she cheated on her King, she also makes sport with pillow talk words about how Knight Trustworthy is the father of her baby. And King Thicklog is to raise him as his very own son.

Queen Best laughed at her former King and Husband. She fantasized about saying to his face what she truly wanted to say to him. Queen Best did not want to break King Thicklog's heart, she wanted to rip it to bloody small pieces and then stomp on them. For what she has had to endure, she deserved to do this in her heart but in her mind, she knew the better not to. If she did, how could she ever become her King's number one Queen once again.

This is what Queen Best wants to say to her sorry bastard of a husband and not almighty King, "Betrayal, my King. Your Queen is a whore. She has had countless times of nasty sex with Knight Trustworthy. And finally my fool of a former Husband, she is even carrying his son to be raised by you as your own son. How's that for payback, you stupid puddle of mud and crud?"

That is what Queen Best said out loud when she was all by herself. It made her feel damn good inside, that she had power over her King and enough power to have her King give back the life she missed so much out of great thankfulness. The best of all to Queen Best, is that the bitch will get what's coming to her and then some.

However this is what Queen Best said to King Thicklog, with hatred in her heart for him and with pleasant, toned words, speaking from her mouth, that has such small and kissable, soft lips.

"My King, I have to speak with you. What I am going to tell you will boil your blood. May I tell you of betrayal?"

King Thicklog wanted to hear his former Queen's words as fast as she could speak them so she could leave that much faster after speaking them to him. What he heard did more than boil his blood, it made King Thicklog turn into a calm, madman that held back his pain and rage until the time he could get them all out of himself and at the same time. "Yes my Queen, tell me of betrayal."

"My King, I am very un-pleased to inform you that your Queen Fineness has been the very one to betray you. My King she has made Knight Trustworthy her lover and..." Queen Best finished her words of deep and dirty betrayal to her King. Her King stared at her with eyes filled with fire. In his mind there are several blades stabbing at him from all directions.

After Queen number one finished, King Thicklog, grabbed her and gave her a giant hug. After that he asked her if she would like to become his Queen once again. She said yes, he told her she was to be known to him and all of Futick as Queen Best. With tears in her eyes Queen Best walked away from her grateful King with many servants in tow, all of them at her beck and call.

Everything was bad and hard to listen to for King Thicklog, but the worst part for him was when Queen Best said the repeated words from Queen Fineness's evil mouth, "King Thicklog is so weak of a man that he could not even get one of his thirteen Queens pregnant without a great and mighty man like you Knight Trustworthy, doing it for him."

King Thicklog, told himself to be calm and to hurry up and inform Genius of all that has happened to him this day. Genius listened to his disheartened King's words and came up with a plan for him to follow through that had lots of pay back in the end for his Queen Fineness.

185

After Queen Best was dressed like a Queen, she made her way secretly back to King Thicklog's chambers, where she met for the first time the very pleasant and handsome man known as Genius. The two of them hit it off right away and became very close friends before the day was over with.

Back to present day: King Thicklog, waves his hand in the air and down walks from out of the shadows Queen number one, the beautiful, Queen Best.

"You see my Queen, you know her very well. Now keep your mouth shut and accept what my Queen Best has in store for you. You betraying little whore."

Queen Best takes her time walking to greet the King and Queen. When she is in their presence, she hugs her King and gives him a loving kiss on his cheek. She looks at the Queen and spits in her face, "You're in my seat whore. Why don't you sit on the floor and stay silent? You will do this now, if you know what's best for you."

Queen Fineness, says nothing as she sits on the floor beside her King and Queen, like she has no worth to them at all. There Queen Fineness stays all during every game and event that happens the rest of the day.

Sometime during this time the woman who won the race and has a day with Knight Trustworthy, wipes blood from the blade of her killing knife. This special woman was picked by King Thicklog to assassinate Knight Trustworthy, very painfully. She took her assassination of Knight Trustworthy to heart by slicing off his manhood while he was tied up and fully awake to see and feel everything she did to him. After she was through making Knight Trustworthy bleed to death, she collected her bag of gold from one of King Thicklog's Knights and rode off into the sunset never looking back.

In front of everyone at the festival, King Thicklog and Queen Best gets remarried.

Queen Fineness said not one word of complaint to their marriage. But inside her mind is totally another story.

As night falls and the festival comes to a close for the day, Queen Fineness is led to the very top of the castle by King Thicklog, Queen Best, Genius and a few trusted guards. Queen Fineness pleads for her life and the life of her unborn child. Queen Best walks over to Queen Fineness who is tied up and standing on the edge of the castle wall. "Plead all you want whore, you will not see another day. Too bad for you, you don't have a soul. But then again maybe it's better that you don't have a soul. For if you did it would surely fall straight to Hell to burn for all eternity."

Queen Best grabs Queen Fineness by the back of her hair and pulls her head back, so her mouth would be beside her ear, "You should have known your place whore and stayed there. You should have never betrayed me and your King. That job is for a much better woman than you. That job is for a woman like me. I'm a Great woman that has what it takes to see my King dead and buried so I can take charge and rule his kingdom."

Queen Best removes her mouth from Queen Fineness' ear and pulls her head back even further, "Take this whore." Queen Best says as she slices Queen Fineness' throat with the sharp blade of a knife. Queen Fineness stands there shaking in pain as Queen Best shoves her off the top of Castle Thicklog.

All watch from the top of the castle as Queen Fineness falls to the ground faster and faster. When she makes impact there is a smacking wet sound that could be heard all the way up the top of Castle Thicklog. Moments later all began to cheer Queen Fineness' death and then they all go to their bedrooms to go to sleep or to have some hot and needed sex.

Queen Best orders bread, wine and fruit to her and King Thicklog's bedroom.

187

The two lovers have fun eating, drinking, making love and falling asleep in each other's arms, 'til the sun comes up in the blue morning sky and they wake up and say a gentle good morning to the other.

Tomorrow is upon us as this day becomes the day that will be forever known as the day King Thicklog presents, God in Heaven and The Devil in Hell to the people that reside within his kingdom. King Thicklog with peace in his voice for Heaven and war in his voice for Hell, begins to preach to his, gathering closer to him, mass of people. They are hanging on to every word the King is saying, like it is the greatest and saddest thing they have ever heard in their mortal life times.

Next is his proof to his kingdom's people, that every living mortal on Futick has a soul placed inside them at birth by God. One hundred or more men and women start saying out loud that they felt their souls come to life in them awhile back. That all of them were afraid to say anything about the enlightenment they felt inside them until now.

The big surprise is when all of these men and women pledge to the people what they say next is so true, that they will give up their souls to the Devil if they are lying. All of these great people swear to God that they all had a dream last night that God was going to speak of his grand design for all the people on Futick through the voice of King Thicklog today.

The last thing, the great finale, that makes almost all of these people believe King Thicklog's words, is that after God speaks through King Thicklog, God is going to turn on all the souls inside everybody's body on Futick. The cheers of joy are endless as people start to sing and cry. Random people yell out, "Finally we can be saved. Our lives have purpose now. God in Heaven, we love you. Thank you for your precious gift. We can't wait to spend our afterlife's with you in Heaven for eternity."

King Thicklog speaks God's words for over three hours. Very few people that gather here today still believe there is no such thing as a soul or God or the Devil. When King Thicklog finishes his preaching to his kingdom of people, he falls to his knees as if a great presence has just left his body. The people in shock stand there in silence until their Godly King stands back up on his feet tall and strong for all eyes to see the glory of his mighty power.

On command, selected people start to act like their souls are coming alive within them. After this happens to them, they all smile and laugh like life is the most wonderful thing on the planet of Futick.

People that do not feel anything in themselves coming on, start to act like they feel it just like everybody else does. Before long almost everybody has made it known that their souls have come to life within them. The few that do not boast about their souls are gathered up into one group of ungodly, unbelievers.

The first man in line is brought up in front of King Thicklog to inspect for the reason that his soul did not get turned on. King Thicklog takes his time and then he has another unbeliever brought up in front of him, then another until ten men stand before him as unbelievers of God.

With anger in his voice, King Thicklog shouts out that these unbelievers' souls all have been touched by the Devil, Satan himself.

"There is no hope for these men, my good people. No praying for them will save their souls. They all must die by fire. Their souls must be burned free from their bodies so that their souls can fall to Hell, instead of staying on Futick after Death as angry and vengeful evil spirits."

The fires starts up within ten minutes time. All the unbelievers are burnt to death before dusk. There are some unbelievers that try to act like their souls start to come on after the promise of death by fire is given to them by their King. King Thicklog, shouts out that they are faking having their souls come on, "Do not believe these unbelievers my good people. They lie to you to save their mortal lives so that they can live longer on Futick and spread more of their evil ways and thoughts."

The fires take over a thousand lives this day. This was only the beginning. For many years to come in the future many unbelievers will be burned to death for their crimes against God. King Thicklog stands tall and proud watching all the unbelievers being burned alive and shouting out from time to time to burn the unbelievers faster and faster.

Later this night King Thicklog makes love to Queen Best and three other ladies of his choice. Queen Best bites her tongue and does her part in the love making, while having thoughts of the death of her bastard King, that will be coming very soon to him indeed.

Let's return to the Day that Queen Best snuck her way into castle Thicklog. This part takes place after Queen Best and Genius met. The night of this day to be more exact. Queen Best knowing that Genius had feelings for her made him make love to her before she returned herself later that night to her lustful and weak in the loins king. The King would make love to her thinking that it was his seed that made her pregnant instead of the seed that she already carried with her to his bed from Genius.

A few months later as King Thicklog's power of religion spreads across the planet of Futick, Queen Best starts to show the first signs of being pregnant. King Thicklog is so happy, this time nothing will go wrong with his Queen and his child. Nine months has gone by as Queen Best gives birth to twins. Both are male and look different from the other. Queen Best in a hurry has one of her babies taken from the castle without the King knowing anything about it. The second born son, which is Genius's son is given to a farmer and his wife, to raise as their own.

190

The Farmer and his wife give the best life they could to their very special one of a kind, peace loving son. The true son of King Thicklog years later takes his place on the throne at the age of twenty one as Grand King of Futick. The people love him through words but hate him passionately in their hearts. But before this can come to be, King Thicklog has to die first.

On the second birthday of his son, King Thicklog threw a giant birthday party for him. Queen Best talked King Thicklog into preaching to his people before the party started. King Thicklog drank his cup of ale before he went out to greet his people. What King Thicklog did not know was his ale was laced with a herb that was tasteless and very deadly. On the grand stage Genius came out and warmed up the crowd for his best friend, King Thicklog. Before Genius could finish his speech he acted like he fell down and died right in front of everybody's eyes.

King Thicklog ran up to his fallen friend and cried out for help for him. Betrayer is more like it as Genius waited for the herb to kill King Thicklog dead and gone. King Thicklog stood up in great pain and then he fell face first dead on the stage's floor. Genius then started to move his body around like it was coming back to life.

Moments later Genius is telling all the people that he is now the new Voice of God's words and that Queen Best is to take over as Grand Queen of Futick until her son Jesus can take over as King on his twenty first birthday. The people cried at first and then they cheered Queen Best and Jesus' names out loud for both Heaven and Hell to hear clearly. If only Queen Best had a few moments longer, she could have saved Futick from damnation.

Sadly like everything and everyone else on Futick Jesus is the opposite of his name, he reigns in pain and terror instead of peace and love. Rest in peace, Futick.

A Dream Or A Nightmare

One Week ago, "Try to relax Daniel. You are in a place that is calm and peaceful. Nothing will hurt you here. All you have to do is relax and give me your thoughts."

"It is not about my thoughts Doctor Hum. It is all about my dreams. My dreams are beautiful. My nightmares are from Hell itself. Nightmares that you cannot imagine have infected my mind. My waking thoughts I feel are slipping away. One day Doctor Hum, reality will no longer exist, everything will be a dream or a nightmare."

"I find this to be highly unlikely Daniel. You have to focus. Dreams can feel and seem to you as more real than your living life itself. I know the tortures that dreams can have on a person's mind. Yes Daniel, I can help you."

"How?"

"By making you help yourself. I will be your anchor. I will be the stable on this side, the side of reality. You, Daniel with the help from my calming words and a little bit of an concoction I have created to help you open up your mind, you will enter your dreams and learn to take control over them."

"You think I can do this Doctor Hum?"

"Yes Daniel. I have confidence with my help, no matter how powerful it has to be, I will help you so you can live a normal life once again."

"That sounds great to me Doctor Hum. It has been so long, a normal life is but a dream to me as I am now."

"That is great Daniel. That is one step. You have discovered your problem, which is you yourself. Keep going forward like this and your normal life can be had sooner than you might think possible."

"Alright, okay, Doctor Hum. I will put my mind in your hands. Release me, give me back my life."

"That I will Daniel. The only way I can fail is if you fail yourself. You do not plan on doing this, do you Daniel?"

"No Doctor Hum, I do not."

"Good, very good Daniel. Starting today, we will get to know your dreams together. For the next week Daniel you will be put in an almost sleeping state of mind."

"A week? Why a week? That sounds like a long time to me, Doctor Hum?"

"Yes I can understand this. Believe in me, one week is all you will need. Who knows maybe we will work so coherently together we can finish before a week's time." (Inside Doctor Hum's mind, "The real reason you trusting fool, is because a week's worth of my treatments is all the amount your credit card has on it.")

"How do we start Doctor Hum?"

"First go lay down on that couch. Get comfortable, relax. While you are doing this I will fill this syringe with my mental, miracle formula. After this your mind will be defenseless to my probing. I will enter your mind while you are in a state that is very close to waking and dreaming. I will dig in deep and hard to capture the truth of your dreams and not what you want to tell me out of fear that I will discover more than you intended for me to."

"I don't know Doctor Hum. Are drugs necessary?"

"Oh yes Daniel. My mental, miracle formula is so pure, you will love it. Besides there is no other way to get to your truthful dreams. We can go slow, take our time, talk and talk for months upon months and it will get us nowhere. You want fast Daniel?"

193

"Yes Doctor Hum, my life is a living Hell, give it to me fast."

"Then let's begin."

Daniel gets out of the chair he is sitting in and walks over to the couch and lays down on it. Daniel sniffs and smells sex from a while ago upon the couch. He looks over at Doctor Hum and wonders if it was his receptionist or one of his patients. "Good for you Doctor Hum." Daniel thinks and smiles, betting to himself that it was his hot looking receptionist, that he laid down with on this couch.

Doctor Hum hurries and injects his mental, miracle formula into Daniel's vein. Quickly it flows with his blood straight to his heart and brain.

Daniel remembers something he was going to ask Doctor Hum, "Wait a minute Doctor Hum, how can I stay here for a week straight?"

Doctor Hum laughs and enjoys telling Daniel, "Don't worry Daniel, I have a bed in the basement of this building all ready for you to lay in for a week straight. Best of all I have the room you will be staying in soundproofed..."

"What? I don't understand."

"No one will hear us. I will free you from your dreams or I will destroy your mind in the process. I have to thank you Daniel, I am so looking forward to entering your mind and taking over. You are so weak of mind Daniel, your mind will be like clay in my hands ready to be made into something I want it to become."

"No please, I've changed my mind, Doctor Hum."

"I bet you have Daniel and I don't care. To me the cure is more important than the patient. I have waited for someone as desperate as you Daniel for a long time. Now I can finally take another step to genius."

Daniel wakes up a little bit and looks at the lady that is standing and looking down at him. She is hideous, she looks like a zombie. Daniel shakes his head and closes his eyes, when he opens them back up the lady looks much better in fact she looks hot.

"Wait a minute," Daniel thinks to himself. "I'm laying down, I can't move and I'm gagged. What the Hell did I get myself into. I gotta fight. She looks so sexy, she has a needle, she's going to bring me down. I'm even paying for this!"

"Relax Daniel, this will hurt some. I'm not too good at giving shots. But I'm part of the team and that's what counts. You should be very thankful for Doctor Hum. He's going to fix your crazy mind, make you all shiny and normal. This must sound so good to you."

Daniel looks at Doctor Hum's receptionist Mary unable to answer her back, "Look at you wanting so much to speak to me. That gag is to hold back your lies. You need more of your medicine, I can tell. Here's the secret, you're not suppose to be this awake, you're suppose to be closer to dreamland. Shame on you bad man. Do yourself a favor, don't anger Doctor Hum. You ever heard of Doctor Frankenstein? I'm just kidding. No, I'm not."

Mary injects Daniel with more of Doctor Hum's mental, miracle formula. She pulls the needle out his arm as a voice from behind her speaks out, "Give him another half of a dose Mary, his mind is strong of will. A will I will be breaking very soon."

"Yes my love.."

"How many times do I have to tell you Mary. When I am In my laboratory, you must call me Doctor Hum."

"Yes Doctor Hum, I'm sorry, I forgot.

You know how I can't stand to wait until you decide to make love to me."

"Yes I know Mary. I love this about you."

"Will you make love to me for the first time in your laboratory?"

"No I will not. This is a place for science and the mind. My couch will do just fine again."

"How about on my desk? Please, I am so tired of that ugly couch. I like it better on my desk."

"Very well Mary. After I dig into Daniel's mind for a few hours, we'll go back up and I will make love to you on your desk. Now it is time for the Doctor to get to work."

"Yes Doctor Hum, let me inject this crazy man with another half of a dose like you wanted me to do first."

"Fine. I'm going to go wash my hands."

"You just came back from washing your hands Doctor Hum."

"I know Mary. My hands still look dirty to me. I am a Doctor, my hands must always be clean."

Daniel is almost out of it again as Mary looks at him, "Don't worry about Doctor Hum washing his hands so much Daniel. It's just his thing. Now enjoy your ride." Mary injects Daniel again but instead of half a dose, Mary gives Daniel another full dose of Doctor Hum's mental, miracle formula. Daniel feels the sudden rush attack his insides, he knows something is not right with him. He's dreaming, he's dreaming in color, he can hear Mary talking to him.

Daniel cannot understand what she's saying from the outside of his dream but he knows contact has been made.

Mary keeps speaking as her words begin to become more clear, when Doctor Hum rejoins them, Daniel can understand every word. "Please remove Daniel's gag."

Daniel wants them to know what is going on, he tries to speak, nothing, no words are spoken out. Frustrated Daniel tries again, it is no good, Daniel cannot speak out loud. Daniel stops trying to speak and decides to listen to what's going on.

"Daniel is ready for you Doctor Hum."

"Yes I am ready now, my hands finally feel and look clean. Now put my gloves on me Mary."

"Doctor Hum, you don't need gloves you are not going to be touching Daniel. You just going to be talking to him."

"I know this Mary and it does not matter. I want gloves on my hands so my hands will not become dirty while I'm digging into Daniel's mind."

"Yes of course Doctor Hum. I don't know what I was thinking."

Mary puts medical gloves on both of Doctor Hum's hands. She looks at him seeing in him that his mind is a million miles away, "There you go Doctor Hum all snug and tight. Do you still want me to stay while you have your session with Daniel?"

"Yes of course Mary. You know I need you to stay just in case I get stuck inside Daniel's mind. You are my anchor Mary, do not forget this and take notes."

"Yes Doctor Hum, I'll just sit down and watch."

Daniel listens and waits.

"Daniel can you hear me?"

Daniel still cannot speak, "Daniel?" Doctor Hum walks closer to him. "Damn are you out of it, you're drooling man. Your dreaming with your eyes open. What is going on? Mary you did only give him another half a dose, this last time?"

"I think so. No, I didn't. I gave him another full dose."

"Why would you do that?"

"His eyes, he was undressing me with his eyes. So I figured if he had that much still in him to want to get it on with me, well half a dose wouldn't have been enough."

"Mary I am the Doctor. I say how much and when."

"Yes Doctor Hum."

"Very well then, I can still do this. Wait a minute is that the syringe you used on Daniel?"

"Let me see." Mary gets up and walks over to where Doctor Hum is standing and looking down, "Yes it is."

"What! Oh damn!"

"What? What's wrong?"

"You is what is wrong. You used the wrong size syringe. This one is double the size of the one you were suppose to use on Daniel. Let me see that would mean that Daniel received four full doses instead of two. Damn Daniel your head is going to look like dripping marshmallow, that's been heated up on high. Sucks to be you. Well Mary what do you have to say for yourself. I think you owe Daniel a big apology."

"Can he even hear me Doctor Hum?"

"Hell if I know."

"What do you mean?"

"Well Mary I think it might be possible that Daniel here, well his mind might be flying so fast and high that it might never slow down. In fact it might speed so fast, that like a bullet it will puncture the walls of the dream verse. After that? Maybe Daniel's mind might become another life form."

"That's crazy. Can't you do something about it?"

"Yes I can Mary. I've already taken my normal double dose of my world famous mental, miracle formula. All I have to do is try to slow down Daniel's mind enough so that I can quickly plug myself inside his dreams "

"Will you be able to control his mind, Doctor Hum?"

"I don't know, but I cannot wait to find out."

Mary goes back and sits down and hopes the man she loves will start to treat her better. She also hopes he can save this fool's mind so she and Bill can have their evening together after he is successful.

Doctor Hum looks at Daniel and shakes his head, "Damn my luck. Don't worry Daniel, I will do my best to save your mind. Unfortunately like every surgery Daniel, things can happen. Just try to look on the bright side. If your mind snaps at least you will be dreaming when it happens."

Doctor Hum walks over to Daniel and stands right next to him as he is laying flat down, tied up on a cold steel table. With only a thin sheet underneath him to hold back the coldness coming forth from the steel table. Doctor Hum looks over at Mary and gives her a smile with confidence and worrying outlines on his lips. She smiles back and ask herself, if she could do better than Bill. "Call me Doctor Hum! kiss my ass." Then she reminds herself that he is a doctor and one day he will die and leave all his money to her. Mary smiles bigger and whispers, "I love you."

Doctor Hum, pulls a tall chair over to Daniel and sits down on it. (I think we know Doctor Hum enough to start calling him Bill now.) Bill laughs and puts his left hand on Daniel's forehead, "You're healed, raise and seize the day, Daniel. (More laughing.) If only it was that easy Daniel. But where is the payday in an instant. No Daniel success takes time, you better hope I can fix your mind before the week is over. Because my man, you will be out of dough so you will have to go."

Bill looks over at Mary and asks her, "What do you think Mary, should we try throwing hot or cold water in Daniel's face for a shock attack to his mind?"

"Yes I do. Can I be the one to do it?"

"Why?"

"Because he stared at my breast instead of my eyes, when his lustful thoughts of me was going through his drugged out, horny mind."

"That's a little light Mary?"

"What?"

"That's a joke Mary. Light instead of heavy."

"Oh. I get it now."

"Mary, can you get me a bottle of water?"

"Do you want me to nuke it?"

"No I want you to bring it to me so I can drink it."

"Smart ass, I mean Doctor Hum."

Daniel looks at Doctor Hum and Mary and wishes they would go somewhere and fuck off.

Daniel to himself, "If I get my hands on you, you fucked up Doctor. I only have myself to blame, I came to see him. But what could I do? My dreams were driving me crazy. I fell so deep in them. When they were nice and warm it felt close to Heaven. Every night after I receive peace, I get nightmares, filled with nightmare creatures that would love to eat my face. I bleed in my dreams. I haven't died yet, but I've come real close. I need help and this is the kind of help I receive? I think I better try to do something."

Mary hands Bill his bottle of water. He opens it up and takes a big drink as he is watching Mary's ass as she is walking away.

Bill puts the cap back on his bottle of water, "You ready to start Daniel?"

Daniel tries to speak and this time a little bit of incoherent sounds comes out.

"All right Daniel, you're trying to babble. We're in better shape than I thought we were. Okay Daniel, try one more time. Give me just one word."

Daniel says to himself, "I'll give you two words."

Daniel tries again to speak, just some more sounds come forth, "That's okay Daniel, I'll do the talking for now."

For the next hour Bill, no Doctor Hum attacks Daniel's mind with good and bad. At first Doctor Hum's words are calming to Daniel as he is thinking back to his childhood. Doctor Hum had him pick a great day. Daniel was happy then Doctor Hum brought forth a pack of hungry and angry wolves to chase him out of his great day to a very bad day. The day Daniel's parents died in front of him. This is the point when Daniel can now talk back to Doctor Hum.

"I was seven years old Doctor Hum. I was looking out my family's front door...

"Take your time Daniel."

"My parents were backing out of the driveway in their car. They were smiling and waving at me not paying attention to what was speeding up the road at them..."

"Everything is fine Daniel, this is only a memory."

"I tried to stop them. I waved and I screamed at them as I ran barefooted out on the snow covered ground. It was a snow day, school was canceled for the day. I got to the beginning of the driveway, when a speeding, out of control rental truck came sliding into my parents car. The truck smashed my parents car so loudly into wreckage as it pushed it down the road straight into another truck coming up from the other end of our road...

My parents was still in their car when it caught on fire. They were still in it when it blew up. I cried as my older sister stood there screaming at me, that it was all my fault that our parents were dead. I screamed back, where were you. My sister in a rage smacked me across my face. After that she slipped and smacked the back of her head on the driveway. My sister also died before any ambulances or police cars arrived..."

"Within a few moments Doctor Hum, I went from having a family that was alive and doing fine to being dead in front of me. That was the worst day of my life, this is the second worst day of my life."

"Well for me to understand you Daniel, I have to be nice and mean to you. Just think of me as God and the Devil. I will take my roles as far as I have to Daniel. I want the secrets of your dreams. You are special Daniel and after I'm through with you, I'll become famous."

"What about me Doctor Hum?"

"What about you? I'm the one that's important."

"Yes you are Doctor Hum. Where do we go from here?"

"Now I want you to tell me what you are dreaming about, while you are talking to me."

"I'm at peace. I'm looking at a side of a cliff that has a waterfall. It was kinda loud so I calmed the sound to more of a comfortable level. Of course to accomplish this, first I had to slow down the waterfall. If I didn't do this Doctor Hum, I probably wouldn't be able to hear a word you said."

"Very good and very powerful of you Daniel. Since I have already made your conscience mind travel back and forth emotionally. I feel it is time for me to take control over your unconscious mind. I want you to stop dreaming about your peaceful waterfall. Wait, before you do, I want you to make the waterfall normal speed and sound. Then and only then, I want you to slip into the worst nightmare you can think of for yourself."

"Yes Doctor Hum."

A few moments go by, "Well Daniel are you in a nightmare?"

"Yes I am Doctor Hum. But I don't know."

"What don't you know Daniel?"

"I think I can make this nightmare I'm having much more nightmarish."

"Yes Daniel do that. I want you scared out of your mind."

"No problem Doctor Hum, give me a minute. How does a lady monster with two heads, with mouths filled with a hundred man eating teeth sound to you?"

"Wonderful. Have one of her heads eat one of your legs. Your choice."

"I think I'll have her eat my left leg. Should I make her choke on it?"

"Yes Daniel after she eats your left leg off you make her choke and dance around like she needs help. Then make the lady monster fall down dead on her face."

"Okay here I go Doctor Hum. This is going to hurt."

"Just remember it is only a dream Daniel. After the lady monster dies, bring back your leg and create a man monster twice the size of the lady monster. I'm going to make him pick you up and smash you to the ground, until he smashes you into a bunch of bloody, mushy pieces."

"Sounds horrible and painful Doctor Hum."

"As it should Daniel. I have to make you weak so that way I can enter your mind on a sleeping level and take over. To help you of course. I'm not going to take over completely. I'm doing this to help you with the problem your having with your dreams Daniel."

"I understand Doctor Hum."

"You still trust me don't you Daniel?"

"Yes I do Doctor Hum. You are a Doctor. What else would you be doing to me besides trying to help me?"

"Very true. I gave my oath. Your well being is of my utmost concern."

"Thank you Doctor Hum. I feel deep down inside me that I can and will trust you."

"That's all I ask of you Daniel. This is just day one. Think where we will be in a week's time. That cliff you were just looking at Daniel in a week, I will make you strong enough to crush it into a huge pile of gravel."

"I would like that Doctor Hum. Not only do I want to be able to control my dreams, I also want to be able to crush them and form them into whatever I want."

"Not only will you be able to do that Daniel. I will make it possible for you to merge nice dreams and nightmares into one combined dream. Where rainbows are covered in blood and butterflies have razor blades for wings."

Nice and calm is Bill when Daniel screams out in pain, scaring him and making him jump. Daniel sees this. The constant distortion of seeing two things at the same time, one in a dream, the other in reality has decreased to Daniel's eyes. He has almost made it possible for himself to see with one eye within a dream and the other eye in reality. Time is all Daniel needs and he will be the master of his dreams.

"Daniel are you alright?"

"Yes Doctor Hum, the monster lady just bit off my leg. You should see what's left of it. There are strands of hanging meat and skin pulled away so fierce that they have become stretched out of proportion."

"That's awful. I want you to love this pain that you are feeling Daniel."

"I'll try Doctor Hum. Damn does it hurt bad. I'm going to make my leg regrow back now."

"No not yet Daniel. Feel the pain of your missing leg longer. Feeling this pain and lots more like it will be the way for you to build up your dreaming strength to the point where you can die in your dreams and not die in reality."

"Yes Doctor Hum, help me build up my strength. I am so glad I came to see you. I had hope in my mind for a cure to my dreams, which you now have turned into reality for me. Thank you Doctor Hum."

"You are very welcome Daniel. I love it when I can help someone like you. I know pride is a sin and all but I can't help it. It makes me feel good when I help a person out and it shows all over me. I shine with pride and I don't care."

"As you should Doctor Hum. Can I regrow my leg now?"

"Yes Daniel and then kill the monster lady. More pain after that as the monster man beats you down to a pulp."

"I can handle it Doctor Hum."

"Not yet you can't Daniel, but very soon you will."

Doctor hum sits and drinks his water as Daniel goes through tormenting pains for the next hour or so. From time to time Doctor Hum talks to Daniel by either making him feel more pain and agony or by letting him heal his wounds and rest his troubled mind for a small moment.

"Time is up Daniel. The time for our talking is over with. I feel that I have weakened your mind with my mighty power long enough. I am now going to enter your dream. Are you ready for this Daniel?"

"Yes I am Doctor Hum, come on in there's plenty of room. But first if you don't mind?"

"If I don't mind what Daniel?"

"I would like another injection of your world famous mental, miracle formula."

"More? Damn Daniel, you are a gluten for punishment."

"I am pain and pain is me Doctor Hum."

"That is so sad Daniel. It's a good thing my profession allows me to drop that and all the other crap that doesn't matter, so I can carry forth with a clear and free mind."

"Yes it is a good thing Doctor Hum. Maybe you should give yourself another injection of your world famous mental, miracle formula as well."

"You think so do you Daniel? Maybe you're right. What could it hurt? I know I can handle it and it might just make it more enjoyable for me."

Doctor Hum gives Daniel and himself another injection of his world famous mental, miracle formula, while Mary has drifted off to sleep from complete boredom. Bill does not notice this and goes forth without his anchor to help him if he gets into trouble.

One hour later Mary is awakened up by the sound of someone screaming to death. Mary raises her head up fast from the small desk she had it laying on and sees Bill standing up looking at the floor. Mary stands up and looks around Bill and sees Daniel laying dead on the floor in front of him about three feet away from him.

"What happened Bill, I mean Doctor Hum?"

"Call me Bill from now on Mary. I don't know, Daniel's mind just couldn't stand the pressure. I tried all I could but to no avail poor Daniel died anyway. Oh well you win some you lose some."

"Yes Bill. Still I'm sorry for your loss and I'm sorry I fell asleep on you."

"That's okay Mary, there was nothing you could do to help Daniel. Just be glad you didn't see it happen. I have to tell you Mary it was quite harsh for me to watch Daniel die. I just got to know him really good and now he's dead."

"Is there anything I can do to make you feel better Bill?"

"Yes Mary, you can take off your clothes."

"I thought you told me that you didn't want to make love to me in your laboratory Bill?"

"Don't you worry about that Mary, I've changed my mind. I think Daniel would like it that we carried on with our lives."

"I don't know Bill, I don't think I'm into making love next to dead bodies. I think I'd rather make love on your ugly couch or on my desk, if you don't mind?"

"Yes of course Mary, you're right. Maybe we can just throw the sheet over him. How about it Mary, would you like to make love with me on a cold, steel table that a man just fell dead off of to the floor mere moments ago?"

"No Bill, I don't think so."

"Think about it Mary? You can even call me Daniel."

"That's weird Bill and morbid. I know Daniel had no worth to you in the end but still he was a person. A living man with his whole useless life ahead of him... And you killed him dead."

"What are you saying Mary?" Bill responds as he starts to sweat a little bit.

"I'm just kidding Bill, I know you had nothing to do with Daniel's death. It was his weak mind, it just gave out on him. Still let's send flowers to his grave."

"Okay Mary but cheap ones. Now let's head up stairs and play doctor or whatever we're into tonight."

"Play Doctor? Are you playing with me?"

"Well not yet, but very soon I will. I'm going to play with everything you have. I love your ass, you shake it so fine."

208

"Yes I know Bill... But my best feature is my face. Don't you agree Bill!"

"Yes Mary your face, it is so very pretty. I can't wait to make your face flush from my hot loving and hard lusting."

"Damn Bill, what has gotten into you tonight?"

"Well Mary whatever it is I am willing to share it with you. Come on baby let's taste some freecom and love."

Bill takes Mary by her hand and leads her to the desk she was asleep on. Slowly Bill unbuttons Mary's shirt and when he is done he pulls it out of her skirt. Mary is not wearing a bra. Her medium size breasts look so sexy to Bill, it's like he's seeing them for the first time.

"Bill, please not down here. Not with Daniel's dead body over there uncovered and looking so nasty."

Bill touches Mary's breast as he kisses her neck softly and sexy, with the tip of his tongue out just enough to taste Mary's scent, "Right here Mary, I can't wait, take off your skirt and sit on the desk with your ankles resting on my shoulders."

Mary pushes Bill back away from her and looks him in his eyes. She sees that he has lust in them for her but this time to her they look a little different somehow.

"Mary let me have you my beautiful lady."

Mary smiles at Bill and licks her lips as she takes off her skirt. She watches Bill closely as he sees more of her body. When she is completely naked, besides a pair of black high heels that she left on, Bill's eyes look like they are about to pop out of his face.

Mary sits down on the desk and invites Bill to enjoy her. Bill enjoys Mary twice without taking a break in between.

209

When Bill and Mary are through making love, Mary has just one thing to say to Bill, "Who are you?"

Daniel shocked by this tries his best to be cool, "I'm the Man, Mary, that is who I am and that is why you love me."

"Do I? I don't think so Daniel, I hardly even know you."

"Mary you're confused, Daniel is dead. It's me baby, it's your one and only Bill."

"Yes Bill of course you are my one and only. It's just..."

"It's just what darling?"

"I don't know how to say this Bill but just to say it. Okay here it goes. Tonight Bill your pecker was a lot smaller than it usually is."

"What? How is this possible? I have the same pecker. It felt to me that I was giving it all to you."

"I'm just messing with you Bill. Your pecker was the same size as usual but you sure used it differently tonight like you have never done before. Why is that Daniel?"

"I'm not Daniel... Oh Hell with it. Okay Mary I'm Daniel."

"Yes I know you are. I would be very mad right now if you weren't so great at love making. Daniel your pecker saved you from me calling the Police."

"That would be funny. The Police would lock you up for being crazy. No one will believe you when you tell them I am Daniel. It's a lost cause Mary. What do you want to do from here?"

"Well Daniel it looks like I'm single at the moment. Does my body do it for you enough to be my man for awhile?"

"Fuck it Mary, let's get married. After the honeymoon is over with, we will get a divorce."

"We will? Why Daniel?

"To split Doctor Hum's money up fifty, fifty."

"Why don't we just stay married and have great sex all the time. I know enough about Doctor Hum's patients to teach you how to talk to them about their problems."

"So the next patient will not be here for about a week?"

"Why would you say that? No tomorrow you have six patients to see."

"Six? But I thought Doctor Hum was only seeing me for this whole week?"

"No Doctor Hum was going to keep you tied up down here for a week. You were to be his nightly experiment after his last patient went home."

"No I need more time to get into the mind of Doctor Hum. Let's go get married and have lots more hot sex. Next time let's make love on a bed."

"Whatever you say Daniel. I need a wedding dress and..."

"You can have whatever you want Mary. Let's now get rid of my dead body. Does Doctor Hum have an axe?"

"I don't think so. Why do you want an axe?"

"To chop my dead body into many very small pieces, that way they will be easier to dispose of later."

"I can go buy you an axe, if you want me to Daniel."

211

"No that's okay Mary, I'll figure something else out. From now on Mary, I think It would be for the best if you called me Bill. It would be less confusing especially at the wedding."

Bill (Daniel) and Mary cleaned up and canceled all of Doctor Hum's appointments for the next month. They got married in Las Vegas and then flew to Hawaii for their honeymoon. They had a great time making love everyday, getting to know each other and finally falling in love.

From the memory of Daniel one week later: Doctor Hum gives Daniel and himself another injection of his world famous mental, miracle formula, while Mary has drifted off to sleep from complete boredom. Bill does not notice this and goes forth without his anchor to help him if he gets into trouble.

Bill then with some kind of special electrodes he created attached one end of them to his head and the other end of them to Daniel's head. A few moments later Bill entered Daniel's dream.

"Hello Doctor Hum."

"Hello Daniel."

"Welcome to my dream."

"Thank you Daniel, let's see what you are dreaming about." Bill turns around and sees a cliff with a waterfall behind him, that is pouring out water very fast without hardly making a sound, "What is going on Daniel?"

"First let me turn the volume up." Daniel makes the sound of the waterfall come back to full life. "That's better."

"I don't understand Daniel. Is this the same waterfall and cliff I had you destroy?"

"Yes it is Doctor Hum."

"You put them back together without me telling you to?"

"No Doctor Hum. I never destroyed them. I never created a lady or a man monster to cause me pain."

"Why did you lie to me? How could you not follow my every word? Your mind was mine to control."

"At first for maybe a minute Doctor Hum. Really I was just biding my time until I had complete control over my dreams and consciousness at the same time."

"For what reason did you do this to me Daniel?"

"My reason is simple Doctor Hum I read about your experimentation. I'm dying, I have about six months to live. This is where you come in, well your body anyway."

"My body?"

"Yes I'm going to step out of my body and into yours."

"Try all you want Daniel, there is no way you have that much power. Nice try but this experiment is over with."

"Yes it is Doctor Hum, for my mind is already inside your body. Goodbye Doctor Hum."

Bill looks at Daniel whose echo is still standing there, then just like that it is gone, leaving Bill's mind inside the dying body of Daniel. Now inside Doctor Hum's body, Daniel unties his former body with Doctor Hum's mind now residing within it. The shock of being out of his body sends Bill's mind into overdrive, which gives the frail and dying body of Daniel's a heart attack from being over stressed.

Daniel turned away from his former body and screamed bloody murder to wake Mary up. The rest is history.

The Bleeding House

Legends tells of a house that bleeds. The origins of this
house that bleeds comes from folklore in the year of 1313
in a small sleepy village in northern England. It's a little
unclear how this house first got its supernatural powers.
Some say it was after the Lloyd family was slaughtered in
their house. Some say that the house already had its evil
power before it killed the Lloyd family. They were just very
unlucky to be the first ones to die.

Whichever way is true or not, still lies the fact that while the
Lloyd family's blood was splattered all within its walls, their
house had blood running down the outside of it as well. Is
this blood from its victims or does this blood come from
Hell itself? That question has been asked many times but
no one truly knows. Opinions are given like they are facts,
but in truth it's all only speculation.

Let's go back to the Autumn of 1313. The Lloyd's are good
people that go to church and pay their taxes. One Sunday
the Lloyd's did not make it to church. Their dead bodies
were found later by some passing by church members on
their way home. That is the end of the beginning of the
legend, now for the first time here is what really happened
the Saturday before this Sunday's horrible findings.

William Lloyd finds a man that is hurt and covered in blood
deep in the forest while he was early morning hunting. His
two sons who are twins are named Daily and Nightly. The
first twin (Daily) was born when the sun was shining bright
in the sky. The second twin (Nightly) was not born until the
moon was full in the sky. William knowing that his family
needed meat to eat had no time to take the still alive
stranger back to his house, so his lovely wife Christine
could heal his wounds. Being the God fearing man that
William was he ordered his twins to drop their bows and
arrows and carry the stranger back to their home post
haste.

William's twins knew better than to question their father so they did what they were ordered to do without a question but with a hearty goodbye from both.

When Daily and Nightly brought the stranger into their home, Christine had Daily fetch some fresh water, while she had Nightly tear up some old clothes for bandages. The water heated up over the fire and bandages on the floor next to Christine, she cleaned the blood away from the stranger's face and body. Slowly Christine noticed that where there was blood, underneath there were no wounds for the blood to come from.

Frightened and confused Christine ordered her twins to run quickly into the forest and bring back their father. On their way to find their father, Daily was attacked by a wolf. Nightly tried his best by hitting the wolf with sticks to get it away from his brother. Sadly all attempts failed and the wolf killed Daily by ripping out his throat as Nightly prayed to God for the strength to save his brother.

Nightly, a young man of twelve held on to the dead body of his brother, while the killing wolf walked twenty feet away and laid down on the ground like it had nothing else to do, for its work was over with. A few hours later in the afternoon light Nightly walked away after burying the body of his dead brother. The wolf watched with eyes of no mercy until Nightly walked out of sight. The wolf still hungry had waited long enough. With sternness the wolf dug back up the soft grave of Daily and ate his fill of his meat, while drinking down and lapping up the blood.

Nightly does not see through clear eyes and before long his mind began to falter making him turn the wrong way off the path until it was too late he had now become lost, with nothing familiar looking to guide him back to the path. Nightly, tired and drained, sat down on the ground to take a little rest and clear his mind.

William with only hunting on his mind has had a bad day of it. It's now the afternoon and no kill is in sight. William will not stop until it becomes dark. Meat for his family is the most concern on his mind.

This is the Saturday afternoon for William and now his only living son, Nightly. The hours they spent from early morning until now is over with. Let's step back a few hours in time as Christine begins her Saturday, from mid-morning until late afternoon, when Daily and Nightly brought into their home a bleeding stranger and then left to fetch their father.

Christine as she speaks out to the sleeping stranger, "You lay on my floor wiped clean of all blood that was present on your thick, hard body. Who are you stranger? It looks to my eyes. It tells my mind. That it seems the truth is this... You covered yourself in blood. Who did you slaughter Stranger? I fear in my blood that you will not be so kind of a stranger whence you wake up as you are now, sleeping like you owe the world nothing."

Christine walks over and picks up her cup of tea from off their only table. Her tea has grown cold, she drinks it gone just to have a pause away from the stranger. Christine fears to ask the stranger but she believes this stranger can hear and comprehend her words. For the stranger is fully awake and only playing a role. Perhaps from out of a twisted mind accompanied with a brutal, murdering body.

Christine puts her empty cup back on the table and walks closer back to the stranger. "I love my husband. Hear my words, believe them as truth. I love my husband. You will not take from me what you want. Unless you decide to take me. If you did this to me stranger, believe this to be as the truth as well. I would rather you kill me. I'm tired of being frightened of you. Bring forth a simple gratitude and leave after. Or bring forth your evil into my life. I fear you, I fear myself more. I feel passion for you. You have to be from Hell. Yet you smell of no fire and sulfur."

216

The stranger opens up his eyes and farts out nastily a large, long fart, that smells of sulfur. Christine puts her hand up to her nose in instant disgust. "Lord help me. I have never smelled such a foul scent, in all my days."

The stranger gets up from the floor, very strong of being and looks at Christine as if she is his to do with as he will. "That's much better. Damn human meat. It gets stuck in my teeth and gives me a belly that feels of fire and an ass that farts out flames. Damn it stinks in here. Why don't you open up the door and let some fresh morning air in here?"

Christine stares with a pounding heart at the enormous stranger who stands above her two feet or more. "You are foul stranger. Please leave my home and cause no trouble for me and my family. We are good people. We love God. Please leave now, very fast of will and make my memory of you a pleasant one."

"What is your name woman?"

"My name Christine Lloyd. My husband is named William. My sons are..."

"I care not about your sons nor your husband's name. In fact as the truth. I already know your twin sons' names they are like day and night to me. Yes I know your name to be Christine before I asked you. I just wanted to know if you would lie to me for protection."

"I lie never. Lying belongs in Hell with the Devil."

"How true my Lady. Lying and many other evils belong in Hell, where they are welcomed there, like they are part of the family. Hell is their home. At last, Hell was on this world before humanity. Humanity came forth to life, living with and accepting Evil. Christine, it's in your blood, it stains your soul. Evil cannot be that bad. Look at you, you have evil inside you, yet you look as pretty as Heaven."

Christine smiles and blushes. A few seconds is all she allows herself of some arousing drama, before she brings herself back to reality. "You have no right to talk to me this way. I do not belong to you."

"Yes, yes, I know, but you could. Let's, you and I, walk out of your home and straight into another life together. A life filled with love and laughter. I will look at you so happy of heart that you are mine, my sweet Heavenly Angel."

Christine upon hearing these words makes her body feverish and her mind almost willing to let the fever in her body reach it. All out of a needing want that she never let herself have a thought of, until now.

"Pleases stranger..."

"I am Orion. My name is Orion."

"Orion? What an eternity name you have. What is your last name?"

Orion laughs at Christine's ignorance, "I have no last name. I am simply know as Orion the stranger."

"Please your eyes. Stop seducing me with them. Orion, please leave my home and never return. I can never let myself run away and fall in love with you."

"Christine you simple human woman, you amuse me much. I was not telling the truth when I said to you that I wanted your love. I have no need of your love or the love of anyone else. Now your body and soul. Well I would like a taste of your body and to own your soul."

"No, please Orion, tell me you lie. Tell me you are not the devil of Hell. Satan himself standing within the walls of my very own home. Tell me, that you are just a foul human man, with a insane humor inside yourself. "

"No Christine. I'm the Prince of lies, this is the truth. Still I am Satan, the King of Hell. Well a part of myself. Lucky for you Christine, the best part of me is in within your home. The part of me that only wants you to give me your body and soul. Do this and your death will be painless. I will even let your stay in Hell feel to you like paradise."

"Satan I will never let you have my body and soul. Want me all you want. My answer to you will always be no. Besides the thought of having your body upon mine. You would surely catch me on fire from your hellish lust?"

"Silly woman, this is not my body. My body, well my form is in Hell. What you see in front of you is a man's body that has grown larger in size due to part of myself entering it."

"Your body is that of a man's? How can God allow this?"

"Don't say God to me!" Satan roars out in anger, causing Christine to cower back from him in fright.

"I'm sorry Satan, please forgive me."

Satan's growl disperses and a smile replaces it, "Fine woman, I'll forgive you. Take off your clothes. Give your married body to me. Watch me Christine. I'll take off my clothes first. I'll show you why it's great to be Satan inside a man's body."

Satan takes off his clothes. Christine cannot help to watch. When Satan's manhood is revealed, Christine stares at it with her mouth wide open in shock with her head shaking no, "No! You are the size of a monster of a man."

"Thank you Christine. Don't worry, what you see is as real as truth. Christine, today is your lucky day."

"Satan I cannot. You are so... My God the size of you. Never I thought possible."

Satan clears his throat, "No God Christine. I'm all Devil. Do you now give me your body and soul or do I rip your pretty body apart and spread your blood all over the walls of your home?"

"What of my family?"

"What of them?"

"Will you let them live? Will you leave them alone and let them survive free, far from your evilness?"

"Hell no. They're dead, all of them. In fact, one is dead as of right now. Your first born Daily. As a wolf, I ripped his throat, killing him. Then I feasted on his meat and blood."

"No! It is not true. You lie. You're the Prince of lies, you lie to me now."

"No Christine. Daily is dead and eaten. I have to say he tasted delicious. The wolf's belly must feel so full to him right now after I gave back his form to him. Imagine being this wolf. You are hungry, you are hunting for food. Next thing you wake up not hungry anymore. It has no way of comprehending this fact, it just goes on with its life."

"You speak of a wolf whose belly is filled with my son's meat and blood. You find humor in telling me. Satan you have no soul."

"Of course I do not have a soul. I have no need of a soul. To have a soul inside you makes you weak. Life is so horrible, you humans sell your souls to me so I can relieve you from all your pain. From the pain of life. From the pain of carrying a soul within you. A soul is so heavy on a human. Life can be fine and great. Your soul is light, easy on your being. The light of Heaven shines on you. Take that same life and add some pain and death, that soul starts to feel heavy and dark. This soul has no Heaven's light. This soul becomes a target to me."

"Why did you target my soul?"

"Sweet Christine, you and your family did not become targets to me until I was placed inside your home. If only your William would have let me laying there. Your family would have never had to bare witness to my evil."

"Perhaps so Satan. My William is a good man. He saved you for he has a soul inside him that is filled with Heaven."

"Perhaps so. How unfortunate for you Christine, you cannot say the same greatness lies within your soul."

"What lie do you speak now Satan? My soul is pure."

"You humans. It is so easy for you to forget your misdeeds. You Christine, laid down with another man. This man gave you his seed. This man's sons you bore."

Christine falls down to the floor and cries the tears of a betrayer. She knew, deep down she knew that her sons did not belong to their father. She was weak, she was all alone and so cold. He gave her his warmth. Christine closed her eyes and gave herself to the man whose name she did not even know.

"I see clarity in your eyes Christine. Yes the man who you gave yourself to was occupied by my presence. I have felt you before, I have enjoyed you before. Your soul is darkened to the point there will be no Heaven for your soul after death. I am your only way to an afterlife that is not filled with pain and torment."

"My family?"

"Your family is as damned as you. Your sons are my seeds to plant or discard. Your husband his soul will darken enough to fall to Hell, after he witnesses your betrayal and the dead bodies of his sons lying on the floor of his home."

"You stand here Satan, tower over me as I sit on the floor. You care less that your manhood is standing out, pointing at me. I may be damned so my care is less as well. I say to you, what I stare at is much larger in size than that of the man that I, one time only, betrayed my husband with."

"Yes that. The time before I was only interested in giving you my seed. This time it is for fun and sport. You can say that I put more of myself into this dead man's body than I did of the other."

"Satan I have to say that you put too much of yourself in this dead man's body. Dead man's body?"

"Yes the man you are talking to is dead. His flesh, blood and bones are being controlled by me. Yes Christine, the man I was before, the one you gave yourself to was dead as well. Why the hesitation? It's not like you've never done this before."

Christine gets off the floor and wipes the tears away from her eyes. She walks up to Satan and stops an arm's length away from him. Satan smiles as he watches Christine take off her clothes. Satan stands still as Christine walks naked in a circle around him, touching him gently with her fingertips as she goes by.

Satan's dead man's flesh is tingling. He is starting to relax as Christine keeps touching him with her fingertips. She gets closer to his manhood with each complete circle she makes. Satan is full of power as he lets Christine have her fun worshiping his dead man's body. One more circle and Christine will be ready to touch Satan's manhood.

Satan hopes God is watching as he gets ready for pleasure. Christine at the last moment takes her hand off Satan and runs towards the table. Satan is surprised, as he watches Christine pick up a knife and stab herself in her heart with it as deep as she can. "See you in Hell, Satan." Christine says before she dies.

Satan roars out in anger as he stomps around the home of the Lloyd's, breaking random things as he goes by. Satan huffs and puffs, picks up the table and throws it against the far wall of the home.

Satan turns around and stares at the dead body of Christine, "You selfish woman. Your soul I was to use to infect this home with evil. Your soul for all time, I would have used to have my fun and pick up some free souls. One such as I cannot ever have enough fresh souls. Throughout time this home of yours would have transformed into new homes. Year by year, I could have had my fun here on Earth. But no you had to ruin the whole thing. Without our last time together this fun for me will never come to pass."

Christine's soul floats in the air, "Yes soul of Christine Lloyd, I can see you. I am not talking to your dead body as you hoped I was. To Hell you go. You could have been so special to me. Now Christine you are just another worthless soul that will be tortured for all eternity. You are such a fool."

Christine looks down at the floor as a spinning fiery hole appears in it. Christine tries to float away but the force of the hole is too strong and before she can beg Satan no, she is pulled fast into it. Christine's soul is gone and the hole disappears, leaving the floor untouched.

Satan speaks, "This was not the way it was meant to come to be. Christine, she should have loved me. When it comes to women, you never will know the outcome until it comes to pass. I cannot have this home on Earth the way I intended it to be. I may never be able to come back to this house without Christine's soul haunting it but not all is lost as of yet..."

"If I want my evil on Earth to flow through time until humanity's fall, I have to be a little creative. Let me think. I've got it. Rise from the dead, Daily Lloyd."

223

It is now two hours before dusk, Satan sits on the floor waiting, while drinking a hot cup of tea. William Loyd is the first to come walking in the door, with a dead deer in hand. William sees the dead body of his wife on the floor and drops his deer on the floor. He screams out pain of rage and looks around his home and in the corner sitting on the floor staring at him is the stranger.

William puts an arrow in his bow and points it at the stranger with the will to kill him where he sits, "Stranger where are my sons? What have you done with them?"

Satan laughs, "Your sons? No William not your sons. They have never been your sons. They have always been mine. It makes me feel so good inside when I tell you William, your wife was unfaithful to you with me. Not only did I use her as I pleased, I also planted my seeds into her. I have a little sympathy for you William. I'm going to let you have your one chance. Shoot your arrow at me. Kill me and live. You don't kill me, I will kill you instead. Is that fair William?"

"You crazy of mind monster, you killed my wife..."

Satan cuts William off, "I did not kill Christine, she killed herself. You should be proud of her I guess. Christine instead of laying down with me, she took her own life. Then of course I sent her useless soul to Hell. Pardon my manners William, let me introduce myself to you, I am Satan the Lord of Hell. It's very nice to meet you William. Now take your best shot before I change my mind and just rip off your head instead."

William looks at the stranger disbelieving what he has been told, "Your crazy mind and crazy words will not save you from my wrath. I tell you this before you die like the monster you are. I will never help a stranger ever again. Be damned, I still will not. You hear my words Stranger?"

"I could give a a goat's ass less about them William."

"Then die stranger!" William shoots his arrow straight at the stranger's face. So very quick is the stranger, he catches the arrow merely a few inches from his face.

"What a shot William. Here have your arrow back." Satan throws the arrow back at William striking him in his belly.

William grabs the arrow in disbelief and pulls it out of his belly and drops it on the floor. William falls to his knees as Satan stands up and walks over to him slowly. "To Hell with you Satan."

"Very well, the last words of a simple, unimportant man. I could let you bleed to death but I want to end your life with my very own hands. That way your blood will coat them and I can show them off to my twin sons."

Satan smells the air and smiles, "Damn, just in time. Calm yourself William. You no longer have to worry about me taking your life. No that special privilege is to belong to my son Daily. Who, if you don't know, is already dead. I left his soul inside him so he can walk this Earth as the undead. Prepare yourself William. Daily is going to come walking in here and eat you up alive. You will die and he still will eat you 'til you are nothing but a pile of bones."

William looks at the open door and watches his son Daily walk in slow as death walking. Daily looks at Satan then over to William. The smell of blood makes Daily growl like a starving beast.

"Daily eat your false father's flesh off his bones. Drink his blood dry. Rip his soul out of him so I can send it to Hell."

Daily does as he is commanded to do. Daily runs at William like he is nothing but food. Fast on top of a wounded and bleeding to death William, Daily bites down hard on his face, biting off his nose. Daily swallows William's nose and bites him in his throat until he dies.

225

Satan watches and says to William right before he dies, "Boys will be boys. What can a father do?"

It is now an hour before dusk. Satan reentered the wolf that killed Daily at little after Daily came in and started eating William. Quick with four legs Satan runs to find a lost Nightly. When Satan finds Nightly he has once again found the path and is on his way back home. Satan wants to make his presence known to Nightly so he runs up close to him and lays down in his path.

"Out of my way you cursed wolf. I would kill you if I had the strength. Leave my path or by the grace of God I will find the power in myself to kill you with my bare hands."

Satan barks at Nightly. Nightly screams at the wolf, "What do you want of me Hellish wolf?"

Satan turns around and starts walking the path to the Lloyd's home about ten feet in front of a confused Nightly. Nightly follows the wolf without saying another word.

It is dusk as Nightly enters his home and finds his mother and father dead, with their blood splattered all over the walls. He looks over at his twin brother, who is suppose to be dead and buried. Daily is sitting still mauled looking next to the stranger. He begins to grow and snap his teeth together, like a hungry wolf would do.

Nightly is about to speak to the stranger when he is stopped, "Nightly my son come further in and have a seat. You must be tired, here let me get you a cup of water." Satan points to the table that is once again back in its place for Nightly to have a seat. Nightly looks at Daily then he walks over to the table and sits down in one of its chairs. Nightly says nothing as Satan brings him a cup of water. Nightly thirstily drinks down the cup of water with one gulp. He puts the cup on the table and looks at the towering now fully dressed stranger without blinking.

"Nightly I am Satan, I am also your father. Believe me or not that is your choice. One thing you know to be true is that your brother is dead. Well I have taken your dead brother and made him an undead monster that eats the flesh and drinks the blood of the living. Look at William's body, Daily ate him."

Nightly looks at his father's body that is almost missing all of its flesh. Anger has taken a hold of him and he wants answers and he wants them now, "What do you want with me Satan?"

"Very good Nightly you believe me. I simply want your soul. It belongs to me anyway but I want you to give it to me freely."

"Why not just take it? If you are Satan, just reach into my body and rip my soul out of it."

"I could do that very easily Nightly but that is for a last resort. I take and I give. If you want me to put your human eating undead twin brother Daily back to death give me your soul and I will do this for you."

Nightly looks at Daily in disgust, "Take my soul Satan, send my brother back to his grave, dead once again and forever to stay this way."

Satan looks at Nightly and smiles wide from his sweet victory, "Let it be done." Satan walks over to Daily and picks him up by his throat. Satan then begins to rip Daily's undead body into bloody chunks. When Daily is nothing more than a pile of bloody pieces, Satan wipes his hands on a dry spot on the wall.

"Let's finish this now Nightly. This is starting to bore me and I long to go back to Hell to torture the souls of your former happy family. Here take this knife and slice your throat and save me the time of doing it myself."

227

With shaking hand Nightly closes his eyes and slices his throat deep, "Very good my son. Now when you are dead and but a soul, I will place your soul into the house. There it will stay until humanity's fall. You as your home will reappear, everyday reshaped and reformed in other places across this world and welcome strangers into you. When these strangers enter you, you are to kill them so I can own their souls. This is what I command of you. Every day and every night you will kill and send me fresh souls to torture. Now hurry up and die so this can begin."

Nightly looks at Satan not able to say a word and dies with hate inside his soul for him.

"Very good. World let me introduce you to The Bleeding House of Nightly. Where anyone can walk in alive with a soul then die horribly, while their soul falls to Hell."

Satan inserts Nightly's soul inside his new Hell house on Earth as is just about to step out of his dead body when he hears a familiar voice speaking down to him.

Satan listens and begins to become very angry after he is told of the way things are going to be.

"No this is not fair. No cannot do this to me. Alright God what can I do. I hate you so." Satan says no more as he walks out of his home. He floats up to the roof and rips his dead body to bloody pieces down upon it. After that Satan falls back to Hell mad as the Hell he reigns.

God's command is as follows. Since Satan named his home on Earth the Bleeding House of Nightly he cursed himself. Now instead of every day and night that the house can reappear, it is now only during the dark of night. At first light it must be gone and back in Hell until it turns night on Earth once again the next day.

It is rumored that God laughed at Satan when Satan said to him that this was not fair to him.

Since the year 1313, The Bleeding House of Nightly has haunted this world in every country that exist or has ever existed. Nightly sends souls upon souls to Hell after ripping their mortal bodies to shredded looking bloody rags. After each night of killing is done with and after the dead souls fall to Hell, Satan cuts himself and sends his blood from Hell all the way to Earth so it can rain down upon Nightly and re-make is home into The Bleeding House. The Bleeding House that kills and bleeds the blood of its victims back out all over its outside for all others to witness, fear and respect.

Satan had no idea on that same very night that a young lady of sixteen that lived in the same village, was replaced with an Angel from Heaven. This lady Angel watched unnoticed staring through a small crack on the outside of the Lloyd's home. Everything that was said and done was documented. God was very pleased with this Angel's productivity and the bitter, sweet that Satan always plays the greedy fool to its finest point.

Well I'm only speculating that God feels that Satan is always the greedy fool. I'll go back a bit. The Angel that took over the young lady, left all accounts of what happened inside this young ladies mind after she left her body. The next day when this young lady witnessed with her very own eyes the Lloyd's home covered in blood, she knew she had to write all down before it had the chance to become a faded memory.

This is the truest account of this dark tale's beginnings I could find. In my hand I hold a replica of the original diary this young lady wrote way back in 1313.

Many have asked why Satan waited until 1313 to infect a humans home with his Hellish presence. Most that answer this question say that Satan loved Christine. Or perhaps her body and soul combined together made her that very special lady on Earth that Satan could not get enough of.

What just came before this gets burned away to a hot flash of ash, as we fall to Hell to check out what Satan is up to, when he gets back to Hell after bleeding all over the Lloyd's home.

Satan walks into his large throne room that is empty as death, except his four servants and one thousand naked ladies lying all over the floor in various places waiting for big, bad and horny Satan to enjoy them.

Satan sits down on his throne as one of his servants brings him a tall glass of ice cold lemonade, on a tray with very shaking hands. Satan looks at his nervous servant, grabs his glass of lemonade and then shoves the servant out of the way.

"Clean. Servants clean me now. Earth is so filthy. I bet the only place that is more dirty than Earth is Heaven. Well at least since I was asked to leave Heaven that is. God was begging me to stay as I was heading out the door. He kept on and on with I was wrong Lucifer. Heaven will not be the same without you. I told God, too bad. You made your bed now sleep in it."

Satan looks around and nobody is laughing. "Hello you stupid Demons that was a joke. The reason why it's so funny is that God does not sleep. Understand?"

Nobody laughs, everybody just stares at Satan like he has lost his mind once again. Satan is pissed, "Damn it to Hell that was funny. Everybody better laugh or I'll tear all your heads off and throw them into the pit of burning shit."

Everybody looks around at the other and one by one they all start laughing until Satan can't stand their laughter anymore. "Stupid damn Demons! Your laughter reminds me of some ugly human being disemboweled and screaming for their pathetic lives. I just don't now. I need more in my Hell. I need someone that is more human like."

Satan stops talking and drinks some of his lemonade and thinks about what he should do about his boredom with Demons.

"Rise my one thousand consorts. Dance your beautiful naked bodies around. Arouse me. Entice me. Let your dance begin."

Satan watches his one thousand beautiful Demon ladies dance for him and only him. Satan all of a sudden throws his glass of lemonade and stands up with a big smile on his face.

"You, servant bring me Christine Lloyd's soul. She will do nicely. She has not been in Hell very long. Yes, she will become my Queen. I have to tell you my one thousand consorts. Your Demon bodies are wonderful but they fail in comparison in that of a real female human body."

Satan sits back down on his throne. Satan gets all comfortable, then he gets back up quickly again, "Damn what am I thinking. Christine has no flesh, she's just but a soul. Damn it, when she gets here have her wait. I'm going back to Earth and grab a human female and bring her back to Hell with me flesh and all. I have to be quick or God will try to stop me. Let me think..."

Satan walks around in a pace, "I have it You, servant I want you to let one hundred Demons out on Earth to run around and cause trouble. God will take the time to smite them all down and he will not notice when I sneak back on Earth far away from my running around Demons and snatch a female human."

One week later Christine has made Satan get rid of all his consorts or else her human fleshed soul is off limits to him. Satan cursed himself and the great idea he had. Christine swears she will make a new King of Hell out of Satan yet. Even if it takes until the dawn of time.

The Mad Shitter
Chapter One:

The year is 1978, the month is March and the state this
twisted story takes place in is Ohio. Let's go back in time
and introduce the hero/villain of this story, his name is
Marvin Lake and he had a very sad and interesting
childhood. His father (Leo) left him and his mother (Jane)
behind without a notice or a goodbye. Children can be
mean, when some bullies beat Marvin up and at the same
time telling him that he was such a big nerd that his father,
out of shame that Marvin was his son, had no choice but to
leave his big nerd son behind for greener pastures. Marvin
cried, screamed no and fought back as best he could.
Three on one almost every day made Marvin's early school
life a living Hell.

Time went by and Marvin grew up but unfortunately so did
his bullies. One of Marvin's Bullies (Bud) finally moved
away when he was in the tenth grade. The tale is that in
Bud's house someone took a shit and then wiped his shit
all over the house. Bud's father went crazy and blamed
Bud for shitting all over the house. Bud ran down the
stairs as his father chased him at full speed cursing Bud for
being born. Bud was fast and his father was clumsy of foot
and fell down the stairs head first breaking his neck and
dying in the process. A couple of weeks after that Bud and
his mother moved away.

Marvin relieved that it was now only two bullies he had to
contend with, came up with a plan for them and of course it
involved shit. First was to make them mad at each other.
Marvin spread a rumor that Billy bragged about having sex
with Dan's girlfriend. Dan confronted Billy about this at
school and Billy told Dan that he was out of his mind. The
two kept on until Billy shouted out that he wouldn't fuck
Dan's girlfriend even if he paid him to. Dan punched Billy,
Billy punched Dan back, then they both got expelled from
school after the blood was wiped clear from their faces.

The next part of Marvin's plan was to make the two hate the other. Marvin broke into Billy's house and took a shit right in the middle of Billy's bed. Then for fun Marvin pissed all over the turd he just shitted out on Billy's bed. After Billy came home he jumped on his bed without looking at it first and landed on Marvin's still nasty wet shit and piss. Billy went crazy just like Bud's father and went running to Dan's house still covered in shit and piss.

Billy pounded on Dan's front door screaming for Dan to open it up because he was going to kill him. Dan was busy upstairs in his bedroom making out with his girlfriend who swore she didn't have sex with Billy. Dan's mother ran to the door and opened it up with curlers in her hair. Billy ran through Dan's mother knocking her on the floor causing her to bump her head against the wall and straight up the stairs to Dan's bedroom.

Dan was laying on top of his girlfriend kissing her when Billy busted through the door. Dan tried to get up but Billy was on top of him and his girlfriend lightning quick. Billy punched Dan on his back and on the back of his head. Billy stopped punching Dan and got off the bed and pulled Dan up by his hair with him. Dan full of rage somehow got himself away from Billy and pounced on him. The two ex-friends fought and fought until both of the them were back on their feet. The two fought closer and closer to Dan's window until they broke it first then they both fell out of it together arm and arm all the way to the very hard ground.

Marvin watched from the other side of the street as the two fell to the ground very ugly. A freak landing that Marvin cheered with full voice made both Dan and Billy paralyzed from the neck down. Marvin still laughing as he walked home the happiest he'd been since he could remember. This was 1973, five years ago when Marvin was sixteen he is now twenty one and pissed off at the world. So Marvin has decided do the same thing he did five years ago now to people he feels should have some shit added to their lives by his very own ass.

Let's join Marvin in his apartment in 1978 on a Thursday night, when the world seemed so dark to Marvin that he is about to take his own life. The same night he made his resolution to spread his shit around.

All alone Marvin has not turned into a swan. A few ladies here and there, with no, I love you given to him by even one lady. Sad and wanting to feel loved, Marvin sits still in his chair, not wanting to move, with an expression of no emotions on his face. Marvin looks over at the .45 that is next to his glass of whiskey which both are laying on the small table next to him.

Marvin's twitches and shakes as he forces his body to obey him. With a nervous hand Marvin picks up his glass of whiskey, he takes a drink and then another, the burn of the whiskey feels good, it's the only thing that truly feels real in Marvin's life.

Do it! Don't do it! Infest Marvin's mind as the glass slips out of his hand and straight on his lap. Marvin looks down at his lap and slaps two ice cubes off of it, making them bang against the wall. With wet blue jeans Marvin gets up to grab his bottle of whiskey from out of his kitchen. Marvin in a hurry opens the bottle up too fast sending its cap spinning to the floor, where it rolled underneath the stove. Marvin watched this happen said, "Fuck it." Then he drank deeply from his bottle of whiskey.

Chug-a-lug, Marvin has drank enough to feel like putting a bullet into his brain. Marvin sits back down into his damp chair with his bottle of whiskey in hand. Chug-a-lug, Marvin throws the empty bottle on the floor. It does not break instead it slides on the floor until it bounces of the wall and then straight back to Marvin, stopping about three feet away from his feet.

Marvin sighs out loudly as he looks down at the still empty bottle of whiskey and wishes it came back to him fully full of whiskey.

It is now time to hear the last words from Marvin, "Fucked up world you have damned me from birth. Was I so bad? Was it my fault my father left us? So much hate coming at me for so long. Why did I have to be the one that people wanted to beat up and make fun of? I tried. I tried hard to be fun and full of life. Everybody just looks at me like I'm weird and a freak. I just want somebody to love. I have love in my heart, it's not my fault that my soul is damaged. Damn world give me something. I deserve something..."

Marvin laughs out loud, "Yeah world I know my answer. It's a big fat fuck no. Well fuck your no, I have a .45. Watch me you hateful world, watch me point my .45 to my right temple. See world my hand is not shaking now. I can do this. World if you will not give me something, I will give it to myself. I give myself my death. Fuck you world."

Marvin closes his eyes. He changes his mind and opens them back up. Back and forth Marvin opens and closes his eyes causing a strobe light effect to take place. Marvin stops with his eyes wide open and pulls the trigger... Marvin looks around, inside his mind, "Am I still alive? I didn't hear a bang? Am I dead? What is going on?" Marvin removes the .45 from his temple and points it at the empty bottle of whiskey on the floor and pulls the trigger...

BANG! The bottle explodes into hundreds of flesh shredding pieces of shrapnel.

Marvin screams, jumps up on his feet and then he drops the .45 on his bare foot. Marvin is hoping on one foot as he hears his neighbors on both sides stirring around and talking out loud.

"Fuck! What am I going to do? Someone will call the cops. Damn my foot. Stupid .45." Marvin puts his hurt right foot on the floor, "Ouch. Damn it. Ouch, my damn foot. What am I going to do? I can't even run away now. I'm fucked. Thanks world, you really suck."

Marvin tries in his mind to come up with a passable enough story for the cops to believe, "How can I convince the cops that someone broke in... Used my .45 by shooting my bottle of whiskey to pieces... Then out of sheer brutality, this man threw my gun down hard on my foot. Preventing me from chasing him as he ran out of my door... That sounds insane. What am I going to do?"

Twenty minutes later comes a loud banging on Marvin's door, scaring the shit out of him, "Open up the door Mister Lake... Open it up right now. Marvin Lake I am speaking to you. If you are alive open up the door or we are coming in with pistols out ready to shoot you or anyone that is holding a gun or any other kind of weapon in their hands."

Marvin stands still with both feet on the floor, about ten feet away from the door to his apartment, as it comes crashing apart from off its hinges. Marvin still standing watches as cops with pistols out come running into his apartment. Marvin thinks to himself, "Which one of these cops is the one that is going to shoot me?"

"Down on the floor... Get down on the floor Marvin Lake and do not move a muscle." Marvin does not move, Marvin does not even blink. "Get your ass on the floor right now Marvin Lake... What the Hell is wrong with you? Do you want to die?"

Marvin looks at the cop that's doing all the talking, including all the talking on the other side of his door and says, "Yes please. Take me out of my constant pain. Yes Mister Cop, I want to die, and so does the world."

Charles the Cop looks at a man that is not worth saving and says, "Calm down Mister Lake. Life is important. Yours as well. So say yes to life and lay down on the floor. Everything will be alright, I promise."

Marvin shakes his head no, "No fuck that. Kill me."

236

Charles the Cop says in response, "You dumb ass. I'm not fooling around with you anymore. You either lay down on the floor all nice and calmly or I'm going to knock your crazy ass down real fast and real hard to the floor myself."

Marvin frowns at the big mouth Cop and says, "Fuck you Pig! Shoot me you gutless bastard. I'm not scared to die."

Charles the Cop, blinks his eyes a few times in dismay, "That's it you asshole, you're going down hard on the floor." Charles runs towards Marvin and slaps him across his head and face with his pistol. Marvin backs away from the pain, causing Charles to kick him in his gut and slap him across the back of his head, with pistol in hand when he bends down from the gut shot.

"That's better on the floor where you belong." Charles says to Marvin as he pushes him the rest of the way flat to the floor using his right foot.

Marvin on the floor in pain and sobering up, wishes the bullet that hit the bottle would have hit his head instead. Marvin to himself, "Fucked up world, you did it to me again. No peaceful death, just more pain for me to endure. Fuck this. I'm not done yet."

Marvin starts to get up. Charles looks down at Marvin, with eyes of rage, "You stupid son of a bitch. You just won't learn. If you want more pain, I'm happy to give it to you." Charles begins to stomp down on Marvin as hard as he can. In a moment a few more unnamed Cops help Charles out, by stomping down on Marvin's prone, helpless body as hard as they can as well.

"You had enough, you crazy ass bastard?" Charles yells out to Marvin as he calls off the other officers stomping on Marvin.

Marvin pissed and hurting bad, yells out, "Never, you sick pigs. Bring on the pain."

Charles laughs out to Marvin's gumption, "That's the spirit Marvin. If you want more pain, you've got it. We'll give you all the pain you ever will want, plus some."

Charles is starting the count down to Marvin's second stomp down, when from behind them they hear a voice cry out to them, "Stop it. Stop hurting Marvin. Arrest the poor man, don't stomp him to his death." This voice belongs to Mrs. Frost.

Charles turns around, looks at an appalled Mrs. Frost and says, "Calm down ma'am, this man is dangerous. We know what we are doing."

"Well it doesn't look to me like you know what you are doing. I'd like to call the police on you, for your treatment of Marvin... But what good would it do. You're the police. Protect and serve, not beat and punish."

Charles gathers himself and nods his head yes, "You're right ma'am. We lost our heads for a moment, we're sorry."

"Well don't tell me, tell Marvin you're sorry, before he bleeds to death on his floor. Shame on you men. What would your mothers think of your actions here today?"

Charles puts his head down in shame, "Not very much ma'am. Not very much at all."

"Well good. Now remember that. Peace and harmony officer, not pain and death."

"Yes ma'am."

"My name is Mrs. Frost. Now I want you to help Marvin up off the floor and get him some very needed medical help." Mrs. Frost stares at Charles and the rest of the police officers for a moment before she yells out, "Well what the Hell you waiting on? Get moving now."

Charles looks over at his men and says jokingly, "I see where she gets her name from. Mrs. Frost indeed."

"What was that officer?" Mrs. Frost says to Charles like she's out of patience with him.

"Nothing ma'am, I mean Mrs. Frost. I was just telling my men to help up Marvin."

"That's good officer. There just might be help for you yet," Mrs. Frost says as she enters Marvin's apartment without asking first. Inside she watches as some police officers help Marvin up while the rest look around for the gun that started this whole thing.

Mrs. Frost silently looks around Marvin's apartment. Under the chair she spots Marvin's .45, right where Marvin kicked it under, in a lame attempt to hide it. Closer and closer Mrs. Frost walks over to the chair. No one pays heed to her actions as she bends down and picks up Marvin's .45 and hides it under her dress. Why would they? She's just an little, old, bossy lady.

The Police Officers that help Marvin up place him down into his chair. Mrs. Frost tells Charles that she wants to speak to Marvin. Charles tells her to go ahead but to be quick with it.

"Marvin, what have you done, you silly young man? Don't say anything about having a gun because I've hid it under my dress for you. Let the Police look for your gun. Marvin have fun watching when they leave out of frustration because they cannot find your gun. Go ahead and feel free to tell the Police any story about a man with a gun you want to now. But most importantly Marvin remember this, I've done something for you, that nobody would have done for you. Marvin you owe me and you owe me big time. Just nod your head yes if you understand me." (Marvin nods his head yes.) "Very good Marvin, I'll leaving now. Good luck telling your story to the police."

Marvin tells Charles about a man that came into his unlocked apartment with a gun. The man took his radio and thirty four dollars. The unknown man got mad that Marvin only had thirty four dollars on him so he placed his empty whiskey bottle on the floor and shot it. Marvin left out the part about his hurt right foot. Charles asked Marvin a few questions and then had one of his men drive him to the hospital.

Marvin was stitched up and checked out. The doctor knew that Marvin didn't have much money so he told Marvin that his bruises were just that and he didn't need any x-rays. For Marvin's pain, he was given a couple of pills and sent home with a bill that he can't afford to pay.

Marvin walks out of the hospital feeling a lot better. (The pain pills have kicked in.) He looks around and feels the still cold wind of this March night blow upon him with a mighty gust. The cop who brought him to the hospital has long split leaving Marvin without a ride home.

Marvin thinks hard trying to find a day in his past that would make him smile and forget this very bad one. Nothing, Marvin cannot think of a day. Marvin is about to give up out of frustration when the day, five years ago he caused Billy and Dan to fall down and go boom. Marvin smiles really big and then he begins to laugh out loud robustly. "I've taken enough shit, it's time I spread some of my shit around. There is a lot of fucked up people out there that deserves my special kind of payback. Look out world here I come to shit all over you."

Marvin is just about to start walking when he hears a stranger's voice ask him if he needs a ride home from the Hospital. Marvin looks at this stranger, who is an old, tired looking man that looks like he could use somebody to talk to for awhile. Even if it is only the amount of time for a short drive. Marvin thanks the old man and offers him money. The old man declines the offer and walks to his car, while Marvin follows him silently.

On the drive home Marvin listens to the old man tell him about how things use to be years ago when this town was much better off. Back then nobody had to lock their doors. Everything was safe and peaceful, while everybody got along. Marvin listens, while trying his best to believe the lies he was being told by the old man. In front of Marvin's apartment, Marvin shakes the old man's hand and thanks him again twice. The old mad drives away, while Marvin thinks about where he wants to take his first hostile shit.

Marvin walks into his apartment, his door is barley hanging on before it falls completely to the floor. Marvin sets the door back into place the best he can and paces heavy objects in front of it for support.

"Someday I had today, a very fucked up one. Tomorrow, tomorrow will be different. No longer will I take any shit. No tomorrow I will start giving out shit. Mrs. Frost. I owe you my ass. You've got to go. Can't shit all over her apartment it's too close to home for me. I guess I have to invent some mad man that's got something against her. Some hateful letters should be a good start. She's old, I should be able to make her have a heart attack within a few weeks. All the time, I will make her trust me more than she does anyone else including the Cops. I owe her one, my one to her will be to stop the mad man that I invented from hurting her."

It takes nine days for the invented mad man to cause so much fear that Mrs. Frost has a heart attack from it. A very close friend in Marvin finds her body. Marvin calls the cops after he finds his .45 and places it safely back into his own apartment. The final report is, there was no foul play in Mrs. Frost death, she simply died from a heart attack. The coroner told Marvin that she died in peace without feeling any pain. Marvin knows this is a white lie because he watched Mrs. Frost die. In her eyes was terror as she cried out in intense pain for help that would never come.

Chapter Two:

April 1978, around a month after the death of Mrs. Frost. Marvin has already got in the groove of breaking into people's houses (That he thinks are full of shit.) and taking a shit inside the house and then spreading his shit around. Marvin has wiped his shit on beds, on tables, on walls, and on stereos. He has even thrown his shit inside ovens and refrigerators. Marvin so far as broken into ten houses.

Marvin even watched from the other side of the road as one of his victims, Mrs. Greenwood, the wife of an attorney, gave her statement to the police. She stood there crying, holding up her shit stained wedding dress. The more she looked at it the madder she got. She got so mad that she started to shove it closer and closer to the two cops interviewing her, who were trying their best to keep their distance and trying like Hell not to laugh.

This is some of the highlights that Marvin was able to hear, "I want you to catch this sick shitting bastard and lock him up. Then I want you to give me a moment with him so I can wipe my shit stained wedding dress right in his shit looking face."

Marvin laughed along with the few other people that have stopped by to witness this happening. Mrs. Greenwood (Sandra) noticed Marvin and the rest of the other people laughing and got even madder. She looked at the laughing crowd and stomped her way closer to them, "You think this is funny you stupid assholes? Get the Hell out of here or I'll make my husband sue every last one of you for everything you got. You might know my husband? He's a big time Lawyer, named Greg Greenwood."

Someone hides their face behind someone and responds back by saying, "Yeah, he's a dick."

Sandra, with finger pointing demands to know, "Who said that? Come on big mouth, show yourself."

Sandra sizes up the crowd back and forth. She decides to stop at Marvin, "You, funny looking man. You look like you have a big mouth. You have something to say to me?"

Marvin strengthens himself while shaking his head, "I'm not even from around here lady. I just stopped by because I was in the neighborhood visiting somebody. Somebody very special. I was walking and you were screaming so I stopped and laughed for a moment. But I did not say anything, I have nothing against you. Is that mud on your wedding dress?"

Sandra listened to every word Marvin said while her eyes were clicking with I've had enough of you. Just shut up already so I can ask somebody else. Marvin notices this and shuts up in mid sentence.

"Are you through? Are you being paid to talk? Shut the Hell up already, I do not have time to waste on you. Somebody else here said my husband is a dick... And by the way Mister none of your business. It's not mud, it's shit. I have human shit on my wedding dress."

Marvin laughs with everybody else and asks, "It's what?"

Sandra snaps back around and marches over to Marvin and holds up her wedding dress about a foot from his face and happily says, "It's Shit! It's Shit! It's Shit! Do you want to smell it? Guess what moron? It smells like shit!"

"I'll take your word for it lady..."

"I am not a lady. I am Mrs. Greenwood."

"Okay Mrs. Greenwood, I believe your wedding dress has shit on it. But how do you know it's human shit?

"What else kind of shit could it be? I guess you think my dog opened up my closet and climbed up my clothes until it reached my wedding dress then shit on it?"

243

Marvin shakes his head no, "I find that scenario highly unlikely Mrs. Greenwood."

"Oh do you now? Well mister I know all about shit, why don't you tell me who or what kind of shit is on my wedding dress? I mean of all things. Why on my wedding dress?"

Sandra starts crying as she dangles her wedding dress on the ground, like it's been tainted. Marvin clears his throat, "I do not know Mrs. Greenwood. Maybe somebody really hates you or your husband. Try to think. Did you or your husband do somebody wrong recently? Or maybe they feel that you did them wrong. That's it. This has to be about your husband, Mrs. Greenwood."

"How so? Please tell me."

"Your husband is a lawyer?"

"Yes he is. One of the finest in all of the state of Ohio."

"Very good. Now find out who he didn't keep out of prison. And maybe, Mrs. Greenwood. Maybe you will find the vengeful person that did this to you."

"Maybe you're right, thank you. Please, call me Sandra."

"Nice to meet you Sandra. I am Marvin Lake. I tell you what, here is my phone number. Give me a call if you need anything. Or even if you just want to talk. I'd like to know if they catch this person."

Sandra takes the piece of small paper that Marvin wrote his phone number on and places it inside her front left pocket of her the very tight pair of jeans she's wearing. Sandra taps her pocket, "I'd like that Marvin. My husband, due to his work, is sometimes away for days upon days. Leaving me here all alone, with nobody to talk to. Not counting my help." Sandra laughs away, loving her power.

"Well Sandra, you call me when you want. Until then, I've got to be going. It's been nice meeting you."

"You too Marvin." Sandra scoots closer to Marvin, "I'll call you tomorrow night about eight o'clock."

"I'll be home waiting then. Until tomorrow Sandra."

"One more thing, be dressed, ready to go and be ready for anything."

"Why Mrs. Greenwood, I do declare."

"Declare this Marvin. I bite."

Marvin and Sandra, smile at the other. Marvin slowly walks away as Sandra tears into the police officers again.

The next night Sandra calls Marvin, who lets the phone ring three times before he answers it. At eight thirty Sandra picks up Marvin in her new black 1978 Cadillac. Five minutes down the road Sandra pulls over so Marvin can drive. Sandra wants to know what kind of man she picked up for a good time. She wants to know if Marvin can handle her wild loving.

Marvin is driving down a neighborhood at twenty miles an hour. His pants are unzipped. Sandra is nowhere to been seen if you are looking through the windshield trying to find her. Sandra has her head in Marvin's lap.

The ride through the neighborhood takes twenty two minutes from start to finish. After the ride, Marvin pulls over and stops. Sandra is through with taking her nap on Marvin's lap while he was driving and is now ready to have some fun for the rest of the evening.

"Drive me back to your apartment. I need to brush my teeth. After that, I want you to fuck me madly."

245

Marvin and Sandra had five more dates before Marvin called it quits. Sandra told Marvin that he was a cheap living pig and stormed off.

With the filthy and hot sex with Sandra over with, Marvin now concentrates on his shit attacks. Sandra, tells herself that Marvin was nothing but a ship passing by. In her heart Sandra feels love for Marvin. How could he betray her?

May 1978, Sandra has called Marvin twenty times since their last date. Marvin has only answered his phone for her three times. Every other time Sandra called Marvin, he was out breaking into somebody's new home and shit attacking it.

Sandra has had enough of Marvin telling her no. In her mind it has to be another woman. What kind of woman could possibly be better for him than her? This she had to know for herself.

Sandra with a lot of money to get to, buys another car so that Marvin will not know it's her when she follows him. Sandra is parked down the road from Marvin's apartment. She sits listening to the radio and eating potato chips.

"Come on you cheating bastard. This time I'm going to catch you cheating on me. You think you tell me when it's over. A poor dog like you. I think not. You should kiss my feet every time you see me, out of respect. Well I guess just like every bad dog, you need to be trained to be obedient."

Sandra grabs another handful of chips and munches them down. She then takes a drink of her cola and burps.

Sandra is trying not to fall asleep as Marvin is finally making his way out of his apartment building's parking lot in his blue 1967 Chevy pickup truck.

"There you are, you bastard. Lead me to your tramp."

Sandra drives smartly behind Marvin. Marvin drives thirty eight minutes until he comes to a stop on the side of a road. Marvin gets out of his truck and walks three houses down. He enters the yard of the dark house and heads straight to the back of it. Sandra has gotten out of her car and followed Marvin very quietly. Hidden in her overcoat right pocket is a .38 and in her left pocket there is a bright red colored lipstick.

Sandra sneaks around the back of the house and watches as the bottom half of Marvin slips into a window that he has broken into. After Marvin's footsteps tells Sandra that he is gone, she walks over to the broken window and stares into it deeply. Nothing. Marvin's gone.

Sandra to herself, "Great I have to be in love with a thief. The silly fool probably thought that since he is a thief and I'm such a great woman in high regards, he wasn't good enough for me. How sweet, my love. It's true I know. I'm way out of your league. But my love, the heart wants what it wants. Our love will not be denied. I will take care of you. I will give you whatever money you need. You will no longer have to rob houses anymore. Hang on my dear, I'm coming in to save you, from the life you have to live."

Sandra full of saving and love inside her heart makes herself climb up and into the window, nicely. Sandra makes herself through the house almost turning on the lights without thinking. Right at the very last minute she stops herself. Sandra's heart pounds in her chest, causing her to start to have enough of walking around in the dark in a stranger's house. She almost calls out to Marvin but thinks better of it.

"I'll go a little further for you Marvin but no more. You better be thankful. All this I'm going through for you. I wouldn't even do this for my money making, worthless in every other way that counts, husband of mine. Talk about short comings. No one could blame me. I deserve it."

Sandra walks out of the living room into the dining room and sees Marvin squatting on the dining room table taking a shit right in the middle of it.

"My God Marvin, what the Hell are you doing?" Sandra yells out to Marvin scaring the shit out of him even more.

"What the fuck!" Marvin yells out at Sandra, as his shit hits the table. Marvin then tries to straighten himself, by doing this he makes himself slip off the dining room table and land on the floor, with his pants still around his ankles. It takes a few moments for Marvin to stand back up and pull up his pants. As Marvin does this Sandra did not say one word, She just seethed with anger. Marvin smiles and says, "Sandra what are you doing? Did you follow me here?"

"Yes I followed you here. You nasty bastard. Why would you do a disgusting thing like this?"

"You wouldn't understand Sandra. I'm a rebel. I shit on the really bad. I make them pay heavily for their evil misdeeds. I guess you can say it's my calling."

"Your calling? Well Marvin you have a very sick calling. If I was you, I wouldn't have answered it. Wait a minute. I can't believe this. You, it was you. It was you Marvin, you are the one that shit all over my beautiful wedding dress."

"Yes it was me Sandra. You had it coming. You and your husband have done some really fucked up things, so I shit attacked you for punishment. And for the record, I didn't shit all over your wedding dress. I simply wiped my ass on it after I got through taking a shit on your bed."

"You shit on my bed? Who the fuck does this? Let me get this straight. You shit on my bed. You wipe your shitty ass on my wedding dress. Then what do you do? You fuck me, that's what. I feel so sick. It's like instead of fucking me, you shit all over me instead."

"Now Sandra, don't go overboard. Yes I shit on your life and fucked you but I didn't shit on you. The time we shared together was very special to me," Marvin says smiling as he zips up his pants.

"Special! I'll give you special, you nasty, shitting, sick bastard." Sandra reaches into her left overcoat pocket and pulls out her lipstick.

"What are you going to do with that Sandra, paint my lips?"

Sandra looks at Marvin and puts her lipstick back into her left overcoat pocket, "Don't be so full of yourself Marvin." Sandra reaches into her right overcoat pocket and pulls out her.38 and points it at Marvin.

"Wait Sandra. Don't be crazy. Put that gun down right now. I tell you what, hand me your gun and after that we can go find a bedroom and have at it.'

"Have at it? You stupid man. Pick it up."

"Pick what up?"

Sandra laughs out loud a little, evil laugh, "I want you to pick up your shit off that dining room table and wipe it all over your head, face and body. Hell with you, you sick bastard. I want you to even eat some of it. I tell you what, just lick the extra shit you have left over off your hands."

Marvin looks at Sandra and starts laughing his ass off, "No fucking way. I tell you what you sick bitch, you eat it. My shit would probably do you some good."

"I mean it Marvin. Pick up your shit and eat it or I will shoot you in your shitting ass."

"No fucking way."

"Okay Marvin, have it your way."

Sandra says nothing else as she pulls the trigger of her .38. Her aim is high so the bullet hits Marvin right in his left eye and instantly kills him. Sandra looks at the dead body of Marvin for a moment. Sandra sighs out, "Men." She walks out of the house and drives home and pours herself a glass of white wine.

Sandra never gets questioned for her relationship with or for the murder of Marvin. Within three months Sandra drinks wine all day and in between glasses of wine she likes to pop pills two or three at a time.

No one called the cops or even heard the gunshot that killed Marvin so Marvin's dead body did not get found until three days later. Tom and Tori Paper or the TP'S as the neighborhood children call them, came home after a long weekend away. They found Marvin dead on their floor and a dried up pile shit on their dining room table. Very good sources have said that the Paper's were more upset about the pile off shit on their dinning room table than Marvin's dead body lying on their floor. This cannot be confirmed.

Thus Ends Dark Stories For The Mind Volume Two. Thank you buying my second book of short stories. I had a great time writing these and I am looking forward to one day writing more short stories for a third volume of Dark Stories For The Mind.

Peace and be true to yourself.

Keith Starblue

www.ingramcontent.com/pod-product-compliance
Lightning Source LLC
Chambersburg PA
CBHW071500170626
46811CB00007B/2650